X 20

X 20

Richard Beard

Flamingo
An Imprint of HarperCollins*Publishers*

Flamingo
An Imprint of HarperCollins*Publishers*
77–85 Fulham Palace Road,
Hammersmith, London w6 8jb

Published by Flamingo 1996
1 3 5 7 9 8 6 4 2

The author is grateful for the financial
assistance of the British Academy

A catalogue record for this book is
available from the British Library

ISBN 0 00 225405 0

Set in Times by
Rowland Phototypesetting Ltd,
Bury St Edmunds, Suffolk

Printed in Great Britain by
Caledonian International Book Manufacturing, Glasgow

To Dr John Lee

It seems likely that investigators will increasingly use primates in future investigations of the relationships of hypertension, cigarette smoking, obesity, glucose intolerance, physical activity and genetic disorders.

Strong J. P. (ed) 'Arteriosclerosis in Primates'
in *Primates in Medicine*, Vol. 9
(S. Karger Press, 1976)

An addiction is held in place by an elaborate system of deceptions.

Gillian Riley, *How to Stop Smoking and Stay Stopped For Good* (Vermilion, 1992)

DAY

1

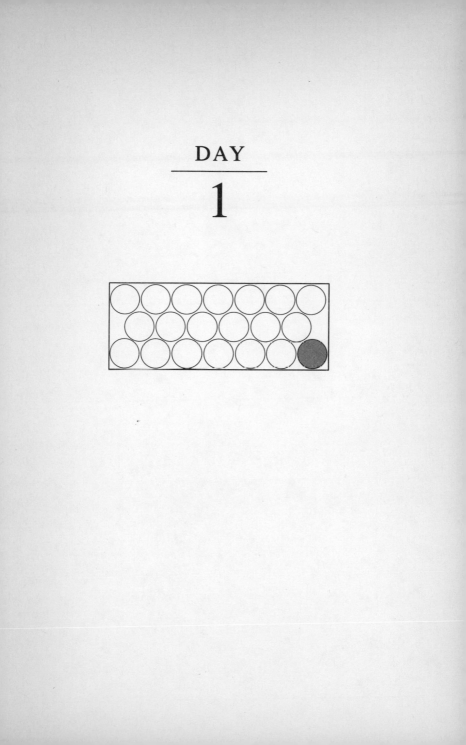

Dr William Barclay, born 7 March 1936, died 3 March 1994, aged 57. Mysterium Magnum. The principle of all generation is separation, he used to say.

Distract your mind. Take up a new hobby. Occupy your hands.

He said that the Mosaic Virus could sweep through a field of sweet tobacco leaves or potatoes or tomatoes in a single day, causing devastation to entire agricultural eco-systems.

Try not to think about it. Spend time in public places. Keep very very busy all day long.

$\{365 \times 20 \times 10\} + \{2 \times 20\}$ (leap years). Equals exactly 73, 040. Plus 17 irregulars. Not give or take, not approximately, but exactly seventy-three thousand and fifty-seven. All the same, it's difficult to prove.

Walter once told me that the old steam-trains in the old days, all steamed up and stretching homewards, used to say Cigarettes tch tch, Cigarettes tch tch. The sound of a train then, an old train on an old track, steaming homewards, smoking.

I knew about this, the concentration. That concentration would be part of the problem. That a restless, dissatisfied mind would rip from one dissatisfaction to the next, like a child stuck in a hawthorn tree in a high wind, on a high hill, in winter. At night.

Lucy Hinton, big-bellied and surrounded by children. The back of her head turns into a chimney, the blackened smoke-stack of a steam train, steaming smoke-signals saying, at the very least, good-bye.

Steer clear of friends who smoke. Repress your desire.

Feeding the dog would distract the mind. Scientists experiment with animals to save people like me from unnecessary discomfort.

Julian Carr, Dr Julian Carr, went to work in his sister's bra.

Breathe deeply. Indulge yourself in every other way.

Always boxes of Carmen No 6, and never soft-packs, although at one time soft-packs were very fashionable, especially in Paris, where I once was.

I hate and despise more things than I can name. My lungs ache. Avoid tense situations. Use public transport.

In the flat where we used to live above Lilly's Pasty Shop, Theo would hop once and jump once and Lilly would bring up a Jumbo Pasty No Chips. He had a range of jigs for different orders, and I swear the cat could recognize the step which meant cod.

I wonder if Dr Julian Carr would have made my parents happy if he'd been their only child instead of me. The Hamburg episode notwithstanding.

Carmen No 6 in endless white boxes, on the beds and tables and chairs, in all the pockets of my life. The logo of black castanets, in silhouette, looks like a split scallop shell. Nowadays, the sign of the double castanet is most often seen beside the air-intake of Formula 3 racing-cars, or discreetly positioned in posters for the English National Opera.

He once said you can change the world and I said no you can't.

There is also hypnosis, aversion therapy, psychoanalysis, acupuncture, electric shock treatment, and possible conversion to the Seventh Day Adventist Church, who maintain that cigarettes are an invention of hell itself.

My name is Gregory Simpson. I am thirty years old. I'm trying to keep my hands occupied.

DAY
2

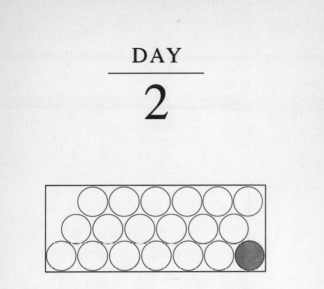

Some time ago, when I was still a teenager, my parents were proud of the fact that I didn't smoke. Each time I promised never to start they would congratulate me on my good sense, then stare silently for several seconds at the memory of my Uncle Gregory. My Uncle Gregory died of cancer at the age of 48, in the winter of 1973.

Every Christmas, before my uncle died, my father used to light a King Edward cigar at the beginning of the Queen's speech. He used to lean back in his chair, four fingers along the top of the cigar, smoking as happily as King Edward. Now, whenever I see the Queen, she smells of Christmas cigar smoke.

Thirteen years ago, in what turned out to be my only year at University, I was allocated a room in the William Cabot Hall of Residence for Men. My next door neighbour was Julian Carr, who smoked Buchanan's Centuries.

The wall between our two rooms was institutionally thin, and whenever Julian had visitors, which was often, it was easy to follow the steep gradients of his impressive voice. The smoke from his cigarettes and the cigarettes of his friends would gradually seep under the adjoining wall, over it, round the sides of it, right through the plaster which held it together. My mother would have called it attempted murder.

Julian Carr was studying medicine. His degree was being sponsored by the Buchanan Imperial Cigarette Company. All his Buchanan cigarettes were therefore free, and he chose to smoke their Century brand, blended and manufactured exclusively in Hamburg.

Almost exactly ten years ago, recently returned from Paris, I met Dr William Barclay in the grounds of the Long Ashton Tobacco Research Unit, just outside the city.

'Call me Theo,' he said. 'Everyone else does.'

It was February and it was cold and we were both smoking cigarettes: the Research Unit corridors and labs were strict No Smoking zones. My cigarette, obviously, was a Carmen No 6. His was a Celtique from a pack he'd bought in French Guyana. It was cold enough to confuse breathing with smoking.

Theo had a tan which made him look unseasonably healthy, and which made a nice contrast with the starched white of his lab coat. But it was his hair which was always the most striking thing about him. Already greying, it stood up from his head like a school performance of surprise. Different sections gave up growing at different lengths, and some bits just kept on going so that his head looked completely out of control, the hair escaping the skull in every possible direction. I noticed he also had a small vertical scar on his upper lip.

We walked aimlessly through the landscaped grounds, past the cinder running track and the asphalted tennis court, timing the walk by the burn-speed of a cigarette, an instinct I still admired in others. Eventually, we reached the narrow pond which marked the boundary of the Unit, just inside the security fence. Theo asked me if I was new and I said I was.

'Got somewhere to live?'

I said I had.

He said he'd won the trip to French Guyana in a Spot the Ball competition.

10

Seven minutes and forty-five seconds ago, roughly, Walter arrived. Walter is one hundred and four years old, but he doesn't look much over eighty. He uses a stick and always wears a hat or a cap, inside and out, no matter the weather. What started as vanity, to cover his bald bareheadedness, is now habit, and today it is a green canvas rain-hat. There is an enamel badge pinned to the front showing the ruins at Tintagel with a red TINTAGEL printed in a crescent underneath.

Walter is sitting in his favourite chair beneath the framed publicity poster of Paul Heinreid and Bette Davis in the film *Now Voyager*. He is smoking a pipe, peaceful as an Indian chief, staring into the middle distance of his memory.

He has already asked me what I'm doing.

'Writing,' I said.

'Writing what?'

'This, that, anything.'

'Why?'

'Distracts the mind. Keeps the hands busy. You know.'

'Thought I'd just pop in. See how you're bearing up.'

'I'm fine.'

My lungs are shrinking and my heart aches: I am about to suffocate from unrequited desire. 'It's really a lot easier than I thought it would be.'

But Walter isn't listening. He's looking round the room.

'When was the last time you went out?'

'The funeral.'

'Oh. Well, the less said then.'

My parents waved me off to University as though I was embarking on a single-handed sail around the world, when between the two of them they knew full well that the world was flat. It had always been flat: in their own lives they had found it nothing but flat. They stood cardiganed together in the frame of the doorway, in primary colours, waving imaginary handkerchiefs.

Unexpectedly, unwillingly, I found I missed them.

My mother used to write a weekly letter in which she hardly ever used full-stops. Mostly, she wrote exclamation marks! She had therefore discovered how to make the events of her life tremendously exciting, not through exaggeration or alcohol or drugs, but simply through punctuation.

Scared that I might choose cigarettes to perform the same function in my new life at University, she often sent me cautionary items from the papers. Attached to her letters with a coloured plastic paper-clip I would find neatly-trimmed columns from the *Daily Express* or the *Guardian*, and sometimes from *Cosmopolitan*.

Half of all smokers expected to die from smoking-related illnesses.

One hundred and ten thousand premature British deaths caused by smoking.

Smokers' chance of lung cancer increased by 980%.

I read endless columns of percentages of danger, and learned from them the equal and equivalent measure of parental fear, always fearing the worst. In my occasional written replies, and always on the telephone, I promised my mother I still wasn't smoking and didn't plan to start. The repetition of the promise became a kind of ritual, a habit it was hard to break. More importantly, it became my easy and English way of saying I loved her.

Even though I didn't smoke myself, I soon discovered that I enjoyed the company of smokers. It was a kind of rebellion by proxy, each smoky room a moment of passive rebellion. I was particularly impressed by Julian Carr, who could smoke before breakfast and in the middle of meals, and who could light matches into his cupped palms like Humphrey Bogart in Paris in *Casablanca*. I lent him sugar and gave him my last rasher of bacon. When he ran out of matches, I let him light his cigarettes from the glowing tube of my electric bar fire.

I learnt how many brothers (one older) and how many sisters (one older) he had. He openly admitted to a happy childhood, which made it sound true. At school, he'd lost his virginity at fourteen and been elected captain of the rugby team. He'd sold marijuana to the fifth-form girls. He was reading James Joyce. I gave him my last egg.

In return, he invited me to the parties he was invited to, which were always the best parties. They had the biggest barrels of beer and the loudest music and the blondest girls, most of whom, at some time, came back to his room and smoked quiet cigarettes far into the morning.

Which is how I met Lucy Hinton. Who had black hair.

Starting in his sleep, jumping and spluttering to attention in the trenches of the First World War, Walter wakes up suddenly, spilling the triangular ashtray perched on the arm of his chair.

I tell him it's alright. I calm him down. I pick up the ashtray and give it back to him.

'I was dreaming,' he says.

'I should hope so. I'd hate to think you were getting senile.'

'Did I ever tell you,' he says, 'about this monkey-skin pouch I once had, dyed the colour green, which I lost during a boar-hunt in the forest of Compiègne in 1903? I was only thirteen.'

But his heart isn't really in it, not like it used to be, and he remembers the Compiègne forests without telling them, stepping off alone into the vast protected reservation of his past.

Among other distinctions, Walter has the largest cigarette-card collection in the county. Sometimes I ask to look at a particular set (*Kings and Queens of England*, for example, or *Great Stories of the Opera*) as a quick and always reliable source of historical reference.

'You're pregnant,' I said.

'Well bugger me, so I am.'

Lucy Hinton lay on the floor beneath the curtained window of Julian Carr's room in the William Cabot Hall of Residence for Men. Her shoulders and her head were cradled in Julian's beige-coloured bean-bag, and she was wearing a denim maternity dress fastened up the front with big black and white yin-yang buttons. Her hands, fingers splayed, rested on her swollen stomach. She had a single feather stuck into a thin beaded headband.

'It's difficult to make an effort,' she said, 'considering.'

Her voice was languid, throaty, like a code which when deciphered always read a breathy *Hello Baby*, a message her pregnant body did its best to confuse. It was as if she was speaking two languages at once, making no sense at all.

I was sitting on the bed, watching her, ignoring Julian who had passed out next to his record collection while searching for the latest Suzanne Vega CD. He was now using the head from his gorilla suit as a pillow, and had unzipped and peeled down the top half of the gorilla to show a T-shirt which said *Buchanan's Silverstone Spectacular* on the back. He was breathing deeply, evenly.

I was dressed as a doctor, with a white coat and a head-torch and a stethoscope round my neck.

'Bung me his cigarettes,' she said. 'I'm dying for a fag.'

Julian's cigarettes were on the floor by my feet.

'Is it due soon?' I asked, 'how long is it before it's due?'
I didn't reach for the cigarettes. 'I mean, how long is there to
go?'

'Well, let's put it this way,' she said, 'I only go to parties
with a full complement of medical students. The cigarettes?'

'You're not really going to smoke, are you?'

'Why not?'

'Smoking by pregnant women can result in foetal injury,
premature birth, and low birth weight.'

At the last minute, I managed to erase my mother's exclamation mark.

Theo finished his Celtique. He looked at the filter, then
looked over his shoulder, then flicked the filter into the grass
at the side of the pond, disturbing a duck which splashed into
clear water. He offered me a cigarette, which of course I had
to refuse. I noticed one of the cigarettes in his pack was turned
upside down.

He smoked, then swore, then clamped his new cigarette
between his teeth and waded down towards the water, found
the previous filter, which he wiped against the grass and then
dropped into the pocket of his lab coat. As he clambered back
up the bank, he said,

'The tiresomeness of conscience. They told me at the desk
you didn't have anywhere to live.'

'I'm in a hotel.'

'Company paying?'

'Yes.'

'I've a room free at my place.'

I retreated instinctively and immediately, making excuses.
I explained at some length how I had to have my own room,
with its own lock. How I absolutely had to be left alone. How

15

I needed to use the kitchen and the bathroom when no-one else was there. How what I wanted most of all was just a simple uninterrupted life, with no intrusions and no involvements and with the minimum possible peripheral activity.

I wouldn't even want to talk to anyone very much, to be honest.

Lucy Hinton gasped and slipped down the bean-bag, her fingers splayed wide across her belly. 'Oh!'

'What?'

'I think it's . . .'

'No!'

'No,' she said, breathing heavily but managing to push herself back up the bean-bag. 'False alarm.'

'Spontaneous abortion,' I said, 'is another well-documented risk.'

'Medical student.'

'History.'

'Give me the pack of cigarettes,' she said. 'I won't smoke one, I'll just hold it, for old times' sake.'

'Promise?'

'Promise.'

I passed her the cigarettes. Our fingers touched, briefly, and I was even more disturbed by the difference between the *Hello Baby* and the baby baby. I glanced at the denim straining at the yin-yang buttons. I thought of the tense surface of a snare drum and had the idea that if her skin were tight enough it might achieve translucence in the last days before birth. All the workings of the baby and the belly would then be visible like television.

'Did you want to get pregnant?'

'I wanted to have sex.'

16

She took a cigarette out of the packet. She held it up to the light, then ran it along under her nose, her eyes closed.

She asked me if I smoked and I said no.

'It's only I was thinking,' she said, 'you could smoke the cigarette and I could just kind of *smell* it.'

Uncle Gregory died when I was nine years old.

It is breakfast time. Uncle Gregory has come to stay. I'm about to leave for school and he is going to take me in Mum's car. Mum is washing up at the sink under the window facing the garden. Uncle Gregory is in the garden, lighting a cigarette. Mum shouts out to him that it's almost time to leave for school. He can't hear her so she taps on the window. Still smoking his cigarette he steps round the whirligig washing line, spinning it like in a musical, and says 'What?' with his mouth moving very clearly. He cups his hand to his ear. Mum shouts at him that it's almost time to leave for school. Uncle Gregory mouths, 'What?'

He eventually understands what she's saying at the exact moment he finishes his cigarette. I can't remember if we were late for school or not.

I did nothing about finding a place to live. I could hardly see the point. Then the Company said they'd stopped paying for the Bed and Breakfast.

In those days I still had to go up to the Unit twice a week, and on the Thursday I took my break when I saw Theo kicking the dew off the grass as he sauntered down towards the pond, smoke sometimes enveloping his head like an extension of his hair. I caught up with him and took a light for my Carmen. I asked him if we were the only two smokers in the place.

'Looks like it,' he said.

'Don't they give them free cigarettes or anything?'

'Sure. But most of them have seen what it does to the animals.'

'You'd think they'd need a fag after that.'

'Yes, you would.' Theo smiled. 'I said almost exactly the same thing once. To somebody I have successfully forgotten. They told me it was in bad taste.'

'Do you? I mean you yourself, are you, experimental? I mean do you personally work with the animals?'

'It's not a wildlife park.'

He lit another Celtique and I opened my mouth to say I'd been thinking about the room in his place when

'Shhhh!' he said. 'Did you hear that?'

'What?'

'Shhh!'

There was a rustling in the reeds by the pond. It was like the sound a blackbird makes in forest undergrowth, pretending to be a rat or a badger, fooling passers-by, exciting them for no reason.

'It's only a bird,' I said, but Theo was already half-way down the bank.

'You *have* smoked at least *one* cigarette before, haven't you?'

She had the unlit cigarette between her lips. She pulled off the beaded head-band, and caught the feather as it swooped towards her breasts. She placed it on her belly, where it quivered as she breathed.

She took the cigarette out of her mouth, looked at it.

'Would you smoke *this* cigarette, if I asked you nicely?'

'Really, I don't smoke.'

18

'Have you ever heard what a womb sounds like?'

I looked at her belly, rising and falling, the feather trembling, the denim warping to the yin-yang buttons.

'Would you like to? You can put your ear against my skin.'

I'd stopped breathing through my nose some time ago and the air in my mouth seemed coarse, clogged with seductive impurities. I slipped off the bed and onto my knees so that I could shuffle towards her, not really trusting language anymore, certain that I was about to experience . . . about to HAVE AN EXPERIENCE. This was life. And living. As advertised.

She held the cigarette out to me, filter first. In her other hand she had a disposable lighter which she scratched into life, the flame lighting up her face, religiously.

'Smoke this cigarette for me,' she said. 'I just want to smell it. Then you can listen to my baby.'

For thirteen years my Uncle Gregory worked as foreman in a factory which made industry-standard fire-proof doors. He supervised the delicate process of sandwiching a layer of asbestos between two layers of wood. This type of door is believed to have saved thousands of lives, both in civil and military specification.

My Uncle Gregory smoked filterless Capstan full-strength. When his legs were playing up, he often used to cut down to forty a day. His hobby was motorcycle racing.

Theo's death makes me angry. Or, I don't know, I'm angry all the time and I'm thinking about Theo being dead and therefore I think it makes me angry.

Visualizing him is easy. He comes through the door in his white coat stained with the residues of strange experiments.

His hair is utterly mad, as usual, and he creeps up behind Walter's chair, motioning All Quiet with a finger to his lips. He nudges Walter slightly and then whispers in his ear: 'Prussians!'

His bad teeth, his terrible teeth and, his teeth excepted, his obvious good health from the toes on up. His body looked like it had miles of life left in it. It was only his head that made him look like a crazed professor, eyes wide and full of old mischief.

Theo's dog also makes me angry, lying on my feet and whimpering occasionally, purely out of habit. I could never understand why Theo liked the dog. The dog is disgusting. In fact, the dog is like a particularly pure idea of idle disgusting dog, and it has never been anything else but useless and disgusting. It has no feelings, this dog, only appetite: it whines constantly at the length of familiar time between now and dinner, not even knowing what's familiar about it.

If I fed him now, I could both distract my mind from cigarettes and fool the foolish dog. Unfortunately, this wouldn't distract my mind from the dog.

Every day since Theo died I have received at least five letters of condolence. Today, there were seven, six of them pushed through the letter-box by hand. One woman carried her baby all the way from the Estates to hook a wreath of braided dandelions on the brass door-knocker, next to the polished sign which says The Suicide Club.

'I don't smoke,' I said.
'Please, just this one, for me.'
'I'm sorry, I don't smoke.'
'Don't you want to hear the baby? Don't you want to touch it?'

20

She flicked at one of the buttons and it popped open and there was her belly tight against a kind of ribbed undershirt.

'Don't you want to?'

'I don't smoke.'

'Oh for God's sake,' she said.

She put the cigarette between her lips and lit it and drew in deeply, tossed the lighter aside and stared at me. She drew in again and exhaled smoke through her nose.

Then she started to cough.

Her body bucked forward and now she was coughing and choking and staring at me, her eyes surrounded entirely by white, her tongue curling into a cylinder every time she coughed.

I tried to take the cigarette out of her hand and she screamed, 'OH MY GOD!'

And I was on my feet and I was fussing over her and I was leaning over her and my hands were alternately grabbing for the cigarette and for her hand to comfort her and for her shoulders to keep her still and pinned back against the bean-bag and to try and get that damn cigarette off of her and out of her hands.

The coughing died down and she grabbed at me, the filter of the cigarette crushing between her fingers. She was breathing very heavily, her body trembling.

'What?' I said, 'WHAT?'

'SPONTANEOUS ABORTION!'

She ripped open her dress and one of the buttons flew off and whacked hard into the CD player. She clawed at her stomach, tearing at her dress, her undershirt, her guts, at her baby, her very own baby, throwing out towards me an endless ream of red intestines, screaming at me to save her aborted baby.

21

There was something moving under the long grass on the bank which led down to the pond. It was trying to free itself, or trying to hide. Theo pulled back a handful of grass: something brown, alive, like the brown feathers of a female duck. It was trying to escape.

Theo cleared away more grass, and the half-blind thing blinked in the daylight. It was a kitten, its fur matted with damp, its small red-rimmed eyes too weak to open properly.

Theo picked it up. It didn't have the energy to struggle, and instead it hid its small face in the lapels of his white lab coat.

'No,' he said, 'I don't do animal experiments. I'm strictly a plant and natural history man.'

She was laughing so hard, she wouldn't have seen me pick the still-lit cigarette from where it was burning a hole in one of Julian Carr's plastic-backed medical textbooks. I crushed it out on the inside rim of the metal waste-paper bin. She was laughing so hard, and rolling around the floor, that the vest she was wearing under the dress had rucked up slightly, letting me see the top of her knickers through the hole she'd made between the buttons of the dress. She laughed so hard I saw her navel prettily indented on her mildly concaved, unpregnant, newly articulate stomach, reaching in and out with laughter.

One by one, I picked up the red nylon rugby socks which had been stuffed inside a pair of woollen tights. I held them in my hands, stupidly.

Walter says:

'It's not the same, is it?'

But I don't want to talk about Theo. I ask Walter how his daughter is.

'Same as ever,' he says. 'Always busy. She joined a new sports club.'

Then he asks me what I'm doing, and I wonder if he's forgotten that he asked me the same question earlier, or whether he only says it for something to say. He whacks out the remains of a pipe.

I tell him again I'm just keeping my hands busy, but this isn't entirely true.

When I was seven years old and in Primary 3, I had Miss Bryant for English Composition. Miss Bryant smoked a single Embassy Regal in the Top Field every day after Period 5. She used to go through the gate and hide behind the high wall where she thought no-one could see. I have a vague but insistent memory of Miss Bryant in English Composition teaching us that the narrator can never die. That if the narrator died at the end of the story, then how could he possibly tell it?

So this is the second reason I'm writing, the reason I don't share with Walter. I'm hoping that Miss Bryant was right, and the narrator can never die.

DAY

3

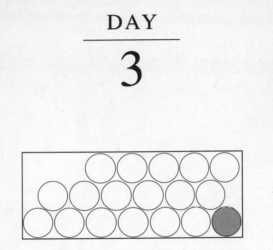

Dr William Barclay (call me Theo, everyone else does) lived in a two-bedroomed flat over a Pasty and Chip shop owned by an enormous Cuban lady called Lilly. If I'd had as much money then as I have now (and the money I have now was inevitable even then) I would have moved out within a week.

As the days went by, he kept on *giving* me things. At night, back from the labs, he would give me records and magazines and an old rainbow jumper he said he didn't wear anymore. He gave me a jigsaw puzzle minus its box and with a piece of sky missing. He said Hacmoglobin had eaten it. He gave me the daily paper at the end of every day.

'Don't you want to know what's going on?'

'No.'

If he had nothing to give me, he might describe some incredible meal he planned to cook for us both, where all the ingredients were colour-coded or began with the letter T. I said no no no, leave me alone, please.

'Yes, you're right, it's a silly idea. I don't feel much like cooking anyway.'

And then as I was closing my door he'd hop and jump, smiling his closed-mouth smile which hid his bad teeth, and before long Lilly would bring up Something Large Chips, depending on the dance. Except now the order was always for two and I felt I had to eat it because Theo had gone to the trouble of ordering and paying for it.

This weakness was my parents' fault.

'I'm sorry,' Lucy said. 'I thought you knew it was fancy-dress.'

I was standing in the doorway with my arms crossed, watching her rub her hands down the front of her T-shirt and then over the pockets of her faded jeans, where there was the clear outline of a cigarette pack.

'Obviously I wouldn't smoke if I was pregnant. Can I come in?'

I wanted to say yes because I wanted to fall in love with her. However, I also wanted to say no because I'd heard her knock at Julian Carr's door before she tried mine. He wasn't there.

I stood aside and let her in. She carried out a quick inspection of the narrow bed and the brown carpet-tiles and the underused pinboard on the back of the door.

'You should get a bean-bag,' she said. 'I love bean-bags.'

And then she said,

'Do you mind if I smoke?'

Walter is here again, out of sympathy. I imagine he also intends to smoke several pipes safe from the disapproving glare of his daughter, Emmy. He seems to believe that the house in general and this room in particular are about to be seized by bailiffs, and he acts as though each day will be the last. It eventually occurs to me, for the first time, that he has no idea the house belongs to me. He wants to know what will happen to Theo's pictures and paintings.

'Where did he get that lung anyway?'

Walter is referring to a grossly enlarged photograph of a cross-section of dissected lung which hangs to the left of the door. It is mostly pink. It is longer than it is high and Theo had it framed in a black-plastic frame. It looks like a wad of chewed bubble-gum recently spat onto a hot road. Someone has picked up the gum and stretched it flat, then photographed it, tar and all.

The hanging of this photograph was Theo's idea of a joke. It set the tone for the whole room, a kind of colourful irony, which was later to become a founding principle of the Suicide Club.

It wasn't my idea.

Julian Carr never doubted that he was going to graduate with a first class degree which would qualify him for a research doctorate at Duke University in Virginia. After publishing his PhD he was going to return to a brilliant career in medical research at a Buchanan's lab somewhere in Europe. During a brief apprenticeship to a famous man he would discover a cure for cancer.

In the meantime, he set about becoming memorable as an undergraduate. In November of that year, he broke into the cold-store at the School of Medicine and stole the heart and lungs of an Indian corpse imported for the dissection tables of first-year students. He opened up the corpse from the back, below the shoulder-blade, so that the body looked untouched from the front. When one of the students eventually discovered the absence of two major organs, she said,

'I think it's disgraceful. All the bodies illustrated in the textbooks are European.'

As my next-door neighbour and friend, Julian Carr was also the first person to tell me the rumour about the gullible history undergraduate, the Hall's only non-medical student to have witnessed a birth. I took his gentle mockery as a sign of affection, and concentrated all my attention on the idea of wrapping my arms around the idea of falling in love.

The first thing I refused absolutely and categorically and without any hesitation was the kitten, the one we'd found up at the Unit. I stood there blocking the doorway to my own and only private room with my arms crossed.

'I don't want it.'

I lit a Carmen for extra emphasis and inhaled deeply.

'It's a present,' he said. 'I've brought it a new feeding bottle and everything.'

'No.'

'With a pink cap and a picture of Bugs Bunny on the side. Look.'

'No.'

'But I've got a dog. I can't have a cat *and* a dog.'

Haemoglobin the dog padded heavily into sight, whining at some memory or some anticipation of food, knowing there was something he wanted, not entirely sure what it was. He gave up trying to remember and climbed onto the sofa, turned two circles before settling.

'I can't have *both*, can I?' Theo said.

'No,' I said. 'Absolutely not. Not under any circumstances whatsoever.'

'I'll tell you what,' he said. 'I want to be fair, so we'll toss for it. Heads you keep him.'

'I don't want the cat, Theo.'

'Tails you hit him on the head with a big stick until he's dead.'

My mother came to visit.

I opened the window two days before she arrived. Then I hid

the Courage ashtray Lucy had stolen from Drake's Wine Bar and emptied my bin of the remains of Julian's filter-tips. The night before, I re-considered, and spent twenty minutes scrubbing the inside of the bin with lemon washing-up concentrate.

Luckily, Julian was away for the day on a Buchanan's placement. The company had invited him to an animal-testing centre where monkeys were taught how to smoke. Lucy was in London demonstrating against Mrs T, so in the end I managed to avoid introducing my mother to any person who had any meaning for me. I surrendered nothing personal and betrayed no place of specific interest.

In fact, my mother was so pleased with her day out that she offered to buy me something special to cheer up my room. We went to the city's oldest department store and had tea in the non-smoking section of the restaurant. Then she bought me a black corduroy bean-bag, paying a little extra for the triangular BSI label stamped NON-FLAMMABLE.

Walter says he was at dominoes last night in the General Gordon, and Humphrey King was wondering whether it was alright to pop in from time to time, like in the old days.

'It's not that long ago, Walter.'

'When you're my age, all days are old.'

I tell him of course it's fine.

He says old Ben Bradley and Jonesy Paul were there as well. And one or two of the others.

I have to laugh.

'All of them,' I say, 'and more, if any more want to join. Bring a whole domino league, Walter, if they've got the lungs to take it.'

'Well *I* can't keep him. He still has to be fed from the bottle and I've had complaints at work from Mrs Cavendish the receptionist.'

'No.'

'She's allergic to cats.'

'No.'

'Also, I'm out every Wednesday night and I can't take him with me.'

'You found him so you should keep him. Tossing a coin is stupid.'

'I've given him a name.'

'I'm not having your cat.'

'Bananas.'

'You can't make decisions by tossing a coin.'

'His name is Bananas.'

I looked at the kitten curled and purring in Theo's arms. Its brown markings still reminded me of a duck. It rubbed its cheek against the wool of Theo's tank-top and a pink tongue stuck out a fraction from the middle of its mouth. I know that cats don't smile, but when he closed his eyes like that Bananas made me think I might be wrong.

'OK,' I said, 'I'll look after him and feed him on Wednesday nights. The rest of the time he's yours.'

'No, no compromises. Here.'

He passed me Bananas, who lay on his back in my arms like a baby and made me feel ridiculous. Theo went off to the kitchen and I followed him, wanting to protest, but in the kitchen he'd already lit a cigarette and was flexing a broom handle across his knee, testing its strength.

I asked him what he was doing.

'Big stick,' he said.

Whenever anyone asked Do You Mind If I Smoke? I always felt like saying No But My Mother Does and seeing whether my mother's views made any difference. Lucy Hinton would have said My Mother Does Too, before sucking a full centimetre and a half of tobacco and Marlboro-brand cigarette paper down her long throat.

Lucy was a student of English literature. She liked writing and acting. She liked singing and dancing. She liked *performing*. She was going to be in a stage adaptation of *The Magic Mountain* for two women, where she was cast as the entire Half-Lung club. She was editing a poetry magazine called *Filter*. She was going to front a swing band called Lucy Lung and the Carcinomatones. She wasn't really: she was just teasing me, plucking tunes on the anxiety I stifled each time she lit up.

I was easy to tease, because after the mistake of our first meeting I was never entirely sure when she was being herself. She was always changing the way she looked and sometimes I used to scare myself with the thought that in fact she was never out of fancy-dress, disguising a permanent pregnancy which was the truest expression of her character. At one stage she liked to pile her black hair in a chignon which she tied in place with transistor wire. She said she was going to get it cut when the play was finished.

'What play?'

'*The Magic Mountain*.'

'I thought that was a joke.'

'The director wants to set it on the Shenandoah.'

'Sounds mad,' I said. 'Who's the director?'

'Julian.'

What's the point of telling *anything* to a man who is one hundred and four years old? He isn't going to *learn* anything.

33

I *told* Walter not to put the ashtray on the arm of the chair. *Silly Bugger*. Now he's knocked it off I shall have to go to the cupboard. I shall have to take out the hoover, fix on the special ash attachment, plug in the hoover, unwind the flex, bring the hoover over to Walter's chair, vacuum, then repeat each inconvenience in reverse order.

Added to that Walter offered me a cigarette can you believe that?

He said he found it inside the band of the grey trilby he's wearing today.

'Must have put it there to hide it from Emmy, then forgot about it. Did I ever tell you,' he added, 'about the pipe-smoking Jesuit on a mission to Greenland?'

He pushed the trilby back a little on his head, took a puff on his pipe.

There was this missionary. Jesuit. Greenland. Igloo. Barest essentials of life, pipe included. Annually, a papal message. All missionaries to sacrifice one more luxury to the holy virgin. Fine.

Several years pass. The missionary is naked and without fuel but he still has his pipe. Raw fish. Ice. Again the message arrives from Rome and again the Pope begs one final sacrifice.

Walter settles the grey trilby back on his head. His darkly stained and dexterous fingers fumble confidentially in his leather tobacco pouch.

'Alright, Walter. I give in. What happens next?'

'He gives up Christianity of course.'

'That's not a true story, is it, Walter? How could he buy tobacco from an igloo in Greenland? It's not TRUE, is it? It's totally meaningless.'

'Oh well pardon me,' he said, filling his pipe. But he must have been chortling quietly to himself, he must have thought it was *funny*, because it was only because he was laughing that he knocked the ashtray off the arm of the chair.

'For God's sake, Walter!'

'Well pardon me for living.'

Julian scrapped his Shenandoah production of *The Magic Mountain*, claiming that nobody understood the geographical irony. Ever since his visit to the animal-testing centre he seemed subdued, disappointed. It was as if just for once his life had failed to live up to expectations and he would sit in his room for hours, refusing to answer the door, listening to Suzanne Vega on Repeat. He turned away several blonde girls who came to visit. He took long walks without a coat. When I asked him if anything was wrong he said,

'Even if I told you you wouldn't believe me.'

At the beginning of December, sixteen cynomolgus monkeys broke free from their cages at the animal-testing centre in the Long Ashton Tobacco Research Unit. Instead of escaping through a fire-door that was mysteriously left open, they smashed every breakable piece of equipment they could find. The next morning the sixteen monkeys were found huddled in a corner of the wrecked lab, shivering and sick after ripping open eleven cartons of 200 cigarettes and eating the tobacco inside.

My parents are good and decent people, which mostly accounts for the faults I find in them. However, theirs were the ideas which reached me first, so I've always been constrained by a sense of original decency which leaves me feeling ill-equipped for life. They believe in gratitude and kindness, and have burdened me with a stubborn residue of both, a sense of good faith which required me to trust that all Theo's gifts

35

were generously offered. Mostly because, as my mother likes to say, if you begin by assuming the worst then where does that lead you?

At University, I sometimes made a real effort and wrote a letter home. I passed on the news that my degree was going fine, even if I was frequently intimidated by the facts of history and all the people and places I was supposed to remember. On a more practical level, I said I sometimes struggled to afford the textbooks I needed, just to keep up with the others.

By return of post my mother sent me a ten-pound book token. After checking that I couldn't exchange it for cash, I spent it on paperback novels.

'So tails is the big stick, agreed? Or a bag, what d'you think? Or an electric shock? A bread-knife? No, bag or big stick. Big stick would be more humane. Harder to do though. But the bags I have are plastic, and they might float. For a while, anyway. Or Bananas would suffocate and that's a bad way to go, all breathless and scrabbling against non-porous polythene. While sinking.'

'Theo, this isn't fair. It's stupid.'

'Well if you refuse to have him we can't let him run around the kitchen until he starves, can we? It wouldn't be hygienic.'

'We could just let him loose, let him go wild.'

'Things don't go wild, Gregory. They get eaten by dogs. Would you like to check the coin? Okay, here's praying for heads. Take this.'

He passed me the broom-handle so he could toss the coin, and it must have disturbed Bananas because he raced up my jumper and tried to claw his way through my neck. Seeing as I was trying to escape with my life, I didn't see the coin land.

'Oh dear,' Theo said, picking it up from the carpet. 'I'm sorry, Gregory, but it's tails.'

I asked Lucy Hinton why she smoked and she said it was because she came from a family of non-smoking fat people.

Her mother had been a teenage beauty queen in Weymouth in the early fifties, with an hourglass figure pinched in the middle by rationing. She met her husband when she was nineteen, and they married in February 1953, three months before sugar was released from the ration.

'Then she inflated,' Lucy said. 'She spread, she bloated, she loaded down, she bulked up. She thought she couldn't have children, but eventually I came along. She was seven months pregnant before anyone noticed.'

For Lucy's mother, eating was both a proof of having grown up and a reward for the rationed years.

'She learned to cook,' Lucy said. 'She tried to feed us into submission.'

'She's a good cook then?'

'You can be very dim, Gregory.'

She lit herself a cigarette, filling the light in my small room with angular grey smoke. She always sat in the black bean-bag. I used the bed, leaning back against the wall, my knees pulled up to my chin.

'Fat is the contract,' she said, waving her cigarette around. 'She wants everyone around her to be fat so they feel at ease with her. My sister's already gone.'

'Gone?'

'Fifteen years old. Five foot four. Fourteen stone. She squelches when she walks.'

Lucy was slimness itself. She used to smoke her breakfast and most of her lunch. She smoked all her snacks. Every cigarette was a weapon in her ongoing rebellion against her mother, and already, even though she was only eighteen, she had a special talent for types of combat like these.

A restraint-based inhalation system. The face-mask is rigid and oral breathing is ensured by inserting a metal bit between the jaws and blocking both nostrils. Cigarette smoke is drawn into the face-mask at regular intervals, and a technician fits a new cigarette each time the test cigarette burns down to a length of twenty-two millimetres. Electrodes connected to ECG monitors are clipped to chests and temples because everything has to be measured. Tubes are stuck in penises and collection boxes under bums because everything has to be measured. Everything has to be measured so you can be sure of the results.

'It's all so pointless,' Julian said.

He was drunk.

'It's not even as if the results have any value, because the stress of restraining the things can never be measured. Unless they enter the test voluntarily it's worse than useless because you can't measure the effects of the tying down. You do see, don't you? Maybe getting tied-up causes lung cancer.'

I asked him why they didn't just find volunteers and ask them politely how much they smoked. They could then take nice peaceful measurements of heartbeats and be done with it.

'Because smokers *lie*,' Julian said sourly. 'Smokers are always lying about how much they smoke, so you can never be sure of the results.'

Every Tuesday and Thursday I was scheduled to jog from the flat above Lilly's Pasties to the Unit. It was about five miles in all, up the hill and over the suspension bridge, and then straight on all the way to Long Ashton.

Just on the city side of the bridge, set back slightly from the road, there was a brace of iron gates hinged in a high brick wall. At that time, nine years ago, the green paint was flaking and the rust was pushing through from beneath. I only noticed the gates because they had the letters GS woven into the ironwork.

They were padlocked, shutting off a gravel drive and chestnut trees spaced randomly in long grass. Through the leaves I had momentary jigsaw glimpses of a house. It appeared to be entirely ordinary, in plain brick with no intricacies at all, and as far as I could see it was completely detached, walled off from the road on one side and looking over the drop of the gorge on the other. The small windows were boarded.

I stared through the ironwork and fantasized about freeing myself into the solitude of the undistinguished house, imprisoning the world behind those gates.

Lucy always insisted that I must have tried it at least once, and she was right.

At primary school, after fifth period, my friend John Rolfe once set off the fire-alarm by flipping a king-size marble called Murad the Cruel at a piece of glass in the gym called Break In Case Of Fire. It was while I was watching Miss Bryant smoke her Embassy Regal in the Top Field. When she heard the bell she said Fuck and threw her cigarette onto the grass and strode off towards Fire Assembly.

I went and picked up the cigarette, which was only half-smoked. I was struck by how evenly it burnt and by its strong adult smell. There was a bracket of Miss Bryant's red lipstick on the filter.

Partly because I wanted to, and partly because I'd heard Miss Bryant say Fuck, I sucked on the cigarette like Uncle Gregory always did. It tasted horrible. I tried to get the smoke to come out of my nose, like with Miss Bryant, thinking this might be the fun of it, but it wouldn't come. I blew all the smoke out, and then kept on blowing until I was sure it was all gone. I said Fuck and threw the cigarette away and ran down to Assembly.

'Simpson!'

'Present, Miss.'

The taste of the smoke was still bitter in my mouth. I was very confused. I'd always assumed that adults smoked because it was nice to smoke, but this was clearly not true. It was at this precise moment, perhaps, that I lost my sense of the certainty of life.

'Look, I'll just keep the cat.'

Bananas was still on my shoulder, but he seemed less keen to draw blood. He'd almost stopped moving.

'Sorry Gregory, but it was tails. It's the big stick for Bananas.'

'I'll keep the bloody cat, alright? You've made your point.'

'Gregory, Gregory. I know you want to push everything away, and I see no earthly reason why you should have an innocent and adorable kitten forced on you against your will, especially after the coin came down tails. Much better to put him out of his misery.'

'I've had enough of this.'

I lifted Bananas off my shoulder and he suddenly became placid so I held him in my arms again. Theo looked at me very carefully. He tossed the coin and caught it without looking.

'I know what you're doing,' he said.

40

'Sorry?'

He looked at the coin in his hand. 'Tails again. Up at the Unit. I know what they're asking you to do. How much are they paying?'

'I don't want to discuss it.'

'Starts low and then increases according to how long you stick at it? That's how I'd do it.'

'It's confidential.'

'You can't push everything away, Gregory. It's always too late to clear that kind of space.'

'That's not what I want,' I said, but I was lying. I wanted to have more money so I could buy the big detached house on the way to the Bridge. I wanted to shut the gates and wall off the world behind me.

'Don't worry,' he said. 'You can keep the cat.'

'Fine,' I said, 'thanks. I'll keep the cat.'

He handed over the feeding bottle with the picture of Bugs Bunny on the side. Then, as he took the broom-handle back to the kitchen, he said,

'It was heads really.'

DAY
4

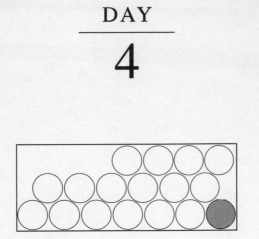

Theo's French Guyanan Celtiques had run out ages ago, and now he tended towards either Camels or Buchanan's Special. He always turned one cigarette in the pack upside down and, I noticed, he always smoked that cigarette last.

Sometimes he didn't leave for work until noon. Sometimes he left in the morning and was back by one, or didn't come back at all. This meant that I could never be sure, leaving my own room, that I wouldn't find him lurking, waiting to give me something.

I discovered that there were only two moments of definite commitment in his week. Thursday evenings at seven-thirty he would sit down, light a cigarette, and watch *Tomorrow's World*. And every Wednesday evening at about six he filled two large shopping bags with cartons of 200 cigarettes, not only Buchanan's, but all the popular brands. I would agree to feed Haemoglobin, who was never grateful, and Theo would call a taxi.

He never told me where he went or what he did when he got there, but he always came back at about eleven and the shopping bags were always empty.

It was none of my business.

'I don't understand you, Gregory. I have no idea what you want. My friend Kim wants to go to Hollywood to earn a limousine so big she can put a Chesterfield suite in the back. Julian wants to find a cure for cancer. What do you want?'

'I don't know, what about you?'

'Right now?'

She lit the cigarette she wanted. 'You don't even want one of these. Any desires at all?'

I could never separate my idea of Lucy from her cigarettes and the way she smoked them. She could lick smoke from the corner of her lips like sugar. Often, she exhaled from the side of her mouth only, turning her head slightly but keeping her eyes fixed on mine. The way she held the filter of the cigarette between the final joints of her index and middle fingers, flexing her hand backwards slightly as if she was always about to inspect her nails. The repeated movement of thumb to filter-tip to dislodge ash which hardly ever had time to form. The archetypal co-ordination of hand to mouth, the same as a sudden thought or a cautious tasting or the blowing of a kiss.

She made it a skill, both the smoking and the promise of a kiss.

I looked at a brown carpet-tile, then at my shoes, my knees. I looked up at the ceiling. I saw a cobweb. I saw a spider. I said to Lucy I'd like to kiss her.

She tasted her cigarette, she remained beautiful, she smiled.

'Never kiss a smoker,' she said. 'All the literature says so.'

As she left she inhaled and blew me a smoky kiss all in the same motion. I was desperate, despairing at my inexperience. I knew nothing. I didn't know if she'd ever come back. I didn't even know how to follow her.

Walter is beginning to believe that I might succeed. Instead of saying 'Still stopped?' he now asks me if I'm still writing. Well clearly yes.

This morning I asked him why and when he started smoking

but he began to tell his Firing Squad story so I stopped him and asked the question I really meant to ask instead.

'Were you never scared of dying?'

'Always.'

'I mean from smoking.'

'No. You mustn't forget Theo and the Estates.'

Walter is wearing a Kill-Me-Quick hat, designed and distributed by his daughter and her anti-smoking LUNG movement at the height of their campaign against us. The No Smoking symbol above the words Kill-Me-Quick is starting to peel. From a distance, the hat might look like the sailor's hat on the packet design of Player's Navy Cut. That particular hat has HERO written on it.

I ask him about his daughter, Emmy, and her new sports club.

'It's Outward Bound,' he says. 'She's thinking of taking up hang-gliding.'

'Good luck to her.'

'Feeling any better?'

'Tip-top,' I say.

'Liar.'

I asked Julian if he would ever give up smoking for a woman.

'Why should I?'

He was thinking of blonde girls and their eager entry to his room. I think he found it hard to imagine having to change to please them.

'I mean if you really loved someone, and they would only sleep with you if you stopped smoking, would you stop?'

'It's a bit hypothetical.'

'Would you though?'

'I suppose it depends how much I wanted to sleep with them.'

'A lot.'

'I suppose I could pretend to give up.'

'No, you love them *and* you want to sleep with them.'

'How many of them are there?'

'I mean her. One woman.'

'Sure. It's just that if I had to make such a big sacrifice to please her, I'd have to wonder whether we were compatible in the first place. Maybe I should be looking for someone who didn't mind me smoking.'

'But if you really loved her?'

'Then I suppose that would be one way of knowing I really loved her. If I was prepared to do that.'

'So would you do it?'

'If I really loved her I would.'

Before long Bananas grew out of bottle-feeding and started eating meat from tins. After each meal he used to come into my room and sit in a sphinx position, his head slightly inclined over my double castanet ashtray. His nostrils would twitch and then, after several seconds, he'd begin to purr, very loudly. Curious to find out whether a cat could become a nicotine addict, I sometimes used to hide the ashtray. He'd look at me suspiciously, still licking catfood from his whiskers. Then he'd prowl around every surface in the flat which had a memory of ash. He tried to push open Theo's door. Eventually, when he found nothing, he'd jump up behind the sofa and start shredding it to bits. He stopped as soon as I surrendered and offered him an ashtray, and then sat calmly with his nose over it, sphinx-like, sniffing serenely.

This was before he got into the bad habit of actually licking the ash itself. If I left a box of Carmens lying around, he liked to use it as a pillow. Later, he learnt how to nudge his way into Walter's tobacco pouch.

The rest of the time, apart from two symmetrical bald spots on the top of his head between his ears, he was a perfectly normal cat.

I went home for Christmas and my mother said I looked thin. I found I missed the company of smokers and I missed Lucy, but when I imagined introducing her to my mother it led to the problem of whose side I would take the first time Lucy reached for a cigarette. I reminded my father of the King Edward he used to smoke during the Queen's speech, and he said yes, he remembered.

That was the Christmas I kept on finding myself alone with him, wondering why we had nothing to say to each other. I think it was because we were largely in agreement about things. Our particular type of closeness was that we had roughly the same idea of what a father and son should expect of each other. He gave me the same amount of money I would receive on a grant, for example, and I never asked him for more than that. He put me under no obligation to follow him into the family business and I had no intention of doing so.

When Uncle Gregory left home to join the RAF, my father had been persuaded to take sole charge of the business. Because his position wasn't achieved by merit, he worked unnaturally hard to convince others, and himself, of his own worth. There are periods of my childhood when all I remember about him is the smell of Cherry Blossom shoe-polish, but by the time I went to University he'd added seventeen shops to the original three passed on to him by his father. This meant that in our area almost every main street was made familiar

49

by the reassuring orange sign, <u>Simpson's Tobacconist and Newsagent (est 1903)</u>.

I like running. I enjoy the solitude of it, the way the effort of it turns into a series of compromises between different parts of the body, working towards an agreement called rhythm. For once, the body is allowed to express itself on equal terms with the mind, instead of staying quiet year after year, and then suddenly blabbing out a great big secret, like cancer, like Theo's cancer.

On the way to the Unit I always used to stop for a moment at the gates in the high wall. The G and the S were at exactly the right height for me to lean against, arms straight, and flex my calf-muscles as I tried to piece the house together through the trees. Its thoughtless solitude reminded me of running.

I pushed myself away from the gates and jogged off towards the bridge. The slight incline made me breathless and I already craved a cigarette as reward for the effort. Instead, I distracted myself by calculating how long it would take before I could afford the house. According to the system they were using to pay me, I reckoned about six years, provided it cost not much more than a hundred thousand pounds.

In the New Year it became common knowledge that the Vice-Chancellor had finally discovered who was responsible for leaving a human heart and lung on her lawn, cut and shaped into the word **Hi!** The Vice-Chancellor had also been visited by the police about the incident at the testing centre with the monkeys.

However, Julian couldn't see the Vice-Chancellor because he was ill. Several University doctors came to see him, as well as Lucy Hinton. I hadn't seen her since the time I'd asked for a kiss, but as soon as I heard the slopes of her voice through the wall I could remember why I'd asked. Her voice disappeared for a while, then re-appeared in a different register I didn't recognize. I tidied my room while I was listening, but she never came.

I went to see Julian once myself. He was sleeping. There was a nurse sitting with him who said he was worse and I couldn't stay. When I asked her why he wasn't in hospital she said it wasn't that kind of illness and anyway, he wasn't in any danger. I went back to my room thinking my mother was right. If you smoked as much as Julian, then something just had to give.

The Tobacco Mosaic Virus is a highly infectious plant disease which renders tobacco leaves useless by mottling them a mosaic of different shades of green.

Theo said that if he could find a way of eliminating the virus then the world would change beyond recognition.

'You can't change the world,' I said.

'You can if you're a scientist.'

Because of the Mosaic Virus, tobacco has to be grown in areas with the highest standards of agricultural hygiene. This despite the fact that otherwise it's a highly resilient plant. Without TMV, tobacco could be grown in window-boxes.

If they learnt how to eliminate the virus, the big tobacco companies could grow tobacco wherever the workers were cheapest. Regions currently dependent on the plant would have to adapt or collapse, while farms in areas with low labour costs would flourish. The economic balance of the tobacco industry would alter beyond recognition.

'Change the tobacco industry and you change the world,' Theo said, 'because we all share in the one weed.'

Theo presented this in a very matter of fact way. It was something he calmly considered at work every day of the week, and he had long accepted the truth of it, and the responsibility. For me it was only science, and because I didn't fully understand, it scared me.

I immediately assumed she'd come to see Julian.

'He's in,' I said. 'He's just not answering the door.'

'I didn't come to see *Julian*.'

She thought about this for a moment. 'Then how do you know he's in there?'

'I hear his lighter.'

Lucy nodded, satisfied. 'So you know I've been to see him before?'

I didn't reply. She wanted to know if I could hear conversations through the wall, actual words.

'I wasn't listening.'

I still hadn't looked at her properly. She was wearing suede rockers' shoes with a red and black Paisley design.

'You know you *ought* to smoke. It would do you good.'

'I'm not the smoking type.'

'Yes you are. You're so damn *anxious* all the time. You just need the right motivation, and the right situation.'

I asked her if she wanted some coffee.

'Yes, coffee's good,' she said. She walked past me and settled herself in the bean-bag. 'After meals is also good, especially breakfast. After sport is okay. Waiting in a cinema queue is hard to resist. Before and after an interview, or a performance of any kind.'

I asked her how strong she liked it.

'The best time though, is always after sex.'

I missed the cup with the water, drenching a carpet-tile.

'Or is that something else you've never tried?'

My lung-ache has lessened. I'm sure of it. I breathe in, I breathe out. I feel fine.

My heart, however, is worse. The outside of my left shoulder flinches when I edge back my arm. It could be a strained muscle, but it could also be the arteries in the limb closest to my heart hardening irrevocably, sclerotically, damming my blood.

The room ticks with the stick-stacking of Walter's dominoes. It is one of those moments ushered into an annexe to the side of normal time. I can hear a bird singing outside. I can hear trees. I can hear the silence of the gorge. We are as we were and as we always have been, and then I remember that as we were includes a Carmen No 6, twenty times a day, and I swallow. I bite my tongue. I envy Walter his pipe. His one hundred and four years of life. I envy him his luck.

The least I could do, when Theo asked, was to tell him how I spent my days.

I was reading history books again. After Paris I'd intended to do absolutely nothing, but there was only so much time in a day. Weeks and then months passed by, and doing nothing except smoke cigarettes was not, strictly speaking, a full-time job.

I justified the history books by thinking of them as something unfinished retrieved from the past. It wasn't a new departure of the kind I'd promised myself never to make again. It didn't involve meeting any new people or even leaving the house, and

I was always careful to monitor my reading for any sensation resembling enthusiasm.

With this in mind, I worked my way through the *Oxford History of England*, smiling from time to time at its gloriously comic central idea that there are always connections to be made and causalities to be found. The comic perfection of rationalized coincidence (what timing!) and the final slapstick desperation of the historian with eight fingers in eight separate dikes and his thumbs up his bum, smiling nicely as he demonstrates to passers-by how the past is under review, under control, wholly understood.

We went dancing and she danced like a mad woman, on drugs. I watched my feet forget themselves in the presence of her feet, surprising the rest of me. We cycled into the city-centre together. We sat together in the refectory, and at the end of each meal she would light a cigarette and I wouldn't know what to do with my hands.

'In English we study love,' she once said. 'We think about it all day long, disguised as poems. Then in class we always come to the same conclusion. Love is action, not words. I don't suppose you think about love much, in the History department.'

Our best conversations always happened in my room, her in the bean-bag, me on the bed. I think it was because of Julian. Knowing that she could easily slip next door made me more eager to please her. It made me remember my luck.

'Do you like thin women, Gregory?'

She was stretched out in the bean-bag. She'd pulled up her T-shirt and was looking down at her waist.

'Yes.'

'Do you like me then?'

54

'You know I do.'

'And do you like me more because I smoke?'

'No.'

She pulled down the T-shirt.

'I don't believe you. If I didn't smoke I wouldn't be thin.'

I asked her if she wasn't afraid of dying and she said she was only eighteen years old for God's sake.

Most of all, I liked to watch her being sad, staring at the flame of her lighter until it became too hot to hold. It was then that I wanted to squeeze her into the bean-bag and make love to her, but instead I just looked. I dreamt about her. I never told her that there were also love stories in the History department. I mean ones which actually happened.

The asbestos factory where Uncle Gregory worked was in Adelaide, South Australia, and he used to save his salary to pay for an annual pilgrimage to the Isle of Man Motorcycle Time Trials. In the early years he worked as a mechanic for a team of his old RAF pals. Then, between 1958 and 1963, and again in 1965, he rode the TT himself.

He had many friends among the racers. In 1960, he was up in eighth place in the Senior 500 when he dropped his Triumph at the Gooseneck. Later, in hospital, he was presented with a trophy made of old kick-starts welded together. Both his legs were broken. Two years later, he knew the names of the wives of all three riders who died at the Devil's Lunge.

When TT week was over, he put his bike on a trailer and came to stay. He used to tease Mum about riding me to school on the Triumph, and when she gave him the car-key he'd put on a big show as if he didn't know how to drive, as if driving a car was so boring he was bound to fall asleep at the wheel. Once, he lit two cigarettes at the same time, as a way of promising mum he'd stay awake. When she didn't laugh, he put the cigarettes in his nostrils.

At this time the Isle of Man TT was sponsored by Wills Woodbines. Uncle Gregory had CAPSTAN across his green petrol-tank. Even today, as far as I know, he remains the only partially-sighted rider ever to compete on the senior circuit.

Julian Carr was in trouble. Some Marxist ecologists had circulated a flyer condemning him for taking money from a tobacco company. They implicated him in the destruction of the rain-forests, the murder of unborn babies, and the economic weakness of the Third World. They therefore proposed his expulsion from the Students' Union.

Added to that the Vice-Chancellor still wanted to see him, and although the nurse had gone, Julian hung on to his doctor's note and rarely left his room. I went to show him the flyer and he looked awful, his eyes dark and somehow unfocused. He said he was fine. He rolled up the flyer, touched it against the bar fire and used it as a spill for his cigarette. He threw the paper into the bin, where it singed a milk carton before I stamped on it. He said,

'Did I ever tell you about those monkeys?'

He stumbled against the wall. He put his cigarette down on the desk and steadied himself. I thought he might be drunk, but the only smell on his breath was tobacco.

'Should have burned the bloody place down,' he said.

He concentrated hard and focused on me, then remembered his cigarette and picked it off the desk and stuck it in his mouth.

'How's Lucy?' he said. His voice was slurred. 'Any luck?'

'Are you sure you're alright?'

'I'm fine.'

I briefly wondered if he was jealous. He screwed up his eyes and tried unsuccessfully to get another cigarette out of his pack. He gave up and just waved the pack generally in my direction. One of the cigarettes was upside down, tobacco showing.

'Cigarette? Or not yet?'

I doubt he even noticed that I took one. I put it in my pocket.

Stay cool, stay calm, think of the tarspots in the lung on the photo by the door. Don't think of the double castanet or the air intake of Formula 3 racing cars or posters for the ENO. Remember that when Theo put up the poster of Popeye, smoking himself into strength, it was a joke. (Remember the spinach.) He didn't frame the Yalta photo of the century's three greatest men because they achieved peace by smoking. If Winston had surrendered his cigars there would still have been peace, surely (Roosevelt was a fag man and Stalin loved his pipe – Hitler never touched the stuff). Look instead at the enlarged acupuncture diagram of a human ear (next to *Now Voyager*), locating the exact point E which relates to smoking.

I tug at my ear, at the exact point E: it doesn't help. Think of Julian Carr, and remember the real reason for disdaining your pain. Remember Hamburg.

More immediately, try very hard indeed to ignore the straight-forward implication of the words painted above the door in thick black italics, Theo's old and useless mantra:

There are no poisonous substances, only incorrect doses
PARACELSUS, *Paragranum*, Basel 1536

I placed the cigarette I'd stolen from Julian on my desk next to a box of Swan Vestas, the smoker's match. I switched on the

Anglepoise. I sat down at the desk and squared my shoulders. I didn't want to be slouching at the moment my life changed for ever.

I had resolved, due to the vehemence of my love, to perish with her.

I studied the cigarette carefully. Fine-cut leaves of tobacco packed into a thin roll of paper, fixed to a synthetic filtering device. An object contrived to spring a small pleasure in the brain. It was such a simple idea, so clear in ambition and so neat in execution. I rolled it along the desk. The paper had Buchanan's printed on it, just above the filter. That was good thinking. I rolled it back again. A cigarette rolls nicely.

It was a kind of cowardice to prepare for Lucy by smoking the cigarette now, alone. But I was scared I might cough, or feel sick, or even vomit, any one of which would be unfortunate if Lucy were there, otherwise impressed by my proof, at last, that I was prepared to die for her.

I put the cigarette in my mouth. I was surprised by how dry it was and I took it out of my mouth and it stuck to my lower lip, tearing the skin. I put the cigarette down, tried to light a match into my cupped palms like Humphrey Bogart in Paris in *Casablanca*, but I couldn't. So I lit the match by striking it towards me and a spark flew off and burnt a hole in my shirt.

I took a last deep breath. I wet my lips and put the cigarette back in my mouth. And for some reason remembered an article from *Cosmopolitan* which said that cigarettes were a substitute for the mother's breast, so I thought of Lucy when she was pregnant, and then I thought of my own mother and the countless promises made and impossible to unmake.

I took the cigarette out of my mouth. I watched the Swan Vesta burn itself out.

I was scared of dying.

DAY

5

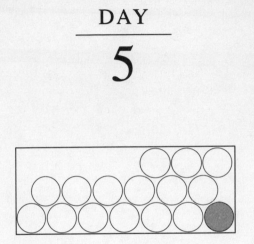

Philippus Aureolus Theophrastus Bombastus von Hohenheim (1493–1541), also known as Paracelsus. Personal doctor to Erasmus and Theo's hero. John Donne is known to have considered him an innovator of greater importance than Copernicus.

Paracelsus believed that in the beginning there was primal matter, the *Mysterium Magnum*, which could generate life by transforming itself. The principle of all generation was therefore separation, and every object separated from the MM was impressed with an identifying signature. It is from this idea that the concepts of micro- and macrocosm were later developed. The particular discovery Paracelsus made then, was that everything around us, however small and seemingly commonplace, is a microcosmic expression of the macrocosm, or EVERYTHING.

He considered that the aim of natural research should be to identify the signature which explained the connection of any particular object to the primal source. For Paracelsus this was synonymous with the search for God, and by applying these ideas to medicine and the human body he became the first European doctor to suggest that diseases were located in specific organs. He also discovered that poison could act as an effective remedy, and was rumoured to have accelerated his research by experimenting frequently on himself.

She introduced me to the Olympians of smoke. She taught me its mythology through black and white cinema, showed me its gods and rituals and villains. I marvelled at Greta Garbo and Sam Spade and the way the smoke of cigarettes made sophisticate the silver of the silver screen.

She took me to see the Gitanes series of pre-war film-noirs at the Arts Cinema, where a sign in the toilet said No Smoking Rauchen Verboten Ne Pas Fumer Non Fumare while the screen filled with unrepentant images of the twentieth century's most proficient smokers. Their lives and our lives were enhanced by tobacco, confirming beyond doubt that in times of stress like love and European war the only fully human action was always a smoke. Smoking was as decent a response to hysteria as it was to boredom. It was as reassuring in victory as it was in defeat. And most comforting of all, it was absolutely one hundred per cent safe. I saw nobody die of lung cancer, not on screen. Nobody even coughed or had a sore throat, except perhaps Marlene Dietrich.

Lucy told me that all this could be mine. That smoking and not smoking was the difference between entry and no entry into a cinematic world where post-coital cigarettes were shared in king-size beds in all the premier hotels of the world. By people like us. She held out cigarettes to me like an apple. It was love and desire. It was knowledge and everything.

Walter, on top form, is wearing his light and dark blue Jack Straws cricket cap, paled by countless seasons of April rain. It is his sporting cap and he is expecting Jonesy Paul and old Ben Bradley for a session of dominoes. Amounts of money will change hands. There will be cursing.

So Walter is feeling chirpy, braving up his luck by filling each of his pipes with a little extra tobacco. I ask him if he ever tried to give it up.

'Never willingly.'

He rocks back in his chair, pipe in mouth, pulls down the dark peak of his cap. He takes the pipe from his mouth and looks into the bowl-end. He exercises his jaw as he joins up the dots of a past experience so varied it can connect into any number of stories.

'I once had a friend who tried to give up. He lost his wife and children.'

'Irritability?'

'No, nothing like that. It was the MCC.'

'Oh come on, Walter. I'm prepared to bet the MCC has nothing to do with it.'

'What we used to call the Marital Consummation Cigarette, the best smoke of the week.'

Walter rambles a little but he gets there in the end. It was the wife's fault. Wanting to make giving-up easier for her husband, she decided they should forego the marital bed until he learnt not to crave an MCC the moment it finished. The husband became increasingly desperate. He held out for two months before deciding to spend an evening at Walter's house, hoping for some moral support. Walter invited him in, opened several bottles of beer, and later, purely out of compassion, he offered his old friend a Woodbine.

The next day, his friend's wife left for her mother's and took the children with her.

'She smelt the tobacco on his breath,' Walter says. 'And for the wife it could only mean one thing: her husband must have slept with another woman.'

Walter was starting to chortle.

'Mind the ashtray!'

Every Wednesday, without fail, he filled the two shopping bags with cartons of cigarettes and called for a taxi. Every iesday night he came home with the bags empty. It was still none of my business.

He seemed to have run out of things to give me and I hardly ever saw him. I started worrying that he didn't like me and I wanted to smoke extra cigarettes to console myself but of course I couldn't. I asked if I could join him for *Tomorrow's World*, and very politely he offered me the better end of the sofa, the one with fewer dog-hairs. Haemoglobin curled up between us and Bananas went to sleep on Haemoglobin.

Tomorrow's World featured a new computer programme being developed to colourize old black and white films. Fashion experts and film critics had already been consulted on the correct colour of Lauren Bacall's eyes in *To Have and Have Not*. There were other ways the old films could be altered. Brand names on consumer items could be changed or added, which was one way that colourization might finance itself. More interestingly, cigarettes could now be air-brushed into inexistence. By way of example, the team from *Tomorrow's World* had eliminated the cigarettes from a scene in *Casablanca*.

It is evening. Rick's Bar. A piano plays and roulette tables rattle in the background. Humphrey Bogart and Ingrid Bergman sit at a table drinking champagne. Occasionally they smell their fingers, very discreetly, as if wanting to give the impression they are actually doing something else. Neither of them is openly going to admit that there is a funny smell coming from somewhere close, which probably explains why, from time to time, they sigh so deeply at the social delicacy of the situation.

Julian Carr came to my room to practise the speech of defence he was going to make at the Students' Union. He'd made a full recovery from his illness and only referred to it obliquely, by apologizing for acting strangely.

His main point was that the money from Buchanan's was intended to start him on a career-path which would eventually help him research a cure for cancer. It was therefore at least as legitimate as money given to Cancer Research, and probably more so. He argued that cancer charities needed cancer to exist, and therefore they might be interested in a certain *delay*, as it were. Tobacco companies, on the other hand, had more urgent incentives to find a cure as soon as possible. Millions of pounds were at stake, whole regions of farmers, nations of producers, teams of distributors, communities of executives. The salesmen and the tobacconists were entirely dependent. Buchanan's sponsored medical students like Julian in the best of faith and he was determined to justify their confidence in him.

'Evil exists,' he concluded, 'there is no need to create it. Should I keep this bit about the animal testing?'

I went to listen to him at the meeting itself and he was magnificent. He was visibly moved when he described how unequivocally he objected to the use of animals in experiments. After the speech, he stood on a chair and gave out free packs of Buchanan's cigarettes. He was not voted out of the Union.

Some weeks later, using a similar strategy, he was elected President. After a minor stumble, his mission of ambition was back on track. Cigarettes tch tch. Cigarettes tch tch. There goes Julian, steaming all the way to the top.

While we waited for the taxi a beggar came up and asked if we could spare some change or a cigarette. Theo said no and then the taxi nearly ran the beggar over.

It was a London-style cab, with lots of leg-room and plenty of space on the floor for the two shopping bags full of cigarettes. The bags were made of plastic-coated nylon, in red and white stripes. I tried to summon back the unprecedented wave of curiosity which had led me into this taxi with Theo, but I couldn't. I had no idea why I'd asked to go with him.

On the dividing window in front of us there was a copyright sticker made in Hong Kong which said Please Don't Offend The Driver By Asking To Smoke. Next to this was a cartoon of two busty women sitting at a restaurant table. One of the busty women says Do You Mind If I Smoke? and the other one says I Don't Mind If You Burn.

'Not many fares this direction,' the cabbie said.

He glanced in the rear-view mirror and caught my eye but I had no idea of how to start a conversation with him. I was wondering how I could have forgotten my basic principle, since Paris, that inactivity was an honest response to life. Only curiosity was absurd. I hoped Bananas was alright: I'd made sure to leave him out a full ashtray.

We were now skirting the edge of the Estates, and this was the furthest I'd ever been from the bridge. All of the five-storey blocks, without exception, were beige and grey, each one merging into the background ugliness of the next as if their natural state was camouflage, always prepared for ambush and modern war. One or two older, detached houses cowered back from the street, curtains closed, unsellable.

Theo told the driver to stop at a pub where the sign was smashed in, leaving it nameless. The Strangers' End seemed a decent guess. I looked at Theo. He said,

'They've got pin-ball.'

In the car-park a security light acted nervously and blinked on the steam of our breath. I was frightened, very keen to get back in the cab and go home, and Theo looked at me as though he knew what I was thinking.

'Not any old rubbish. They always have the latest machines.'

Uncle Gregory settled in Australia after he was discharged from the RAF. Partly it was for the sunshine, but it was also because of the excellent treatment he'd received at the Royal Adelaide Hospital. His full disability pension meant that there was no real need for him to work in the asbestos factory, but he liked to keep himself occupied. The job also helped cover the costs of his trips to England.

In his final tour of duty for the RAF, Uncle Gregory had flown as navigator in a five-man Canberra bomber. His pilot was Group Captain Ralph Lane, who in 1957 became only the third pilot in the history of the RAF to win a DSO in peacetime. Lane died in 1964 when he fell down the stairs of a house he'd designed for himself in the hills behind Shepheard's Hotel, a small town near Montreal. Despite the fact that he'd been blind for nearly seven years, Lane's fall was rumoured to have been a suicide.

Uncle Gregory went to the funeral in Shepheard's Hotel. It was very well attended. That was the year he missed the TT.

In February the Vice-Chancellor finally summoned Julian to her office. She was keen to discuss the vandalization and theft of property properly belonging to the School of Medicine. She meant the Indian corpse. There was also the small matter of the animal testing centre housed in the Long Ashton Tobacco Research Unit, where sixteen cynomolgus monkeys had caused eighty-five thousand pounds worth of damage in a single night. Julian was reminded, in no uncertain terms, of the air-conditioned audio-room which the Buchanan Imperial Cigarette Company had recently sponsored in the basement of the University Library.

The Vice-Chancellor was aware of Carr's distinguished academic record and his recent election as President of the Union, but she couldn't possibly overstate her personal disapproval of this kind of meaningless and juvenile behaviour. She was therefore left with no alternative but to attribute blame to chemical imbalances in Carr's brain, caused by the clinical tests he'd volunteered to follow on behalf of his Faculty.

Carr's successful completion of the course of drugs, despite certain unwelcome side-effects, had been taken into account. As had his respect for the University's need for confidentiality in such matters. He was therefore excused with a stern reprimand, and a warning that any future indiscipline would be punished with the utmost severity.

Walter is so happy today that he sometimes lets his pipe go out. I watch him playing and winning at dominoes with Jonesy Paul and old Ben Bradley. It's like the beginning of the club all over again, except that I can't share the absolutely incalculable joy which is a cigarette at each and every moment I want one.

Jonesy Paul looks old enough to be a contemporary of Walter's, but he did something in a war with submarines so he must be younger. On doctor's orders he smokes the lowest tar L and B, but he makes a point of ripping off the filter. He is telling old Ben Bradley that if any one of the many ships carrying radioactive waste into British ports were to sink, then cancer would devastate coastal communities for generations to come.

'And they warn you against a little cigarette.'

'Dominoes,' Walter says, and deals.

Old Ben Bradley is only fifty-three. He is called old Ben because fourteen years ago his first son Ben turned professional and went to play Rugby League for Hull Kingston Rovers. Last year, the whole Bradley family had a box at Wembley to watch the Silk Cut Challenge Cup final. The Rovers were the underdogs and they lost.

At this moment I envy Walter his pipe. I envy Jonesy Paul his filterless L & B and I envy old Ben Bradley his JPS. At this moment I envy everybody everywhere everything, which I know is stupid but that's how I feel.

Lucy was gradually wearing me down, wearing out my resistance. Sometimes, she deliberately provoked me by going next door to smoke a cigarette with Julian. I could hear their voices through the wall, interrupted by silences the length of an inhaled breath or a snatched kiss. I asked Lucy what they talked about.

'Cigarettes.'

'But what do you do?'

'We smoke.'

When I insisted she tell me what they really talked about, she just threatened to go next door again. She made me nervous. With her slim fingers she made a point of pulling each Marlboro from her pack like a Lucky Dip where the prize was always the same, and always satisfactory. She coolly lit each cigarette and left me to fidget between different weapons of defence: a folder of statistics sent by my mother; the foul taste of Miss Bryant's Embassy Regal; Uncle Gregory dead at 48; the ransom of my mother's love.

But there was little comfort in being well-armed now that Lucy spoke only the one smoky language, the *Hello Baby*, easy to understand. She had cast herself in the role of a medieval princess who could be wooed and won, where smoke-a-cigarette was her modern version of swim-a-lake, climb-a-mountain, kill-a-dragon. She worked on making me believe that cigarettes could be the one moment to change everything, as if all I had to do was smoke like Humphrey Bogart to end up with the girl and my own piano-player.

I began to wonder whether cigarettes had changed since Miss Bryant. Otherwise, how could Lucy Hinton and Julian Carr and 33% of the population (!) who I'd never really thought about before ever have learnt to smoke with such an impression of pleasure?

We walked from the pub across a failed area of open space towards a five-storey block at the hub of the Estates. Theo handed me one of the shopping bags and I was surprised by how light it was. I looked around for muggers and thieves but it must have been too cold. I kept looking, just in case.

Surprisingly, the pub had almost been fun. Theo had the invisible but convincing invulnerability of the slightly strange, the uncommon man. He made me feel safe and I stayed close to him. We played pinball, and the ends of the longest strands of his grey hair trembled as he tried to tilt his ball into favourable alleys and nearly always succeeded. He beat me by two hundred and nineteen million points.

Inside the block we took a wasted shudder-proof lift to the fourth floor. There was an outside walkway with numbered doors spaced by frosted windows. In front of the door furthest from the lift-shaft there was a queue of three or four women, and I followed Theo towards them. Under his breath, Theo said: 'Call me Dr Barclay.'

He said hello to all the women, and introduced me as his

new assistant. Nobody took much notice. Then he took a Chubb key from the pocket of his coat and opened door number forty-seven. He invited us all inside.

I never really understood why Julian did it. It wasn't as though he needed the money.

He looked at me seriously, his square jaw jutting slightly.

'It was a matter of principle. They would have tested the drugs on animals otherwise, which would have been totally pointless.'

'Because of the restraint again?'

'No. Because rabbits are not in the market for a male contraceptive pill. You know, if you wanted to do some tests I could set you up.'

'Well thanks, Julian, but all the same. Considering.'

'You can earn up to fifteen hundred pounds for a ten week course.'

'No really, Julian.'

'I know you're short of money. You could take Lucy on holiday with fifteen hundred pounds. You could take her to the Caribbean.'

'We're not going on holiday together. And anyway, we're just good friends.'

'Any family history of madness? Any cancer in the family?'

'I'm not going to do it, Julian. Look what happened to you.'

'No allergies? No drink problem. Solid and dependable. You'd be perfect. Look, if you ever find yourself short of cash, just think of the animals you'd be saving.'

I could always tell which of my mother's letters were more important to her by the number of exclamation marks, each

71

one a wide-eyed whoop!! on the page. There was one particular letter where I counted thirty-seven, along with four separate articles about smoking, which was also a record.

The bad news was that 15–20% of all British deaths turned out to be smoking-related.

Limb amputation due to vascular disease was a newly discovered risk.

Reference was made to Buerger's disease, to Chronic Mucus Hypersecretion and Obstructive Lung Disease. There was Benzo-a-pyrene. There were one hundred thousand dead every year in the hidden holocaust. And it could at last be confirmed that children who regularly attended religious services were less likely to smoke. It said so in one of the articles.

There was no good news. Only vitamin A, which is found in carrots, made a tiny recordable difference in efforts to combat lung cancer.

Of course I immediately recognized the letter and the cuttings as a special barrage of love. My mother was letting me know how much she loved me. It wasn't until the end of the third and last page that she let slip the supposedly confidential information that my father (Mr Simpson the Tobacconist! Of all people!!) had been provisionally nominated for an OBE, for services to the community.

This morning, on my fifth day without cigarettes, Dr Julian Carr telephoned for the first time since Theo's funeral. He knew full well I knew it was him. I could hear him in the silence, inhaling.

He let me listen to him smoke. I had nothing to say to him but I didn't put the phone down. Eventually, he whispered, very softly:

'Feeling a bit squiffy, are we?'
Then I put down the phone.

In a way, the films were right. If I smoked a cigarette and made love to Lucy then I wouldn't drop down dead before the night was over. But dreamers find it hard to reduce the world to its todays and calendar tomorrows, and I was also worried about collapsing in the middle of an awards ceremony many years in the future.

For all I knew Lucy could be toying with me. She might be using me as an early experiment in her masterplan to seduce Julian. She may have slept with him already. She might still be sleeping with him. Perhaps when she went next door they never talked at all, just fell into each other's arms and made mad passionate love and the noises which came through the wall only *sounded* like conversation. The time she spent with me could be a trick like her pregnancy. And if I committed myself to her by a simple act of breathing that wasn't a breathing of air, then how could I be sure she wouldn't turn on me and laugh, perhaps while the smoke was still settling in my lungs?

The time she'd acted pregnant: it was late and I was drunk but she'd fooled me. She'd made me feel gullible and inexperienced and stupid. I didn't want the same thing to happen again but I didn't want to smoke a cigarette either. I asked her if she knew what she was doing to her health.

'I know, I know. I'll be dead at thirty and so will my babies. I kill passers-by in the street and total strangers in restaurants. I am personally responsible for the murder of children in public parks. It could hardly be worse, could it?'

It was a flat with two rooms, one behind the other, then a kitchen, and then behind that a bathroom. All the rooms were

73

in a row like train carriages. In the first room there were chairs around the walls and magazines on a low table: a waiting room. The clinic itself took place in the inner room. I made coffee and lit the gas-fire. Then I sat behind Theo and watched.

They came in one by one, and each stayed for between five and ten minutes. Theo sat on one side of a table in the middle of the room, and with his 'patient' sitting opposite him it reminded me of prison-visiting the way I'd seen it on television. Everyone who came in called him Dr Barclay, and in the three hours we were there every visit followed the same pattern. Someone would come in, sit down, tell Theo why they started smoking and why they carried on, and then at the end he would give them cigarettes. It was all formally done, and there was no show of gratitude.

At the end of the clinic we were left with a single carton of 200 Kensitas. I called for a taxi which would only come as far as the pub, and as we walked back across the open space, Theo said,

'Best keep it quiet.'

'Yes Theo.'

'Doesn't look too good. Tobacco men handing out cigarettes.'

'No, I can see that.'

'Freud's early work was on fish. He specialized in the noses of fish.'

'I didn't know.'

'Nobody likes Freud anymore.'

'No.'

'But he was right about one thing. Everybody has a story.'

'Yes,' I said. 'I can see that too.'

Outside Lilly's Pasties, the beggar was still begging. Theo gave him the carton of Kensitas.

DAY

6

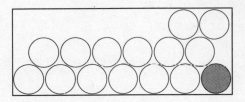

Time, memory; the usual problems.

I remember her bones. When I dreamed her she had no bones at all, and I hadn't expected her pelvis and her hips to be so hard. I hadn't expected her to *move* so much.

But that was later. First I had to surrender, which was inevitable once I reached the stage where every morning I woke up with a nagging sense of dissatisfaction. It was as if all the dreams I never remembered had secretly ended unhappily, and only Lucy could change the endings. But then Lucy was also the smoking of a cigarette.

Once too often, she stood up and shook out her hair and threatened to go next door.

'Why?'

'Julian watches me smoke without frowning.'

'Wait.'

'What now?'

'Come to dinner.'

'Where?'

'Here. On Monday, no, Tuesday.'

'I'm getting very impatient, Gregory. Pretty soon I'm just going to give up.'

'Great news.'

'You know what I mean. Give up on you. I've tried everything and I don't believe you even like me.'

'You know I like you.'

'Then prove it.'

'If you say yes to dinner, I will.'

'You'll what?'

'You know what. I promise. We can make it a special occasion.'

She lit a cigarette and smiled.

'Please, Lucy.'

'I'll dress up shall I? If we both know what it means.'

The more often I went to the Estates, the more radically I had to revise my opinion of Theo. His approach was disciplined, rigorous, the exact opposite of his hair. I concluded he wasn't entirely confident he was doing the right thing.

His prescriptions for cigarettes were never automatic. There was once a lank young man, in a surplus East German combat jacket and blondish dreadlocks. In a bad teeth contest he would have run Theo a close second. He didn't sit down, and his head bobbed in a reflex memory of years viced in a walkman. Or maybe it was just because he was completely stoned.

'It's like they told me you hand out cigarettes.'

Theo said he was a doctor.

'Like to the oppressed, man.'

'I conduct counselling clinics.'

'That last woman had 200 Raffles. I saw her.'

'Tell me how you started smoking.'

'I'm a traveller. I could really handle a few fags, you know?'

'Do you like travelling?'

'Yeah, well. Like it's the only honest response?'

'Sorry.'

'A couple of hundred would be fine.'

'I'm mostly just an endurance man. I'm sorry.'

Another time a young boy said his mum had sent him to pick up a packet of Embassy Legals. The boy had the face of an apple-eater and a milk-drinker. He had freckles and a hard, cheeky look that in adults becomes a kind of endearing bluntness. Theo told him to sit down and unrolled the photo of the diseased lung. When the boy understood what it was his eyes opened wide and he stood up and backed towards the door. He couldn't keep his eyes off the photo. He said:

'I don't believe you.'

'Believe me.'

'It's just a piece of bubble-gum.'

Then he ran through the waiting-room and away, leaving the door wide open so that we could all hear his trainers slapping along the walk-way.

'The youth of today,' Theo said, shaking his head.

She took off her clothes. When she was naked she shaped herself into the bean-bag. I remember her bones.

Tuesday arrived. I pulled my desk into the middle of the room and covered it with my spare blue duvet cover. I bought two red candles and stuck them in lumps of Blu-Tack. I went next door to borrow Julian's desk-chair. I was very nervous.

'You need hot food for a seduction,' Julian said.

He thought he always knew best. I planned to give Lucy three courses, all of them cold so I wouldn't have to leave the room once while she was with me. Julian pointed out that I'd also chosen the wrong colour wine.

'You could take her out for an Indian,' he said.

Lucy had once told me that I shouldn't upset myself about Julian because he didn't fancy her. But anyone can change their mind, and I thought he might be jealous and getting worse at hiding it, which was one more worry to add to the already considerable anxiety which was gathering in my chest, making me linger too long in Julian's doorway, still holding his desk-chair. I asked him if he thought Lucy liked me. I mean really.

'Of course she likes you.'

'How do you know?'

'She told me.'

'Did she?'

'She said she liked you because you were straight.'

'Straight?'

'Square.'

'I'm not square.'

'You hardly drink. You don't smoke.'

'Did she really say that?'

'Why should I lie about it?'

'You told me that all smokers lie.'

'I was lying.'

The Marlboro cowboy never had conversations like these. He was totally unhurried, unworried, unmodern. He was exactly how I imagined myself, tomorrow.

Some months before he died Theo gave a plant to Emmy Gaston, Walter's daughter, as a present. Today Walter has brought the plant back and it doesn't look very healthy. It is about a metre high, but the broad leaves look sorry for themselves, slack in the mouth, in full contemplation of death. There are no flowers on the plant. Theo told Emmy there would be white flowers.

'She wants you to save it,' Walter says. 'She imagines Theo passed on the secret. And she gave me a message but I've forgotten what it was. I think she wanted you to meet somebody.'

I tell him not to worry, and he doesn't. He settles in his chair and starts puffing at his pipe, flicking through a *National Geographic* feature about cash crops in the Pacific basin. He is wearing a tweed flat cap, with a crimson-feathered fishing fly attached to the cloth stretched over the peak.

I move the plant slightly to the left so that I can see him better. He looks up and asks me what I want. I'm embarrassed that he catches me looking so I say nothing and bend my head over the desk and write this sentence and will carry on writing it until he goes back to his magazine as if none of this ever happened and now he is reading the magazine again and I think I can stop.

She was very generous and she refused to let me fumble. Her limbs curled out of the bean-bag, wrapping me in.

Faced with the possible intimacy of the evening, I felt friendless. I wasn't sufficiently close to anyone else to take the risk of explaining how much Lucy meant to me. I couldn't ring home, obviously, and either I was feeling guilty in advance or my mother already suspected something. The last time I'd phoned I'd asked her about Uncle Gregory's cancer.

'Are you sure he got it from smoking?'

'Of course I am.'

'I mean, are you absolutely positive that this is factually accurate?'

'Gregory. Your Uncle Gregory smoked sixty high-tar ciga-rettes every day of his adult life. What else did you want him to die of? You're not thinking of smoking are you?'

'Of course not.'

'Promise?'

Julian didn't understand either. He became arch and sugges-tive when I wanted him to be sympathetic, as though Lucy was just another blonde girl. He said the important thing was to stay calm and not to worry. I asked him if he was going out for the evening and he said he didn't know. I was terrified, abject before my desire.

I lit the candles with my Swan Vestas. I turned off the electric light. Wanting something to do with my hands, I opened the bottle of wine. Julian had said it needed to breathe. I was wearing a tie. I was a boy dressed up and pretending to be a man in one of the smallest rooms in the William Cabot Hall of Residence for Men, and I suddenly realized that nothing here could possibly match the incomparable success I'd imagined for the evening. I felt out of place, absurd, worthless.

And anyway, it was too late. She wasn't coming. She would have found something more interesting to do than dinner on this evening with me, like watch television. I licked my fingers to snuff out the candles, and then decided it would be less dangerous to blow them out instead when there was a gentle knock, three times, tap tap tap, on the door.

A club for smokers is not a new idea. At the end of the nineteenth century there were a number of smoking clubs thriving in London. They were called Divans and among the most famous were Whites in Devonshire Street and The Slipper Club in the Strand. Divan as a word derives from the Persian. It has vacillated its way through the English language swerving in meaning from a collection of poems to a courthouse to a room entirely open on one side towards a garden to a type of long seat but at one stage stopping at a club for smokers. The word divan then, is a good example of how a single point of departure, in this case a word, can come to mean many different things and travel far beyond itself.

The Divans of the late nineteenth century allowed gentlemen to smoke in peace (see Disraeli, *Endymion* XX 1880). They were also places of refuge from women, who were strictly excluded from membership. It's different now of course, at the end of another century. Smoke has been democratized, and it features in everyone's photographed past. It has become a sign of the commonness of our humanity, the link between a Maori and a Mau-mau. It has been the century's open addiction, the world-wide admission that breathing by itself is simply not enough.

But it's different now, like I said. It turns out that pleasure kills, as the strictest of history's theologians always promised. A hundred years ago it must have all seemed so splendid, such an innocent pleasure so cleverly packaged and so obviously harmless that with hindsight it almost convinces, as feared by the Seventh Day Adventists, as the most perfect invention of hell itself.

'When I first wake up and feel depressed. When I'm tired and worn out or when the children get a bit stroppy. When I'm violently mad and about to throttle them. You know.'

'Here. Take these whenever you like. Do not exceed the recommended dose.'

It was mostly women who came to Theo's clinics, often with young children. They had a lifetime's habit of sacrificing their own desires to please other people, and smoking was the solitary repeatable indulgence that could be called exclusively their own. Small comfort through it was, it was still a comfort.

'I was sort of on my own, and you can't really sit and read a book so you think what the heck can I do and instead of twiddling your thumbs. I don't know what made me do it. I just went round the corner, bought a packet of cigarettes and smoked a cigarette.'

'Here. Take these whenever you like. Do not exceed the recommended dose.'

Most of them were unfamiliar with the blind optimism needed to give up anything as consoling as cigarettes. One woman said that at least finding a match was a reason to get up in the morning.

'Sometimes I put the baby outside the flat, shut the door and put the radio on full blast and I've sat down and had a cigarette, calmed down and fetched him in again. Then I give him his tea. I think it's all in the mind really, you know like it calms you down, just in your mind.'

'Here, take these.'

Her hair, released, fanned into the black of the bean-bag. The allelujah of eyes closed and open, open and closed. Her shoulders.

'The carrots aren't glazed. They're more alert than that.'

It was going brilliantly. Lucy was dressed as a gypsy, with Creole hoops in her ears and her black hair tied back. She was wearing make-up which brought her features into focus like a portrait photograph, and she had a wraparound top thing and a long red skirt, threaded through with gold. The candle-light flecked deeply in her eyes and I realized this was the point and I hoped it was doing the same for me. She was laughing a lot, which made me think she was happy. Her teeth gleamed. She touched my arm when she wanted me to really *visualize* her sister in a wet-suit, trying to water-ski. She was happy about everything that ever was. She was absolutely bloody fantastic.

After the starter (grated carrot salad), she lit two cigarettes at once. I drank some wine and watched her hands. She offered me one of the cigarettes.

'This is a magic cigarette,' she said.

She leaned towards me. 'It's enchanted. Whoever smokes

this cigarette will fall in love with the next person they see.'

I took the cigarette from her hand.

'Will they live happily ever after?'

'Yes.'

I offered it back to her.

'Why don't you smoke it yourself then?'

'I will, once someone falls in love with me first.'

I looked at the magic cigarette and watched it burn. Then I placed it carefully in the Courage ashtray so that the filter rested in the indentation designed for just this kind of emergency. I dropped a twenty-pence coin over the glowing ash and watched the smoke dwindle and die. Just like Lucy had taught me.

'Inevitable,' I said. 'But we haven't even had the main course yet.'

'Oh we're still a long way from the main course.'

I poured more wine, and she complimented me on the way I'd arranged the slices of avocado at right angles to the smoked chicken.

Between 1945 and 1980 there were 423 publicly recorded atmospheric nuclear tests. There are thought to have been at least the same number again which were never announced. Radioactive fallout from these explosions is mostly in the form of Carbon-14 and Plutonium-329. Carbon-14 converts to carbon dioxide and is taken up by plants and then incorporated into organic material and the food chain. It has a half-life of 5,730 years. Plutonium-329 has a half-life of 24,400 years. Between them these two isotopes are expected to cause 2.4 million deaths from cancer, 670,000 of them before the end of the century.

In July 1962, the US exploded a 1.4 megaton bomb in space, 400 kilometres above Johnston Atoll. As a result of this explosion nitrogen oxides were injected into the stratosphere, where they continue to catalyse ozone destruction. The breakdown of the ozone layer is a primary factor in the increase of skin cancers in the southern hemisphere.

Statistically, by comparison to the effects of nuclear testing, cancers caused by known carcinogens such as asbestos or the polycyclic hydrocarbons in used engine oil are negligible. Between 1945 and 1980 there were also 1,400 nuclear tests conducted underground, the full consequences of which have yet to be calculated.

The Estates confirmed most of the conclusions I'd reached in Paris. It was better to have money than not. Don't involve yourself because the worst will always happen. And if the worst doesn't happen then you can still be run over by a bus.

Since de-regulation there had been no bus service to or from the Estates. There were still fights and broken-bottles and sometimes even petrol-bombs. But worst of all was the sheer bus-crushing tedium of the repeats of underfunded days and the kids crying their eyes out and the other one hundred and ninety-nine people in exactly the same position as you and all of them after the job you wanted, which you only wanted because it was the only one on offer. Have a fag. Calm down.

Once, Theo sent me down to the Estates on my own. He had a cold.

'You should see a doctor if you're ill.'

'I'm not ill. Never been ill in my life.'

I went down to flat No. 47 by taxi and handed out the familiar advice and the cartons of 200 cigarettes. I acted like a doctor and kept my mind on the great mercy of the thin white tube which could communicate the idea of what it meant to want something and also be able to have it. It offered a small proof that desire wasn't exclusively a source of pain. Theo had taught me this.

There was a new girl I hadn't seen before. She looked very tired and her thin brown hair hung stranded over her face. She was younger than me and she was carrying a small child wrapped in a V-neck sweater. She looked over my head when she spoke.

'I was meant to be with her dad, but he left me when she was one day old.'

'Here,' I said, 'take as many of these as you like. Do not exceed the recommended dose.'

Her eyes met mine for the first time.

'I don't even smoke,' she said.

It was as if what we'd done was exactly what she'd wanted to do. I remember her bones and everything else I mostly speculate because I can never remember it clearly enough. Her hair, her shoulders, her bones. Her legs, I think. I think it was over very quickly and it was never over. It was too soon and too late and she was unhappy and never happier.

After the dessert, a crême brulée I bought at the Co-op, she went and made a show of collapsing well-fed and content into the bean-bag. She had the ashtray with her and she lifted up the magic cigarette. There was a little kink where the twenty-pence piece had been. It was time to fall in love with the next person I saw and live happily ever after. I said:

'You once said the situation had to be right.'

'Yes,' she said, 'but it's a little late to go looking for a cinema queue. Now is now.'

'No, I mean another situation you said.'

'Sport?'

'Lucy.'

'Cigarette first, my darling.'

'After, you said. You said it was better after.'

I knelt down beside the bean-bag and kissed her. The literature was right. She tasted like an ashtray.

Uncle Gregory was hospitalized in Adelaide after the first
British atomic test at Maralinga in South Australia. He was
the navigator in the Canberra bomber detailed to take re-
connaissance photographs of the atomic cloud. The crew of
the Canberra on 27 September 1956 had been issued with
special protective goggles, which were ordinary goggles fitted
with smoked glass.

When the bomb detonated, the Canberra was at five thousand
feet and one mile from ground zero, as planned. Uncle
Gregory, who was responsible for the photographic equipment,
and Captain Ralph Lane, the pilot, were both blinded instantly.
Lane was subsequently awarded his DSO for flying the Canberra back to Woomera rocket station following only the
instructions radioed through by the control tower.

After three weeks in the Royal Adelaide Hospital, Uncle
Gregory recovered limited vision in both eyes, thanks largely
to the skill of the Australian doctors. Captain Lane never recov-
ered his sight. Both men were honourably discharged from the
RAF with full disability pensions and a copy of the Official
Secrets Act.

For the rest of his life Uncle Gregory would blink excessively. This made him look as if he never believed a word
anyone said. As if constantly, day after day, he couldn't believe
his eyes.

I miss Bananas like vitamins. I miss him terribly. There is still Haemoglobin, for what a dog's worth. When Walter lights up his pipe Haemoglobin lurches towards him, salivating. 'Good dog,' Walter says, patting him on the head, 'good Pavlov's dog.'

Bananas had an addiction to nicotine which was altogether more intense. It made me proud of him, as if it was equivalent to fetching my slippers or jumping through hoops. I haven't filled an ashtray for nearly six days: he'd probably have left me by now.

I've watered the plant. Before nodding off, Walter spent some time explaining to me how life was better when he was younger because there were no statistics. He'd just read in the *National Geographic* that more people had now died this century than in both World Wars, thus proving that peace was a terrible and dangerous thing.

The *National Geographic* didn't say that, Walter did.

'I don't smoke,' she said, 'and I've never smoked, so don't bother asking. I don't intend to beat around the bush. Are you a real doctor?'

She was very different to the women who usually came to Theo's clinics, if only because she was wearing extraordinary make-up. She had spectacular black crow's feet and dark lines either side of her mouth. Her hair was in a tight bun whited with talc, but her grey eyes were bright and defiant.

'I'm a real doctor,' Theo said.

'What about him?'

'He's my assistant.'

She examined us both very closely. 'Have you ever given any cigarettes to an old man?'

'I have never given cigarettes to an old man,' Theo said.

'I shall be brief. I live with my father, who is increasingly frail. Despite my protests, he insists on continuing to smoke, ignoring the harm it has done to his health. I personally consider smoking an illogical, irrational and stupid habit, as do most reasonably intelligent people. However, it has come to my attention that you and your assistant have been giving out free cigarettes to the inhabitants of these estates and this area generally. I have no idea why you are doing this, and I can find no sympathy in my heart for either of you. I shall be straight-forward. My father is the only person I have left and I object to him killing himself.'

'I'm sorry,' Theo said. 'I didn't mean to offend anybody.'

'I am not yet offended. However, if I catch you giving cigarettes to my father I shall personally put an end to all this.'

She looked derisively at Theo, at me, and then at the various posters Theo had pinned to the walls. 'You should take this warning seriously,' she said. 'I have a great many friends. Do I make myself clear?'

'Yes,' Theo said, 'I'm sorry.'

'Don't mention it.'

We made love on the black corduroy bean-bag with the triangular label saying NON-FLAMMABLE. I remember her bones. Candle-shadows. At some stage, in its real life version, it came to an end. And there were no tricks. At the last moment she didn't transform into a cackling hag, laughing at my presumption to desire her. She didn't fool me. She wore no disguise, under her clothes.

She smiled, as if we'd done exactly what she'd wanted to do. The bean-bag rustled as she relaxed back into it. Her face was flushed, and so was her neck. She blew some hair from her cheek. She pushed herself up onto her elbows, making me

90

raise myself up on my arms. She stretched over for the magic cigarette and came back again.

'Let's both smoke it,' she said. 'Let's smoke it between us. I'll show you how.'

I remember how kindly she said that. It was a beautiful thing to say. She lit the cigarette and drew in deeply, instantly falling in love. And I remember what I did next. I slowly withdrew from her. I looked at the cigarette. I wiped my eyebrow. I asked her if she wanted some coffee.

'You just put it between your lips and breathe. You'll like it.'

I said I also had tea.

'Not too deeply at first.'

English Breakfast.

'Come on, Gregory, don't be a bastard. Take the cigarette.'

Lapsang Souchong. Earl Grey. I turned away from her and fumbled with cups and various tea-bags. One of them broke, spraying my hand with tea-dust. Darjeeling. I knew she didn't want any tea.

'You total total bastard.'

DAY

7

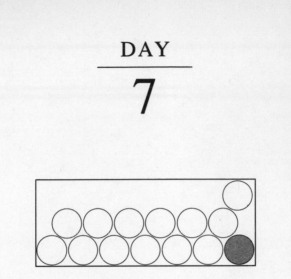

Even the weather hates me. The wind is furious and the rain bends the windows. Sometimes, there are hailstones. A hurricane is not out of the question. A typhoon, a tidal-wave, a flood, a deluge, an end of the world or worse. Probably worse.

I have no idea where Walter is. It is mid-morning and nearly one week since I stopped smoking and I'm alone in the middle of the weather with only an empty house around me. A dog for company. Haemoglobin keeps turning a figure of eight, one loop on the seat of Walter's chair and the other on the carpet. He misses his morning pipe and I consider throwing him out into the rain, because I miss tobacco too and what has he ever done for me?

Calm down. Write some words. *Substitute.*

Walter is like a Carmen No 6, and so is my old black bean-bag. Theo is like cigarettes, and so is Lucy and so is Bananas, and so are all the ashtrays Bananas would have hoarded. All of them are absent, all gone. I am left deserted, abandoned, blameless, and I feel deeply sorry for the person I am now, my knee drumming the underside of the table, foolishly trying to exist without hourly satisfaction.

Reduce the craving to its basics: I do not want a cigarette. I do not want. I do not. I do.

He never used to be scared of the weather. Haemoglobin, while circling, has started to whine and I wonder how it would look if I smoked a cigarette out of kindness to an animal. I wish Walter was here. Just the one. If Walter was here I promise I'd even listen to his Firing Squad story.

95

Everyone sympathizes with kindness to animals.

Theo inhaled his first cigarette the day he was born, though only passively, and he claimed this as the reason he loved the morning smell of tobacco smoke on clothes. It reminded him of his mother. He didn't smoke a cigarette of his own until he was twenty-six.

His mother's side of the family was dominated by non-conformist Scottish Calvinists, none of whom ever doubted their pre-destined place in heaven. It was a family of preachers and missionaries and martyrs, strangers to doubt, and Theo's mother was no exception. She smoked forty Black Cats a day and sometimes drank excessively while smoking. Frequently, she crossed the road without looking either to the left or the right.

Theo's father ran away while Theo was still a child. Complaining of smoke in the curtains and ash in the butter, he took a steam-train to Edinburgh and was last heard of living in Morningside with a non-denominational croupier.

This last detail might have been a joke. Theo often joked about his mother. He told her life as a story and withheld the secret of how she acted and how she felt in the quiet moments when her story wasn't happening to her. For all I know they were never still, the two of them, together and unhurried, with nothing particular on their minds.

She called me a bastard several more times and refused to look at me while she dressed. She turned away. The bean-bag had impressed her back and her buttocks with thinly-spliced parallels of corduroy. I asked her to stay. I asked her why she was leaving.

'Fuck off,' she said.

She slammed the door on her way out and I heard her go into Julian's room. I heard the word bastard again, through the thin wall. I pulled on my shirt and trousers thinking, I mean, it was only a matter of a little cigarette. Compared to her decision to be naked in my bean-bag. It was only a cigarette. I just needed to follow her and talk to her, and even though I didn't really understand why she was upset I considered this my first lesson (as a man) in understanding that women were impossible to understand. Of course she'd come back, or she wouldn't have slept with me in the first place. Obviously. It was only a little cigarette, a tube of paper full of *dead leaves*. For God's sake.

I didn't knock. She was sitting on the edge of Julian's bean-bag, which was a kind of khaki colour and didn't match her hair. She inhaled deeply from a cigarette and hugged her knees.

'Hi there,' I said.

'Go away.'

'Lucy, I don't understand.'

When she sneered, her face became heart-shaped.

'You can't even tell when a girl's pregnant.'

Julian was shuffling about, head down, patting his pockets, looking under his pillow, opening the drawer in his desk.

He slammed the desk-drawer a little too hard and swore.

'Here,' Lucy said.

She passed him her lit cigarette.

'Lucy, please!'

Julian took the cigarette and inhaled deeply, as if at last he had in his hands and his mouth and his lungs the only thing he'd ever wanted. He blew the smoke up to the ceiling in rings, then looked at Lucy to say thank you. She smiled blankly, reached out her hand, took back the cigarette, inhaled.

97

And then I realized. Julian Carr and Lucy Hinton, right in front of me, in the room next to my own, with no regard whatsoever for my feelings, were sharing the magic cigarette.

I kept to a kind of twenty-hour clock. The Carmens measured the hours which paced the days, and the Estates and *Tomorrow's World* marked off the weeks and the months. I counted my birthdays past, 23, 24, 25, glad that Paris had cured me of caring.

I played a lot of pinball, until I hardly ever lost by more than five million points, and then in flat No. 47 we listened to other smokers' stories, often the same stories, and handed out cigarettes. There was never any sense of heightened experience about the transaction. Instead it had a kind of necessary English drabness to it, as if to disguise the fact that it was necessary.

Sometimes there were other visitors. Every two months or so the small boy with the apple-eater's face would try again for cigarettes. It was like watching him grow up, evolving different solutions to the same problem, and he once came with a girl who looked like his sister. He pushed her into the room in front of him.

'This is Mary and she wants 20 Player's Navy Cut for her mum.' He looked at us hopefully. 'Her mum's in the Navy.'

'Don't be stupid,' the girl said, 'and I don't want any cigarettes.'

'Shut up you.'

'Well I don't. It's a disgusting smelly habit and it kills people.'

She pushed past him and left. He looked unhappy and dissatisfied for at least ten seconds, and then he was thinking about something else.

'Can I look at the bubble-gum picture again?'

Theo told the boy he could have a poster of Popeye, if he kept a lookout for an old woman with grey eyes.

'My real name's Jamie,' the boy said.

By nature, I worry. Today I worry that Walter has been blown into traffic. I worry he has been battered to death by a rogue squall of hail-stones. That the wind has tumbled him along the street like paper, breaking every brittle bone in his body. I just worry, because without cigarettes I am more natural.

It was here in this room that we celebrated Walter's one hundredth birthday with an EGM of the Suicide Club. Actually it was one day after his birthday because his family had claimed the day itself. Walter's daughter Emmy baked three cakes in the shape of one zero zero, and to prove the continued strength of his lungs Walter insisted on blowing out all the candles by himself. Later, as they were leaving the party, three of his great-nephews and a cousin complained that the icing tasted of St Bruno.

On behalf of the club, Theo had wanted to blend a hundred strains of tobacco into a special anniversary smoking mixture. However, there weren't a hundred different strains of tobacco, so instead he compiled and bound in calf's leather a collection of 100 interesting facts about smoking. He pinned a dark-brown tobacco-leaf, like the dry-veined wing of a giant moth, into the inside-back cover.

Walter didn't dare take the book home and I have it here on the desk. Inside, used as a bookmark, is Walter's telegram of congratulations from the Queen. It smells of King Edward cigars.

The last time I saw Uncle Gregory, in 1971, he was as brown as a varnished boomerang. He was so brown that his tan almost masked the dark moles on his shoulders and back. He'd spent the Australian summer travelling from city to city following the Ashes Test series and the Benson and Hedges one-day internationals. Whenever England were batting he made a point of taking off his shirt, closing his eyes and tipping his face up to the sun. In the second Test England occupied the crease for almost two days and Uncle Gregory didn't see a single ball.

That was the last time England won the Ashes in Australia, but back in our summer, watching the rain scar the windows, Uncle Gregory shocked me when he said he'd been supporting the Australians. He didn't even have a good word for John Edrich.

He stayed with us for nearly a month, sitting shirtless in the back garden under the whirligig washing line, blinking furiously, mending the motor-mower and the washing machine and anything else that Dad was too busy at work to mend. He clamped his cigarettes between his teeth and stubbed out the ends in an old puncture repair tin from the shed.

'You're just feeling sorry for yourself.'
'Can I have more coffee?'
'Stop moping, Gregory. She's not coming round.'
'I never said she was.'
'You've been moping for weeks. Go and see her.'
'I'm not moping.'
'Don't be frightened, Gregory. She's only a girl.'
If I'd been a character in one of Lucy's old films I could have laid siege to her, eventually climbing up the drainpipe to her window on the third floor, thereby saving her forever from

the terrible mistake of ignoring me. As it was, I had no history of visiting Lucy's room. I'd never been comfortable there, either because there was no Julian Carr next door, or because her walls were covered with postcards of male torsos which only roughly approximated to mine. I don't know.

'Go on, Gregory, grab destiny by the throat and shake it.'

So I went to see her, and for once I found myself standing in an open doorway trying to get in instead of keeping someone out. Lucy's friend Kim was there, and neither of them made me feel very welcome. Lucy looked beautiful. Her black hair was tied back and it looked very clean. I asked if I could talk to her on her own and they both said no.

'I really am sorry, Lucy.'

'Oh for Christ's sake,' Kim said. 'You still don't get it do you? It was only a bet. And now it's finished. Over.'

'Sorry?'

'It was a bet. Now why don't you just fuck off?'

An old white man in a woolly Rastafari hat. It wasn't always the same.

'Have you seen an old woman?' he said.

'What does she look like?'

'Brownish hair. Energetic.'

'Your wife?'

'My daughter. On the warpath.'

'Sorry. We haven't seen her.'

'Well never mind. How about some fags instead then?'

I think Theo refused because Walter was altogether too cheerful. He wasn't even disappointed when Theo said no. Instead, he asked if he could stay and smoke a pipe. Then he sat there and told us all about the Estates, which used to be full of proper houses like his, sensible and two-storeyed so that you could throw the cat out of any window in the house without killing it.

'In the old days it was all equally crap of course,' he said. 'But we were promised something better than this. That's what hurts.'

In those days, Walter wasn't even a hundred years old.

'Your daughter,' Theo reminded him quietly. 'Is she about my age? Very striking eyes? Very grey, very handsome eyes?'

Sometimes, she would spend the last of her monthly salary on cigarettes when Theo needed new shoes. This never occurred to either of them as a genuine option. When they went shopping, unable to afford cakes and tea-shops, they would rest and warm themselves in the public library, and while his mother argued with the tired librarian about whether cigarette smoke damaged the pages of books, Theo read his way through the science shelves. After insisting on her right to smoke in a public place, Theo's mother would flip through the index cards in the catalogue, looking for the pseudonym of her runaway husband. First she tried variant spellings of the name Barclay, and then anagrams of the variant spellings. Then she would just flick through at random, sometimes stopping at a name or title which interested her, working on the principle that if her husband had published a book she was sure to recognize his pseudonym as soon as she saw it.

This was all part of her exhaustive effort to trace him, which was motivated by the desire to tell him that he had not been, and therefore by definition never would be, chosen by God. She wanted him to know that God had annulled their marriage for precisely this reason. As for his new life, with a croupier or without, God wasn't sufficiently interested to have an opinion. This was all she wanted to say, so as to save him from labouring under any false hope of salvation.

These afternoons in the library were largely responsible for Theo's extraordinary progress at school. Three months after his sixteenth birthday he was accepted as an undergraduate in the Faculty of Natural Science at the University of Glasgow, where he decided to specialize in botany. He and his mother therefore moved to Glasgow, where his mother found an early-morning job on the Underground trains, sweeping flattened cigarette filters out of the carriages and onto the platform, where it was somebody else's job to scoop them into dustbins.

There is a thought trying to surface which I am trying equally hard to subdue. It is not a nice thought.

As it was close to Christmas we had crackers at Walter's hundredth birthday party and he wore a silver and green paper crown all day long. He and his best friend Humphrey King stayed so late that in the end there were just the four of us, finishing off a birthday bottle of Captain Morgan's. I smoked an illicit extra Carmen because it was a special occasion and Theo was smoking Cartier's. In his pipe Walter had the special blend of four tobaccos that had been an unexpected gift from Julian Carr.

Humphrey King was the only one not smoking. He hadn't smoked for fifteen years, ever since he realized that he only smoked when he was depressed, and in forty years it had never once cheered him up. Now, whenever he smelled cigarette smoke, it automatically depressed him. He was sitting by the fire reading Theo's compilation of smoking facts. He looked at each of us in turn.

'One of us four is going to die of cancer,' he said.

'Cheer up, Humphrey, it might be me,' Theo said.

103

'It says here that twenty-five per cent of smokers die of cancer. That means one of us four.'

'Let's hope it isn't the one in four who's Chinese,' Walter said. When he chortled he had to take his pipe out of his mouth.

'John Wayne died of lung cancer,' Humphrey said. 'I used to really like John Wayne.'

I remember looking at Humphrey and hoping it would be him. Or if not, then Walter. It ought to be Walter, at his age, or Humphrey, for the simple but convincing reason that I knew him the least well. But I didn't really mean that about Walter. I didn't mean I wanted him to die. I just meant that he was old and I was young, and I have more of a right to see the other side of the year 2000. I intend to astonish children with stories about the twentieth century, stories which Walter will be far too senile by then to remember.

That nasty thought just won't go away.

On television, on every channel, Superman was regularly crushing the evil Nick O'Teen. People started jogging. The Clean Air Society experienced a revival. Cigarette taxes were increased and medical research confirmed that filtered cigarettes led to no significant decrease in the incidence of heart disease. The first papers were published on passive smoking, and more than 600,000 British children were awarded Superman certificates attesting their personal commitment to the fight against tobacco products.

Everywhere, tobacco was in retreat. In the portrait gallery at St John's College Cambridge a pipe was painted out of the hand of Dr Samuel Parr, a hot-tempered, cricket-loving cleric whose proudest memory was of the tobacco he once shared with the Prince Regent at Carlton House. Smoking was banned from cinema auditoriums, and a year later every window of every carriage on the London Underground had its very own No-Smoking sticker.

All the same, if you smoked a cigarette the nicotine still reached your brain in seven seconds and made you feel good. This was one of the reasons a hundred and forty different cigarette brands remained on sale in tobacconists throughout the country. It also explained why none of the adverse publicity made any difference to the Long Ashton Tobacco Research Unit. Theo still had his job. I still jogged up there twice a week and was regularly given clean bills of health. I watched my money pile up in the bank.

The Buchanan's people were most reassuring. They emphasized that statistics only indicated correlation and not causation, which meant, just as an example, that incipient cancer might be causing people to smoke. Equally encouraging were the discoveries being made at Buchanan's own labs in Hamburg, where Syrian Hamsters proved as likely to contract cancers from exposure to distilled nicotine as they did from a leading brand of hair-gel.

Walter is dead.

The weather knows this, and hacks frenzies of anguished rain against the windows. Walter has been run over by a bus, like in one of his stories. He would have called it The Centenarian Smoker Run Over by a Bus story. Probably while on his way to buy tobacco. Yes, just like one of Walter's stories.

He could have been run over by a bus, all the same.

He has been run over by a bus.

He has toppled into the radiator grille of a Leyland Cityhopper travelling at thirty miles an hour which has scorched his coat and then bundled him under its front axle.

Or. The wind has pressed him, ever so gently but irresistibly (a man of his age) over the railings of the bridge and down into the gorge. He is so old and frail that instead of falling straight down he is blown some distance up-river before making contact with the water.

Or struggling against the wind his heart has failed. Or he died of an undiagnosed cancer of the brain, lung, larynx, pancreas, oesophagus while unlatching his front-door. Or he choked to death on a strand of half-inhaled pipe tobacco. I don't know. I don't care. I just want him dead.

Walter is dead. I weigh up this fact carefully. Without doubt it is a major disaster. It is worthy of wailing. It almost certainly constitutes a shock of sufficient magnitude to justify, in order to cope, the lighting and smoking of a cigarette. Even the severest non-smoker would understand. Nobody would blame me, surely, not after such an unexpected tragedy, not after the unbearably sudden death of a close close friend like Walter.

What I'm trying to say is that in my mind I am killing Walter for a cigarette. It simply isn't true that giving up smoking is good for your health.

He was bigger than me and stronger than me. He'd been captain of his school rugby team and his torso wasn't unlike those on the postcards in Lucy's room. He was less frightened than me and more clear-headed, so that when I tried to punch him he grabbed my head and put it under his arm. Then he squeezed my neck until I begged him to stop.

He was now walking me calmly round the small garden in front of William Cabot Hall, as if I'd asked him for advice. He was *counselling* me. In the middle of the garden there was an over-sized statue of William Cabot sitting on a chair looking out to sea. There was a seagull, a real one, sitting on his head.

'Now listen to me,' Julian said. 'Just listen. There was never a bet.'

'Kim said it was after the time with the socks. That you had a bet with Lucy to see how gullible I really was.'

'She's just trying to get her own back.'

'Kim said you bet Lucy a pack of cigarettes that she couldn't get me to smoke.'

'*Gregory.*'

'What should I do, Julian? Just tell me.'

'Go and see her. Be nice to her.'

'I *was* nice to her.'

'Hell, Gregory, if you really like her buy a pack of fags, break down her door and smoke every single one of them in front of her face.'

'I mean apart from that. You're sure there wasn't a bet?'

'Do you really think she'd sleep with you just for a bet?'

'I never told you she slept with me. Who told you we slept together?'

'Go and see her, Gregory.'

'There must be something I can do.'

'Sure. You could give up everything and go to Paris or New York, packing only your self-pity. When you arrive unwrap it carefully from your cardboard suitcase and mould it into art objects in the tradition of suffering lovers since the eve of time.'

'Come on, Julian, be serious.'

'Imagine it. Gregory Simpson in New York, the man who even gets worried about leaving his room in the morning.'

'It was a bet, wasn't it?'

'For God's sake, Gregory.'

'Well fuck you. Fuck everything.'

'Gregory, come back. Where are you going?'
'New York. Where d'you think?'

He was always cracking jokes and larking about. When we were playing in the garden he'd pull me aside and ask me what did the big chimney say to the little chimney and I'd say, I don't know, what did the big chimney say? And then I'd run off on a circuit of the lawn, turning my arms into wings and banking heavily into corners while dropping atomic bombs on Australian opening bowlers. By the time I landed I'd forgotten what the joke was.

Uncle Gregory and my father spent a lot of time that summer talking in private. They once called me into the dining-room and Uncle Gregory solemnly gave me an envelope with my name written on the outside in capital letters. My father then took it away from me before I could open it. He said there was money inside so it was better if he looked after it for me. It was a very thin envelope, so I didn't think it could be very much money.

Uncle Gregory spent the next summer in the Royal Adelaide Hospital, and I used to send him a different Get Well card every month, because Mum told me to. They never worked. At Christmas, to hide the fact that there was no present from Australia, I had an extra present from Mum and Dad. It was an Airfix 1/20 model of a Canberra bomber with a detachable observation turret.

Uncle Gregory died in hospital before I finished making it.

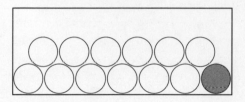

She knocked on the door for the third time and I told her to go away.

'Are you alright? Come downstairs.'

'Later.'

I hadn't unpacked either of my cases. I'd thrown the bean-bag into the corner, but only to clear a space and not to position it. I stayed absolutely still, lying on my bed and hardly breathing until she went away. Of course I wasn't alright.

Then I jammed all the questions she'd asked me into a single senseless lump, like plasticine: What about your exams? Are you hungry? Don't you want to talk about it? Is it a girl? Would you like some tea? Have you heard about your father? Were you being bullied? You're not taking drugs are you? Is history too hard a subject? Coffee instead then?

And when they were all mashed together I tossed them onto the bean-bag and out of sight.

This room was much bigger than the one in William Cabot, with a window over-looking the front garden and the road. It was big enough for a double-bed which didn't touch the wall on either side, and I lay there listening for the neighbours, Seventh Day Adventists who were usually out, standing on other people's doorsteps. I felt so lethargic I could hardly move my head, and the silence wasn't helping. My eyes locked onto a faded Nick O'Teen sticker on the side of the book-case which held my science-fiction novels.

Every day, before Superman found and destroyed him, Nick O'Teen would tempt little children with cigarettes. He used to say: 'If you want to grow up fast, take one of these.'

I can't remember what Superman said.

Theo lived with his mother in two rooms at the station end of Buchanan Street. They often had disagreements, either about botany, which Theo's mother dismissed as a vain attempt to label God, or about cigarettes. She would ask him if he didn't trust God to take good care of her, while all Theo really wanted was some clean air for the aspidistras he was cross-pollinating on the window-sill.

Often, at the weekends, his mother would take bus-trips. Acting on information received from a widespread network of friends and acquaintances, most of them Calvinists, she travelled all over Scotland to check on the latest sighting of her husband. The information was consistently incorrect, but she did think she'd once recognized the slope of his back in the wheel-house of a lobster boat receding from Craobh Haven.

At the age of nineteen Theo was awarded a first-class degree. His mother accused him of getting ahead of himself, but for the graduation ceremony she bought them both a new pair of shoes and stood proudly at the very front of the Assembly Rooms as her son was officially made a Bachelor of Science. Theo then submitted a proposal for a PhD, provisionally entitled *Patterns of Deception in Plant Virus Infections*, and became the youngest research student ever to be accepted by the University, a record he held until the mid-seventies when the Maths department began admitting students from China.

Maybe Walter really *is* dead.

He isn't here again and maybe in fact in reality he really has been run over by a bus.

112

This feeling now is completely different from the feeling I had yesterday. That was just a bad and ugly thought, and dark, and sharp-shaped. But today, on the second day running, I'm thinking that perhaps he really is dead, and what should I do now? Smoke? Pathetic. There is this huge difference between how I think things will be and how they actually are. I have to phone up Emmy. I have to know what's happened to Walter.

Okay, right. So that's settled.

I just phoned up Emmy and after asking me how the plant was getting on and whether Walter had told me about Stella, she eventually understood why I was sounding so worried. Fairly convincingly, she told me that Walter wasn't dead. He was at Humphrey King's house, comforting Mrs King.

'So he's alright?' I said.

'He's fine. It was good of you to ring.'

Walter isn't dead. He hasn't been run over by a bus. I'm so relieved I could almost listen to his Firing Squad story. I'm so relieved I could tell it myself.

This wouldn't be the first time I'd asked for Uncle Gregory's money. I once stole some Lucky Boy chocolate cigarettes from the sweet display at one of my father's shops. A new assistant whose name I didn't know took me into the stock-room for a telling-off, and then I had another one from my parents when I got back home. I nearly cried and I wanted to be tougher than I was, so I imagined being Uncle Gregory in the cockpit of a Canberra or at the start of a motor-bike race.

After the telling off, I stood up straight and said I was sorry and asked if I could have the money to pay for a ticket to Adelaide, where I was going to start a new life as a cricketing airline pilot. My mother said no, I had to learn to be honest if I was going to run a chain of tobacconist shops. Then my father said no. So I started crying after all, and mum hugged me and said I could have the money when I was older if I promised never to steal again. I promised.

'And never to start smoking,' she added.

After that I rarely thought about it, except vaguely when I suspected that only a top skateboard or a motorized go-kart or a decent stereo stood between me and widespread popularity at school.

But this time, as soon as my father came home, I was going to go downstairs and ask him straight out for Uncle Gregory's envelope. He would object, and we'd probably fight, but I was prepared for fighting if it meant I could have the money and therefore be in New York by the end of the week. I'd probably find a new lover within a month. That would show Julian Carr, and Lucy. That would teach them.

And then everything would be alright.

About twice a year he used to get the most terrible flu which he would cough out of his system over a period of weeks. He always refused to see a doctor.

'I'm not ill,' he said. 'Never been ill in my life.'

Then I would go to the Estates on my own. Otherwise, we went together and often Walter would come and join us, though not always in his Rastafari hat.

Jamie was vigilant in pacing the walkway, travelling up and down in the lift, and patrolling the block for any sign of a lady with grey eyes wearing too much make-up. And even though Theo gave him film-posters and Bounty bars, he never stopped asking for cigarettes. At the end of the evening we'd smoke and Walter would tell stories while Jamie flipped through the pages of the waiting-room magazines looking at the adverts. Then he'd gabble on about what he was going to do when he was rich. Jamie and Walter would always set off for home together, both of them convinced they were protecting the other.

And Emmy came to see us most weeks. The Bluebell Drama Club also met on Wednesdays, so sometimes Emmy looked older, and sometimes younger. Her eyes, however, were always the same. Because of the carriage layout of the flat and Jamie's warnings we could always hide Walter by pushing him through into the bathroom, and then into the toilet for good measure.

'I promise you,' Theo would truthfully tell her, 'I have never given cigarettes to an old man.'

However, Theo always acted strangely for at least an hour after any visit from Emmy. He would ask a different type of question to the people who came for cigarettes, like had they really thought *properly* about the danger of an earlier death. The replies were predictable:

'You have *plans* for those extra years? Like holidays, or something?'

Or he'd ask someone if they minded losing their sense of taste, or smell, which always raised a smile.

I sometimes slipped into the waiting-room for a quick Carmen and while I was there I watched the way the others used to smoke. There was an intensity to it which said that each cigarette had to stand for everything – for bread and meat and beer, for shoes and blankets and the tinsel on the Christmas tree and the Christmas tree itself, and for tins on the shelves and something decent on the telly. Something, anything, to look forward to. Something to depend on.

A panacea is a miraculous plant which cures all known diseases. It is a universal remedy, a catholicon, and Pliny ambitiously identified it as lovage. Later, panacean qualities were variously claimed for other plants, among them ligusticum and opopanax, wound-wort and witch-hazel.

The first connection between the elusive panacean plant and tobacco was made in England by Edmund Spenser, author of *The Faerie Queene*, and by the time of Queen Elizabeth's death it was well known that tobacco could cure colds, eye inflammations, involuntary tears, headaches, migraines, dropsy, paralysis, slowness of the blood, apoplexy, death trances, childbirth pangs, hysterical passions, dizziness, memory loss, restlessness, black melancholy, mental derangement, plaque, bad air, and all infectious illnesses known to mankind.

Later, the universal remedy was sought not in a single plant, but instead in a single action, or in a single chance happening, or in a single idea. All our daily dissatisfaction could be turned round in one easy moment of panacean discovery, a hope well served by casinos and product advertisements and the promise of emigration to paradises like Australia. The panacea skipped from plants to chemicals to grand ideas to thoroughbred horses to fortunate combinations of numbers by way of the changeable moods of moody men and women.

But always, even since Pliny, the panacean hope has had a regular home in the miraculous love of the one good man or the one good woman. This is the most common of catholicons, and guaranteed to cure everything.

A group of four or five people with Emmy Gaston, Walter's daughter, at the centre. She wasn't wearing make-up. Her brown hair was pulled back into a no-nonsense pony-tail fastened by a rubber-band. She was probably a few years younger than Theo, and she was waiting in the dark, with her friends, outside the double-doors which led to the lift. There

were two placards, hand-written in black marker pen: SLOW
MOTION SUICIDE and STOP THIS NOW!!, which looked
like it had been used before.

The five protesters, including Emmy, followed us into the lift
and we travelled up to the fourth floor jammed together and trying to avoid each other's eyes. The lift stopped and we stepped
out one by one onto the walkway. It was so cold and there was
so much steam from all our breathing that it looked like we'd
each inhaled a pack of cigarettes in the lift and then left the
packets behind. In front of No. 47 there were a few people
already waiting, and while Theo unlocked the door Emmy was
asking, not to anyone in particular, but just generally,

'Did you know this man gives cigarettes to children? Would
you want your children to smoke? Do you know the probability
of catching cancer if you start smoking before fourteen?'

'Emmy,' Theo said. 'Come inside. Let's talk about this
inside.'

She stood absolutely still and stared at him. She flared her
nostrils and breathed out a long straight plume of breath.

'Who on earth said you could call me Emmy?'

Her back seemed to straighten. Theo developed a small
apologetic crouch.

'I'm sorry,' he said, but mostly he seemed surprised by his
mistake, as if the word Emmy had been through his mind so
many times it had become familiar without him really noticing.

'Please, come inside,' Theo said, recovering some of his
composure. 'Everyone, come inside.'

One of the Estates women said,

'I knew this would happen.'

1916.
The morning of the battle of the Somme. Twenty thousand

117

men die in six hours and not one of them by accident or bad luck. Compared to smoking, Walter decides, this is genuine stupidity and dicing with death.

Walter, a private in the Black Watch, was arrested by an officer's adjutant while walking for no apparent reason in a direction two cardinal points astray of the forward trenches. Within two days, as an example to all other soldiers with a poor sense of orientation, he was court-martialled and sentenced to death by Firing Squad. On the third day, stood against the battered wall of a ruined outhouse, he was faced by a platoon of caterers from the King's Own Scottish Borderers and a second lieutenant from the Blues and Royals. The soldiers were cold and wet and miserable, but according to Walter the officer was oblivious to this because soldiers didn't count as human beings.

Walter is not blindfolded but his hands are tied behind his back. His back is against the wall, from which a greenish type of moisture has begun to seep through his tunic onto the tensed muscles of his shoulders, which are wet anyway with sweat. The caterers load, check and make ready their rifles. The officer, who clearly has previous experience, orders rifles raised, rifles levelled, rifles aimed, one and all at Walter's heart. The officer nonchalantly lifts his arm.

At this point, any number of things can happen.

About a month after Theo submitted the corrections to his PhD thesis (*Deception Patterns in the Tobacco Mosaic Virus*), his mother heard that her ex-husband and Theo's father had been sighted working in the kitchens of the RAF jet-fighter base near Achnasheen.

Above all else, Theo's mother loved travelling on the West Coast Red Band bus service. Perched just high enough above the hedges to see everything, at just the right speed, the buses were big enough to allow cigarette smoke to circulate, unlike the confined compartments of the West Highland Railway.

On this occasion there were only six other passengers heading north from Glasgow. Well before the Erskine Bridge, they were already coughing in a meaningful way and looking darkly towards the back of the bus, where Theo's mother sat contentedly on the very back seat, daring anyone else to join her by smoking one cigarette after another.

By Ardlui, all the other passengers had crowded into the seats behind the driver, and Theo's mother settled down to enjoy the moving pictures of Scotland in the big BSI stamped windows.

Twenty minutes short of Achnasheen, the bus swung round a corner and narrowly missed a head-on collision with an RAF transporter towing the tail section of a Vulcan fighter-bomber. In braking, both vehicles skidded across the road. The articulated trailer of the transporter skewed into the back of the coach, sheering off the right hand rear-wheel panels and crushing the seats inside.

Theo's mother was killed instantly. There were no other casualties.

Earlier than I expected I heard him come in, and then I thought I heard them arguing but that couldn't be right because they never argued.

I went downstairs for tea and nobody was saying very much so I just came out with it and said I was leaving University and wanted to have Uncle Gregory's money. It was the direct approach.

'It's not a good time,' my mother said.

'Let the boy speak!'

I looked up from my plate, wondering how much I could have missed in less than a year. Lucy had once asked me what my father did and I said he went driving on Sundays between his roast lunch and the *Antiques Roadshow*. Then I showed her the exclamation marks in one of my mother's letters, and we both spluttered with amazement, even though neither of us could have said exactly what was wrong with exclamation marks. Lucy had asked me what my mother was like really and I'd said you know. *You know*, as if there was nothing to be said beyond the expected. It had taken such a short time to forget them. I didn't deserve the money.

Mum had pursed her lips and narrowed her eyebrows. She looked a lot like me and she was very worried and I was the one making her worry. Dad needed a haircut. He looked tired and somehow disappointed, as if he could see right through me to the absurd life I projected for myself, where episodes of gratification were punctuated by glamorous catastrophes with my only responsibility the inevitable rescue of the beautiful women involved. It was the idea of life a film-maker might have, but at least a film-maker would make a film of it.

'Fine,' Dad said. 'I'll organize it tomorrow.'

Mum asked him if he'd gone mad. Misunderstanding her, and a little flushed with my success, I assured her that I hadn't smoked once while at University.

'Greg wanted some of the money used for foreign travel,' Dad said. 'He was clear about that.'

'No problem,' I said, 'great.'

'What's the big hurry?' Mum said. 'You can stay as long as you like. Here, I mean.'

'It's ten thousand pounds, a bit more.'

'New York,' I said. 'I was thinking of going to New York.'

'You could maybe work in one of the shops,' Mum said. 'Gregory?'

120

Dad said: 'Not Hollywood then?'
'I know what I'm doing, Dad.'

Emmy, still made-up as Hedda Gabler, had been on her way
to No. 47 to check for Walter when she found Jamie sitting
alone in the lift smoking a cigarette. She'd asked Jamie if
Theo had given him the cigarette and Jamie thought very hard
about the question. After due consideration he said no.

Instead, he said that Theo had sold it to him.

'But I paid with my own money.'

The next week Emmy turned up as herself, with her placards
and her friends.

We went through to the inner room. I lit the gas fire while
Theo asked Emmy if they couldn't just talk this through to a
compromise, like adults.

'You sell cigarettes to children,' she said.

'Look at me,' Theo said. 'Do I look like that kind of person?'

'I have no idea what you look like. I warned you what
would happen. And I know Walter comes here.'

'I can explain.'

'You seem to think all this is some kind of joke,' she said,
slapping her hand down on the table. 'But people die horribly
from smoking cigarettes, and quickly too. It can happen in
less than a year. I doubt you've ever seen a cancer of the
tongue? Well the tongue swells up until it fills the whole
mouth, by which time the mouth is also cancerous, and it could
be your mouth, or Walter's, or Jamie's. Then your soft-palate
starts swelling, followed by the glands in your lower jaw and
finally your neck. You can't speak, or eat. You can't even
vomit, which is something you desperately want to do, most
of the time. You certainly can't smoke anymore. Can't get the
smoke down there, although by this stage the pain doesn't

leave much room for nicotine nostalgia. And it's not just the smokers. There's no statistic which records the spectator's pain of the nearest and dearest. Now you may be perfectly happy about all this but I am not.'

'Oh come on,' I said, and Emmy said 'shut up you,' without even looking at me. She said to Theo,

'This is only the beginning.'

Theo winced as she closed the door firmly behind her. He said to me,

'How can she think I'd do it if I didn't think it was the right thing to do?'

New York City is disdainful nicorette-chewing blondes on dwarfed side-walks hailing yellow taxicabs to luxury pent-houses in awesome skyscrapers negotiating kick-back deals with nicotine-patched lawyers sporting diamond tie-pins from stogie-sucking jewellers mourning runaway daughters starring in pornographic movies directed by cheroot-smoking pimps in sharkskin suits with a taste for disdainful New York blondes, chewing nicorette. And the streets are paved with gold.

Smokers in America, it's said, at least in the upper strata of society, are treated as pariahs.

It seemed a pretty clear choice, an uneven contest between the land of opportunity and a University I didn't like, exams I didn't want to do, and a next door neighbour I never wanted to see again in my whole life. However, I also had the strong feeling that if I went to New York I'd almost certainly never see Lucy Hinton again, and that's probably why I spent most of the rest of the week lying on my bed in my room. I read paragraphs from depressing French novels which sent me to sleep in the middle of the afternoon, and gave me dreams which came out simply as language.

My father was regularly coming home much earlier than I remembered. I sensed him about the house, prowling. He asked me why I hadn't left for New York.

'I'm getting organized,' I said.

'What for?'

'I want to find myself.'

'And you think you're in New York?'

'I want to know who I am, I think.'

He looked at me over the top of his glasses.

'You need to know a lot more than that, son.'

He was joking, of course. I seemed to remember he used to like a joke, sometimes. I said,

'I heard about the OBE. That's great news.'

'Oh well done,' he said. 'Very well done. Bloody marvellously tactful.'

Then he stamped off into the bathroom, taking his newspaper with him. This wasn't home as I remembered it at all.

One possibility is native American folklore. Even while the Enfield 303s are aimed unerringly at the New Testament in his top left-hand tunic pocket, Walter reminds us that smoking originated as a solemn spiritual and diplomatic ritual on the buffalo plains of the Americas. At about the same time, historically speaking, there was a war-cry common to many of the Indian tribes, including the Crow, the Comanche, the Panankey and the Picayunes. We are *people*, they yelled as they rode into tribal skirmish, *we* are people. Everybody else was enemy only.

The officer in charge of Walter's Firing Squad, according to Walter, was therefore no better than a Red Indian savage.

Another possibility, as fingers more familiar with regimental meringue tighten around triggers, is that Walter reminds us this incident is taking place well before passive smoking was even *invented*. Then, after a short ironic aside (if they'd known about passive smoking of course no-one would have smoked in the trenches) he might describe how the officer, still with arm aloft, and using his other arm to slap his swagger-stick against the brown-tan tops of his riding boots, puts his moustache in Walter's face and says:

'Last request, soldier.'

And Walter, who up until then has only smoked once or twice in a purely recreational way, asks for a cigarette. He says this is the first of many times in his life when he has a strong conviction that he isn't going to die from smoking.

He is given a cigarette, a Craven A, and he is about half way through it when the officer from the Blues and Royals, a veteran of too many Firing Squads, drops down dead from passive smoking. Nobody else is authorized to give the order to fire, so the caterers let Walter go. He smokes a second cigarette to celebrate.

The moral of Walter's Firing Squad story depends on its ending. In this version the moral is: 'Don't believe everything you read.' Other versions have different endings and therefore different morals, but among the different versions there is always one certainty. Because Walter is right there, telling the story, the caterers from the King's Own Scottish Borderers obviously didn't shoot him.

DAY
9

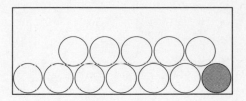

The only tobacco in the house was the cigarette I'd once taken from Julian. I kept it loose in my Helix scientific instruments tin, between the dividers and the compass, loosely partnered by the sharpened butts of HB pencils. My suitcases were now unpacked and Julian was wrong because instead of self-pity I found only socks and pants and T-shirts and sweaters, paperback novels and a Courage ashtray, my Helix pencil-box and a pair of trainers. I hadn't tidied any of it away because I was still about to set off for New York: the week after next at the latest. In the meantime, clothes were strewn everywhere, half in and half out of the opened suitcases.

I kept the Helix tin on the bedside-table so that I could write down the dreams I dreamt as language, but it was always too late and I could never remember them. Instead, still only half awake, I pushed the pencils aside and picked out the cigarette, trapping it lengthways between my index-finger and thumb, turning it in slow-motion arcs through the afternoon light like the disembodied wing of an aeroplane. I watched it from every possible angle, flying it one way and then the other, waiting for inspiration.

I looked at it for so long that in the end there was nothing left to understand. It was just a cigarette, some dried leaf packed into a roll of paper with a filter at one end. There was no other truth to be extracted from it. It had no special moral to offer me, no message to impart. It was just one cigarette among hundreds of thousands of others which could be bought all over the country in shops very much like Simpson's,

Tobacconist and Newsagent, newly famous in our area since Mr Simpson the proprietor had been charged with selling cigarettes to minors.

The Chamber of Commerce were thought to have withdrawn his nomination for an OBE.

Walter is back.

He is wearing an Australian Army Burma Theatre of Operations hat. It is faded almost white and on one side the brim is buttoned to the crown. There is a drawstring pulled tight under his chin which has the effect of bobbing the hat forward on his head whenever he speaks or chews on the mouth-piece of his pipe. Haemoglobin is lying contentedly at Walter's feet and the room smells of tobacco again, the way it should.

When Walter told me that Humphrey King was dead I thought he was going to cry. I was embarrassed for him and looked away. I brushed my hands through the plant on the desk as if I was checking for aphids.

'He was one my best friends,' Walter said. 'The miserable old bastard.'

Walter tells me how he and Humphrey once shared a hookah pipe outside a brothel in Tangiers, and one of the plant's broad leaves snaps off in my hands. He sniffs back a tear and I rip the leaf at its edges, folding it and unfolding it and tearing it again.

The funeral is tomorrow and Walter told Mrs King I'd be there. He noisily blows his nose into a limp white handkerchief, and then whenever tears seem inevitable he sucks on his pipe, swallows, and the tears miraculously dissolve in tobacco smoke.

'In Tangiers he said he wanted to die with his boots on,' Walter says. 'He didn't.'

128

'Natural causes then?'

'Of course not. It was cancer of something. It always is.'

I try to distract him by asking if he knows anyone called Stella.

'Stella,' Walter says slowly.

'Emmy told me you were supposed to give me a message about someone called Stella.'

'Used to be a cigarette brand, years ago.'

'I think it's a person.'

'Humphrey used to smoke them.'

He takes a huge draw on his pipe and I look down at the skeleton of a leaf my fingers have picked out. It is very fragile, very fine. I throw it in the bin. The desk-top is littered with strips of leaf which I push into a neat pile. Then I slide a sheet of paper underneath the pile and tip all the pieces of leaf into an envelope, which I seal carefully and put away in the top drawer of the desk.

I have no idea why. It's an irrational but organized thing to do, which seems about as decent a response to death as any.

In 1960 Theo was 24 years old and a doctor of philosophy. He wasn't extravagant: not smoking and not drinking had always been a limited gesture of rebellion against his mother, but now his mother was dead. There was a small pension from the Glasgow Underground but the money seemed pointless without their ritual bicker over how much should be set aside for whisky and cigarettes. Otherwise, all he had left of her was a wardrobe of clothes smelling of smoke.

Unwilling to accept the random nature of her death, Theo decided to gamble the pension-money as a kind of scientific research into Providence. If he lost all the money, was evicted from the flat, and as a consequence died from exposure or starvation on the streets of Glasgow, then God would only have himself to blame.

He therefore took a train to the race-track at Ayr. It was a mid-week meeting and there were only four races on the card. To prolong the tragedy of it all, he decided to lose a quarter of the money on each race, and he chose the horses arbitrarily. In the 2.30 he had Rocky Bay both ways. It fell. In the 3.00 Doc's Divine Chance came in second, but Theo had his stake on the nose. In the 3.30 Mr Clinamen failed to start and although Theo's stake was reclaimable the bookie forgot to tell him. In the last race he put all his remaining money on a three-year-old gelding and rank outsider called Too Good To Be True.

As the race started Theo was already pushing his way out of the grandstand, dazed by grief, newly orphaned and now destitute, categorically abandoned by his mother's God.

They were lying on the floor of Julian's room, probably. Facing each other, dealing cards and smoking cigarettes. Laughing nearly all the time. With their poker-playing smokers' fingers they were arranging straight flushes of hearts to bluff against each other for small piles of England's Glory matches. Later they would count up the matches and convert them into the harder currency of cigarettes. They were at it all the time.

His plain beige-coloured bean-bag left behind no interesting patterns on her naked back and buttocks. I imagined her face, heart-shaped. It was all a bet. It was only a bet. Or worse, it wasn't a bet at all and she'd really liked me and I'd ruined everything, but before I could work out what this meant they were making love again, without restraint, mindless of absent neighbours.

Afterwards, looking up at the canopy of smoke above the

bean-bag, they amused themselves by picking out the wholly ridiculous shape of Gregory Simpson's face, foolish and innocent, non-smoking, pale and frightened in the street-level reflections of the glass skyscrapers of New York. They bet each other a carton of Marlboro that within a week he'd fall in love and be seduced beyond saving by an intelligent, athletic, gorgeous, and infinitely demanding transvestite.

They were very experienced gamblers, so they were probably right.

There were fifteen or maybe twenty voices following Emmy Gaston in a harmonized version of *We Shall Overcome*, and we'd already smoked two cigarettes each working up enough courage to leave. Jamie had already gone home, flicking V-signs as he ran backwards along the walkway, and Theo was trying to convince Walter that it was alright if he didn't want to come anymore, considering the trouble it must be causing at home.

'I'm a smoker,' Walter said, clamping his pipe-stem proudly between his teeth. 'Always have been. Always will be.'

'You shouldn't have to fight with your own daughter.'

'Never shied away from trouble.'

'Please, Walter. You'll just make it worse for yourself.'

Walter peered at the underside of his pipe, as if he suspected it was leaking.

'Go home, Walter,' I said, 'or she'll think we've abducted you.'

'Can't,' he said.

'Think of yourself for a change,' Theo said.

'I am.'

Emmy had found out that it was Walter who'd given Jamie the cigarette.

'It was in a good cause,' Walter said. 'To pay him for being our look-out.'

'He's only a child.'

'You didn't really think he was doing it for chocolate? Anyway, never did *me* any harm.'

Along with Walter, Jamie was our only other ally. He liked to carry out a rough approximation of his old job, and every Wednesday he ran across the wasteland to meet us, shouting 'she's here again, she's here again.' She always was.

Emmy was much better at allies than we were. She knocked on the doors of strangers and politely described how Theo gave cigarettes to children and pregnant women and old sick dying people. Would they be interested in signing a petition? She made contact with health professionals and anti-vivisectionists and the local committee of ASH, then organized them into rotas.

She christened her collection of anti-smokers the League against Unprincipled Nicotine Groups. Then she had LUNG hats made which looked like sailor's hats with a No-Smoking badge on the front over the words Kill-Me-Quick. She took her petition beyond the Estates and started working up the hill towards the bridge. She made banners: LUNG for Lungs, LUNG for Life, which she waved from the walkway as inside No. 47, listening to the singing, we all decided on one final smoke before leaving.

'She's a damn fool,' Walter said, filling his pipe. 'She's never been the same since she married that Frenchman.'

Theo stopped his lighter halfway to his cigarette. He looked at Walter through his eyebrows.

'It's all fight the good fight with her,' Walter said. 'Fight any fight.'

The standard European wheel has thirty-six numbered compartments, half of them red and half black. There is also a compartment with the value of zero, which is painted green. Ten different bets can be placed at the table, ranging from the single number with a pay-out of 35 to 1, to a line of twelve numbers ('colonne') which pays out at two to one. For less courageous players, bets are available on red/black, odd/even, and high (manque)/low (passe) numbers, although the pay-out on these is an unmiraculous evens. If the roulette ball falls into the compartment marked zero the bank collects all bets.

There is some doubt about the game's origins. Some say that roulette was invented in the seventeenth century by the French mathematician Blaise Pascal, who also invented the digital calculator, the syringe, and the hydraulic press. Others claim it was the exclusive idea, early in the eighteenth century, of the papal legate to Toulouse, Cardinal Joseph-Bienaimé Caventou. More plausibly, however, it was invented in China and transported back to France by Dominican monks.

Although the outcome of any spin of the wheel is decided by chance, gamblers often sense that an element of judgement is involved, dependent on probabilities which are usually calculated as percentages. Unfortunately, too strong a faith in probability will eventually lead to the mathematical anomaly known as the Monte Carlo fallacy. This is the false assumption that probabilities apply to individual events, when in fact they are only accurately predictable ratios. This basically means that successive bets fail to compensate each other.

To a gambler standing at the roulette table then, percentages of probability have little or no value. Anybody can either lose everything or win a fortune, because all gamblers know that mathematical expectation is seldom the only reality. For obvious reasons, roulette players often prefer to trust in destiny.

Variations on the European game of roulette can be found both in the United States and in Russia.

I opened the door, arms crossed, feet apart. But it was only Lilly, enormous at the top of the stairs.

'Oh, hi Lilly. I didn't hear Theo dancing.'

'Let me and this woman in,' Lilly said, pushing past me. Emmy followed her in, looking calm and composed in white trousers and a sweater. Her hair was pulled back and I saw, in this light, that her face wasn't unkind.

Theo came out of the kitchen with a dog-bowl in one hand and a fork in the other. He spread out his arms.

'Welcome,' he said.

'This lady tells me you've been selling cigarettes to children,' Lilly said, ushering Emmy into the middle of the room. 'She wants me to sign a petition against smoking, and she's causing a queue in the shop.'

Emmy stroked Bananas on the head as he sniffed at an ashtray.

'It's all lies,' I said.

'Now you two make it up,' Lilly said. 'Because we're all nice people and I've my customers to serve. If you boys want feeding, just dance.'

She had a mumble to herself as she thumped down the stairs, and Theo said well this was a nice surprise and did Emmy fancy a cup of tea?

'I'm not here by choice,' she said quickly. 'However, I'm quite thirsty.'

Theo put the dog-bowl on the television and I went into the kitchen to make the tea. When I came back I was surprised to see them both sitting on the sofa. It meant that I had to sit on a chair miles away. Emmy was saying:

'But you're sure you've thought about it from every possible angle?'

'Enough milk?' I asked politely. She ignored me so I lit a Carmen and blew the smoke directly at her face. By the time it reached her it had floated well above her head. Theo said:

'Look at Walter, he seems alright.'

'Walter is very frail and always in danger.'

'Walter's as strong as an ox.'

'He is *frail*. If he carries on smoking he will die.'

'He's ninety-eight years old.'

'Precisely. How much longer can it go on?'

She peered closely at Theo and he shut his mouth to hide his teeth. 'When was the last time you had a check-up?'

'Sorry?'

'If cigarettes do more good than harm, like you say, then when did you last see a doctor?'

'I'm fine,' Theo said. 'Fit as a fiddle. Never been ill in my life.'

'That's what my husband always said.'

'Ah yes, your husband.'

She stood up and handed Theo her mug. Theo said,

'More tea? Biscuits?'

'No doubt I'll be seeing you at the Estates. Thanks for the tea.'

'We have biscuits.'

But Emmy was already closing the door behind her. Theo listened to her footsteps on the staircase, then sniffed at the tea left in her mug. He raised it to his lips and sipped. He swallowed, then sighed, almost as if it was the first cigarette of the day.

'You liar,' I said. 'We never have biscuits.'

Dad: 'Well how was I supposed to know? They all look the same and they all wear make-up and they all act so bloody grown-up all the time.'

Mum: 'That's not the point.'

Dad: 'And they all lie. It's not as though I'm selling acid drugs, for God's sake.'

Often, though usually while lying in the bath, I had pretensions to brilliance so extreme and absolute they were brilliant in themselves. Exploring my latent greatness, I became enthralled by long sequences of imagined triumphs which weren't to be disturbed by doors slamming downstairs, or by heated voices rising clearly through the floor-boards from the kitchen below.

Dad etc: 'And I suppose you've never made a mistake in *your* life?'

Mum etc: 'What's that got to do with it?'

'Never peeked out of the bedroom window?'

'That was fifteen years ago.'

'And watched him parade naked, entirely for your benefit.'

'He was never naked.'

'You used to drool.'

'Nothing happened and I never used to drool.'

'Only because you wouldn't kiss a smoker.'

'Now you're being silly.'

'He wouldn't have lasted ten minutes with your nagging.'

I turned on the hot tap with my toes and slipped my ears under the water until all I could hear was the whale-song of the water-pipes. I was the centre of the universe, poised to rescue beautiful women, and in this place there was no death and no loneliness and I believed it was my destiny to live forever.

136

Too Good To Be True came in first at twenty to one, leaving Theo a great deal richer than when he arrived at the race-track. The following day, undeterred by God's perversity, he bet on the outcome of a Hamilton by-election. A surprise win by the Scottish Nationalists meant that he more than doubled his money. He tried to lose it again by joining an illegal black-jack game in a Pollokshaws café, followed by roulette in Glasgow's only licensed casino, the Rubicon. He later moved on to greyhound-racing, bingo, push-pennies, and one-armed bandits.

To ensure that the outcome was uniquely the responsibility of his mother's God, he decided that none of his bets should involve any skill. He could therefore bet on football and horses and the Embassy World Darts because he knew absolutely nothing about them. His second rule was never to back out-siders, so as to avoid the possibility of an enormous win. The obvious disadvantage of this was that it made winning more likely.

He once had a bet on a four-way distance-spitting contest outside a pub in the Grassmarket in Edinburgh. He knew noth-ing about the spitting backgrounds of any of the competitors, so he bet on the favourite. The favourite won.

In two years of gambling he always won a little more than he lost, and there came to be a type of wildness in both the gambling and the winning. He let his hair grow longer. More than once he declined offers of teaching posts at the University, because he was never satisfied that he'd established unequivo-cally the existence of a benign God suffering constant remorse for the injustice of his mother's death.

He therefore carried on gambling even though he missed the more consoling results of research into plant cells. It was only in 1962, after a coincidence completely outside his control, that he was unexpectedly rescued from this desperation of good fortune by the Royal College of Physicians.

'You never used to be like this. Come on, Theo.'
'Maybe she's right.'
'You're the one who started it. You can't just stop.'
'What's the point? Emmy says we kill people.'
'We haven't killed anybody.'
'Make them dependent.'
'You think they're free? They need us.'
'We created the need.'
'Cigarettes help. You've heard the stories.'
'A poor substitute for real help.'
'There is no real help.'
'We addict them.'
'We're all more addicted to water.'
'What?'
'It gets us through the days.'
'We die earlier.'
'Understanding satisfaction.'
'Children suffer.'
'Less than being beaten.'
'There's no connection.'
'In an irrational rage by parents desperate for cigarettes.'
'Yes, well. But. It's still a risk.'
'It's not drugs, Theo. It doesn't break up homes.'
'Increased risk of fire then.'
'It's only one mad woman, and friends.'
'She's not mad.'
'They're all the same.'
'Only married.'
'They hate one smoker and take it out on everyone else.

We just have to keep on going until she gives up and leaves us to our own devices.'

'Would you say she hates me?'

'Who knows? She's not normal.'

'Have you seen the way she waves a banner? Amazing.'

'Stop tormenting yourself. Look, let's have a fag, before Bananas rips up the sofa. *Theo.*'

'Sorry. What?'

'Let's have a fag, alright?'

'I'm trying to cut down.'

'You're *what*?'

'They say that cigarettes are sometimes a substitute for affection.'

'Last request, soldier.'

I blame myself. Feeling sorry for him I actually *asked* for it.

1916 etc. The officer pulls his silver cigarette-case from the upper left hand pocket of his tunic, and then asks Walter for his last request. Walter says nothing.

'Speak up, soldier. D'you want a cigarette or don't you?'

'I don't smoke,' Walter says.

'I don't smoke, *sir*.'

'I don't smoke, *sir*.'

'Of course you smoke. You're about to be shot. Take one of these.'

It wasn't the ideal moment for Walter to point out that he didn't smoke because it was bad for his health, so he took the cigarette from the officer and put it between his lips. The officer then pulled out a silver wheel-lighter and spun the wheel. It was out of petrol.

'Damn,' he said.

He asked the caterers if any of them had any matches, and unfortunately they did. The officer took a box from a pastry chef, who then returned to his place in the line, rifle at the ready.

'These matches are damp,' the officer said. 'Where have they been?'

'In a trench, sir.'

The officer struck a match, just to check they still worked. He threw the first match away and walked back to Walter. He struck a second match and held it in front of Walter's cigarette just as Walter exhaled, practising how to smoke. The match blew out.

'Sorry,' Walter said.

'Sorry, *sir*.'

'Sorry, *sir*.'

The officer struck a third match and was shot dead by a German sniper.

'Can I sit in your bean-bag?'

'No, Mum, please.'

'I've never sat in a bean-bag before. It's a long way down.'

'*Mum*.'

'It's very comfy really. Am I meant to lean forward? Or lie back like this?'

'*Don't* sit in my bean-bag.'

'I'm only *seeing*. Well help me up then.'

She picked up some clothes and folded them. She came and sat beside me on the edge of the bed. She took a book from the bedside table and looked at the cover-picture of a melting clock. Then slowly, as if reaching out her hand to trap a living thing, she plucked Julian's cigarette from the open Helix tin. She held it up accusingly.

'Gregory.'

I said Mum.

'What is *this*?'

'You know what it is, Mum. It's a cigarette.'

'And why is it here in your room?'

'It's mine. And it's only a cigarette.'

I took it away from her and put it back in the pencil-box. Mum said she didn't understand me, and I had the feeling she was making a big effort to be understanding.

'First cigarettes,' she said, 'and then *New York*. It's a girl, isn't it?'

I didn't answer.

'You know you could work in the shop?'

Her arm, by motherly guile, crept around my shoulders as she patiently explained to me that visiting idealists were shot to death every day on the streets of New York, mostly by realists. She also reminded me that I was completely middle-class and therefore totally unskilled. I should remember who I was: Gregory Simpson, son of Mr and Mrs Simpson, tobacconists.

'I don't want to work in the shop,' I said.

'I'll ask your father.'

'I don't want to work in the shop.'

'What *do* you want then? What is it you really want in life?'

'I don't know.'

'Whatever it is you want,' she said, 'you can't have it. Not exactly how you want it. You know that, don't you?'

She gave my shoulder a little squeeze.

'There's always something missing, and feeling dissatisfied is just, well, it's the same for everybody. You could do a lot worse than work with your father.'

'What does Dad think?'

'He thinks he's a drug-dealer.'

141

'It's a tobacco shop. I'd probably take up smoking.'

'As if you hadn't already,' she said, staring significantly at the Helix tin. 'Cigarettes won't help, Gregory.'

'I don't smoke, Mum,' I said. 'I promised, remember?'

She didn't look totally convinced.

'It's kind of a sentimental cigarette,' I said.

She gave me a big hug, jamming my throat against her shoulder.

'I love you, Gregory,' she said. 'Don't forget I love you very much.'

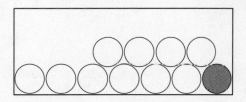

'Surrounded by a wall.'

'Sounds nice,' Theo said.

'You must be mad,' Walter said.

We were in No. 47 at the end of another charitable evening and I'd been describing my dream-house by the bridge. I still ran past it twice a week on my way to the Research Unit, and amazingly it was still empty. It was flat and square, made of brick scuffed orange like cigarette filters. The outside was blank and unornamented, which made it seem like an inside house, discreet, with no outside heart.

I could buy it too, if I wanted. If they gave me an advance on next year's money I could easily afford it. At the very least I could get a surveyor's report, even though Theo was bound to beg me to stay on at the flat.

'Theo?'

'It's haunted,' Walter said. 'That's why they can't sell it.'

'Theo, what do you think?'

'It's a well-known local fact,' Walter added, 'that two previous houses have stood on exactly that same spot.'

I wanted Theo to say something, anything, but Walter was already launched into a description of the original house, a grey mansion with tall spires and a slate roof stained dark by rain. At dusk, from the barred windows, screeching vampire bats flew wildly, desperate for blood.

(I knew all this, bats excluded. The surveyor's report clearly stated that all three houses had made use of the same foundations, making the present brick-built structure inherently more solid. The previous two buildings, by unfortunate coincidence, had both been demolished after fire damage.)

'The old man did it,' Walter said.

'What old man?'

'The mad arsonist professor. He smoked opium like a Chinaman and it scrambled his brains. Then he burned down his house.'

'It was electrical.'

'Then when they built the second house he came back as a ghost and burnt that one down as well. That's why nobody dares buy the place, because who's to say the ghost isn't waiting there still?'

(The surveyor's report made it quite clear that nobody had bought the house because the back half over-looking the gorge was rotten with damp. It was as flammable as a moist sponge.)

'Thank you Walter,' I said. 'That was most helpful and encouraging.'

'Sounds nice,' Theo said, absent-mindedly tapping ash from a cigarette onto his trouser leg, listening for Emmy's voice on the walkway, his judgement and sensitivity to his friends and flat-mate utterly destroyed by the selfish obsession of love.

'Your mother tells me you want to work in the shop.'

'I don't want to work in the shop.'

'Why on earth would you want to work in the shop?'

'I don't want to work in the shop.'

'Over my dead body.'

He told me he hadn't given me Uncle Gregory's money so that I could waste it by staying at home. And what about my University education?

'You never went to University,' I said.

'Precisely. You think I *wanted* to be a tobacconist?'

Or failing that, as a kind of educational second-best, there were foreign countries full of satisfactions far grander than any offered by a chain of provincial British newsagents. He said I didn't want to be dependent all my life and he was right. There was New York City and beautiful women wailing to be rescued from burning buildings.

But then there was also the mole-like suspicion, encouraged by my mother, that mothers were always right and I ought to resolve my life now, while I still could. Perhaps instead of beautiful women my destiny was simply to continue the series of Simpson's, Tobacconists.

I asked Dad if he thought New York was a good idea, really.

'I don't know,' he said. 'It's your decision.'

'But do you think it's the right decision?'

'How should I know? It's your life, Gregory, and it's up to you. There's no user's manual.'

We are waiting for a taxi, black. Walter wears a black Homburg. He is leaning forward on his chair, his hands crossed on the crook of his stick and his chin resting on his hands. I ask him if he thinks I should wear a hat.

'Leave me alone.'

'I was only asking.'

'Stick to your writing.'

I haven't been outside the house since I gave up. This makes me nervous, which makes me want to smoke, so I follow Walter's advice and try to subdue the familiar craving for a Carmen by writing, wishing my blood would hurry up its re-learning of the purely organic life.

'I really don't want to go.'

'I told Mrs King.'

Walter looks at nothing in particular, grimly revising all

147

the stories he ever lived and invented with Humphrey King, wondering why all of them had to have the same ending: Humphrey King dies. It makes the stories weak and uninteresting, predictable from the beginning.

Humphrey King will be buried in the ground, not burnt in a furnace like Theo. Most of the Suicide Club will be there. We will sing hymns and shuffle darkly in our funeral suits. During the service one of us will have an uncomfortable throat just itching to become a choking fit, and Jonesy Paul's memorial address will have to compete with sporadic bursts of infectious smoker's cough. Afterwards, in the weak sunshine of the churchyard, someone will recall the ironic spirit of the Club and attempt to brighten the occasion by observing that it wasn't the coughing that carried him off it was the coffin they carried him off in. Blah.

'I'm coming straight home, mind.'

Walter and the others will go to Mrs King's front room for expert sandwiches and ritual estimates of how much longer they each have to live.

'What about Haemoglobin?'

'He'll be fine.'

At Theo's funeral I smoked thirty-seven cigarettes, one after the other, and I made sure that Carr was watching.

On 1 March 1962, an Ash Wednesday, the Royal College of Physicians published their first ever report on smoking and health. The initial print-run of ten thousand copies sold out, as did the twenty thousand sent to America for re-distribution by the United States Cancer Society. The report received widespread publicity and in 1963 cigarette sales in the UK fell by 14.5%.

The College pointed out that in 1960 10,000 people died

from lung cancer in comparison to 250 in 1920. In an extensive study of British ex-servicemen a 20-a-day smoker was found to have a 14 times greater risk of dying from lung cancer than a non-smoker. As many as 3 out of 10 smokers would die from a smoking-related illness.

Industry spokesmen were quick to respond. No causal connection had yet been demonstrated between smoking and cancer, so the results given in the report were merely inferences from statistics. They had no more authority than mathematical expectations at a roulette wheel. The increase in lung cancer could be explained by improvements in diagnostic method. And a study of ex-servicemen was inherently unreliable because it wasn't random: ex-servicemen might have a higher rate of lung cancer for entirely different reasons. It was all a question of presentation: even according to the RCP, 70% of smokers remained in robust good health. To suggest otherwise was to deny British tax-payers their citizen's right to enjoy a pleasant and perfectly legal pastime.

The RCP couldn't explain why certain smokers were more susceptible to disease than others. It was entirely possible, even after the findings of the Royal College, that a smoker could go through three packs a day for fifty years without losing a single day to smoking-related ill health. Or he could die horribly of lung cancer before he was forty.

What a gamble that was.

'And I've never worn your stupid rainbow sweater and I've never done the jigsaw puzzle and I *hate* Lilly's jumbo pasties.'

'Then why eat them all the time?'

Because I'd never learnt any of the other dances, but I wasn't going to tell him that. Instead, I watched him drop cartons of cigarettes into the nylon shopping bags while at the same time dialling for a taxi and trying to avoid tripping over Haemo-globin. All this fuss was clearly a ploy of his to annoy me, just because I refused to go with him to the Estates. I said,

'I don't feel well.'

'Rubbish.'

'Really. I feel, it's something in my chest I think.'

'See a doctor then.'

'Theo, please.'

I followed him into the bathroom and this was the part I really hated, when he preened himself in front of the mirror. He never really improved anything, like his hair for example, so I suppose he just did it to check he looked like himself. He inspected his face from lots of different angles with his mouth closed, and sometimes stroked the little vertical scar on his upper lip.

'Beautiful,' I said, but I wasn't very good at sarcasm.

'I thought you were ill.'

'I was lying.'

'You shouldn't lie.'

'All smokers lie, you know that. I bet Emmy Gaston never lies.'

'You're in the way, Gregory.'

I followed him into his bedroom where he picked his brown overcoat off the bed, then back into the living-room. I watched his back struggle into the coat, lit a Carmen, and told him I was going to move out. Now he'd *have* to pay me some attention.

'Elsewhere,' I said, 'somewhere else. Another place. Not here.'

The horn of a taxi sounded from outside. He ignored me and went over to the nylon bags and arranged the cigarette-cartons so that none of them poked out of the top. I said:

'I can't just stay in the same place all the time, can I? A man has to move on, doesn't he?'

'You won't move out,' he said, picking up a bag in each hand.

'I will.'

'You won't.'

'Let's toss for it,' I said, but he didn't even laugh.

'Sure you won't come to the Estates?'

'Do you love her?'

'I don't want to be late,' he said, slipping past me.

I watched the door close. The taxi sounded its horn. Haemoglobin sniffed at my hand. Bananas looked round for an ashtray. We all have to be doing something, when we're lost and alone and under-attended. We all have to occupy ourselves somehow.

At my own funeral, well into the next century, few of the mourners will remember cigarettes as anything but curious artefacts from a past millennium.

The cathedral will be crammed with dignitaries who take turns to pay their respects to my coffin of highly polished ash. We are more than half-way towards the year 2100, and for the last decade or so I have been solemnly revered as an ambassador from the twentieth century. Children rarely fail to ask me interested questions about typewriters and frying pans and petrol engines. They want to know if it hurt to suck down the poison smoke from cigarettes and I tell them no, not really, but none of them quite believe me. Instead, they privately conclude that we were all less civilized and therefore tougher in the old days, and I'm not beyond suggesting that maybe we were.

In a less optimistic version of my own funeral I'm only

Uncle Gregory's age, or younger, and the twentieth century is easily remembered. At the graveside there are no personal friends, and in my line of work I have no colleagues. My mother weeps into a black handkerchief. A couple of spring-time strollers in fashion raincoats stop and stare and internally sermonize on the stupidity of smokers. They identify the scene as a moral lesson for their children, and then wonder if it's going to rain.

And me, I wonder if Julian Carr will be there, either today or in fifteen years' time or in fifty. I examine my nails, gauging where best to start biting.

He bought twenty Consulates, just to get himself started. Then he applied for a high-flier's job in a Tobacco Research Unit in England, where he was accepted on the strength of his PhD. He rented a flat above Samson's Turkish restaurant, which later became Lilly's Pasties, and quickly settled into the routines of his new home and his new work. Compared to molecular biology, learning to smoke was easy.

Gradually, he began to lay off the bet of his smoking against acts of kindness. This, if anything, was his little guilty hypo-crisy. He subscribed to charities, saved abandoned animals, and gave life-saving cigarettes to people who couldn't other-wise afford them. He saw being kind as an extension of his challenge to Providence to strike a good man down, a refine-ment to his gamble on the existence of his mother's God. It was as if he wanted to make a conquerable opponent of the unknown, tricking it into revealing itself by gradually increas-ing the value of the prize at stake.

Theo only rarely talked about his past, and if I'd been more busy than I was I might never have succeeded in piecing his story together. The flexibility of his working hours suggested that his research at the Institute was beyond reproach, to the point where he could turn up whenever he liked. I had no idea how much he was paid, but the two-bedroomed flat above Lilly's Pasties was a direct result of his habit of buying more than four thousand cigarettes a week.

He still gambled occasionally, as a kind of unannounced check on the remorse of God. He'd play Spot-the-Ball, or pump money into the fruit machine at The Strangers' Rest until we won enough change for the pinball. He once told me he won Haemoglobin in an impromptu game of 21 in Broseley, Shropshire, but I don't know if that's true.

He would almost certainly have played and won the National Lottery, if his luck hadn't run out.

Monday morning.

I am wearing a brand new and slightly crisp short-sleeved white shirt and an orange tie. The tie has a weave of gold STNs at diagonal intervals. I am wearing grey trousers and the polished black shoes I last wore for my A-levels. I rinse out my coffee-mug (I love Simpson's) and kiss my mother on the cheek.

'I'm proud of you,' she says. 'New York was a stupid idea.'

'Immature beyond belief. Thanks, Mum.'

My father has already left, in a mood so foul he made a point of slamming the door twice. But I can't be worried about that because this is Monday morning and my first day at work as a shop-assistant in Simpson's Tobacconist and Newsagent (est 1903), High Street Branch. My destiny begins today, free of the pain of decisions. My life becomes a set of train-tracks with a timetable and a clear idea of destination and no call for judgements of steering. This morning and every morning until I become area manager I will walk to the shop. Then I shall buy a car. Before succeeding my father to the position of general manager and, generally, Mr Simpson the Tobacconist, I will at some stage engage myself to a slightly plump but always punctual young girl who will delight in bearing me a son called Gregory.

I open the front door and take a deep breath of fresh spring air. A freak ray of sunshine picks me out and I smile at the sun-drenched lawn and a chestnut in bloom. One of the Adventist neighbours, in a charming green dressing-gown, is picking up her milk from the doorstep. I turn towards her and say over the wall:

'Good morning, fine morning, good morning to *you*.'

I stride purposefully into our quiet road, swinging my arms and slapping lamp-posts with conviviality as I pass them by. I jauntily follow a brown-headed spaniel, out on its own, predatory and curious between interesting shits on the pavement. I beam into front gardens full of great klaxon daffodil gangs. On the High Street I overtake a black man and wonder why people don't have curly hair in cold places. I mean countries, of course. I ask myself what is curly hair all about? I turn my head for a pretty girl with thin ankles and the spaniel passes me on its way back home, followed by a thickset man who could have been bred specifically for meat. He has a cigarette pinched backwards into the palm of his hand, but I feel I can safely ignore that.

Everyone is off to work, just like me, and I am entirely satisfied because I have succeeded in completely repressing every single one of my desires. It is therefore hardly surprising that by lunch-time I will be walking home with my head down and my feet dragging, looking at nothing much but my shoes.

Jonesy Paul and old Ben Bradley. Dr Hacket, Marlowe and Whittingham, Drake and Mrs Drake. The Pole Jan Peto, Russell, Gallagher, and Lundy Foot the mariner addicted to all legal substances except alcohol and tobacco. He passes around his latest variety of Ginseng. All of them, at one time or another, have been regular or part-time members of the Suicide Club, and a general restlessness is therefore inevitable about mid-way through the funeral service. I watch them trying to occupy their hands.

Later, outside, lighters click like insects and there follows a general inhalation of tobacco smoke, like the exact opposite of a sigh. It is a sound expectant of imminent satisfaction, which is realized in every case within seven seconds. Lundy Foot swallows some Sanatogens and I put my hands in my pockets.

'Nobody told me it was lung cancer,' Drake says, and Jonesy Paul says it wasn't.

'It was too,' says Lundy Foot, gum-chewing.

'He hadn't smoked in fifteen years,' says Dr Hacket.

Walter says: 'Nothing to do with smoking at all.'

Everyone agrees that this must surely be so, especially since Humphrey's lengthy participation in the North Africa campaign exposed his lungs to irritant and probably fatal sand particles. Jonesy Paul and Lundy Foot then support each other at some length on the dreadful modern dangers posed to the lungular health of one and all by radon, volatile organic and inorganic substances (from walls and floor-coverings), concrete sweat, ozone from electrical machines (notably computers and printers), heat radiation, humidity, static electricity, bacteria, fungi, fungal spores, house dust, mites and mite excrement, and the incalculable problem of all other people and their terminally flaking skin.

The air was so dirty, Jonesy Paul said, he was surprised

anyone bothered to breathe it. He asked me if this wasn't so.

'Sure,' I say, 'he could have died from anything.'

Old Ben Bradley says, 'He could have died from old age.'

There is a moment's silence and then a general shaking of heads.

'No,' Walter says. 'It was definitely his lungs.'

And it was then, or perhaps a little later, that I saw Julian Carr. He was some distance away near the entrance to the cemetery, his hands in his pockets, leaning against a solitary tree like a bereaved and secret lover.

At my back, the gorge. I moved into the front half of the house. I had no curtains. I had no chairs and tables. I had no socket for a television aerial but that was alright because I had no television. I found myself living in the largest room of the house, ground-floor-front, surrounded only by the things I owned.

From a call-box I phoned home for my bean-bag. Mum sent the bean-bag and asked me one if I was still smoking, two if I had a girlfriend, and three did I want anything else.

'No, I'm fine,' I said, and then had nowhere but the floor to stack my history books. I bought a cooker and some rugs to quieten the floor-boards. I bought a Calor Gas heater, and then sat on my rugs in front of the fire listening to noises from outside, reading my history books and sometimes laughing out loud, frightening myself with echoes. I bought a fridge with a freezer compartment and laid up frozen supplies.

I often talked to Bananas. He was an amazing listener, as long as he had his ashtray somewhere near him, and I reassured him that Lilly would keep an eye on Theo, the poor old man, the old mad scientist. He wouldn't waste away, living all on his own, without friends. Then I introduced Bananas to the

156

bean-bag and from then on the bean-bag belonged exclusively to him. Neither of us missed Haemoglobin one tiny bit.

I sat on the floor, watching smoke curl to the ceiling, listening to the house creak and wondering how to distinguish the rattle of a window-frame from the cackle of a ghost I didn't believe in. For the first few weeks I smoked all my cigarettes before night-fall, and spent the evenings re-heating frozen pasties.

Behind the counter I was visible from the waist upwards, a white shirt and an orange tie and a happy face against an unbroken background display of cigarette packs.

Chesterfield, Camel, Kent. Stuyvesant (for sporting events worldwide), Philip Morris, John Player Special (Black to Basics). Lucky Strike It's Toasted. Buchanan's Century, More, Raffles, Richmond Straight Cut, Royals 25 because a change is as good as a rest. State Express and Sullivan No 1 and Salem Lights and Silk Cut purple blue red and green. Lambert and Butler if there was really nothing else. Rothmans (airplane pilots), Winston (USA), and a Benson and Hedges after breakfast. 555 (555 *what*?). Carmen No 6 and Embassy No 1, Embassy Regal, Embassy Extra Mild, Embassy Extra Extra Mild (depending on her mood and the time of her life, say). Virginia Slims. Du Maurier in the theatre at St Moritz while Sobranie shares a Cocktail with a Black Russian Viceroy. Maybe. Fortunas (Spanish beaches and the cafés of Madrid). Caporal and deep blue packs of philosophic Gitanes. Kool or Craven in Piccadilly and Mayfair. Down at the Kanif Club with the entire Senior Service. Triple A. And then finally, just to round off the evening with another new lover, a consummate Consulate menthol.

It was like being surrounded by Lucy's plans for the future.

It was like a vision of endless but calculable days without her, measured in cigarettes by the twenty and my fear of each and every one of them, because Cigarettes Kill and Smoking When Pregnant Harms Your Baby and Tobacco Seriously Damages Your Health and surely it must be true because on every single packet it says so.

I grabbed a pack, any pack. It was a soft-pack of Gauloises and I tried to stare it down. The door opened and I stuffed the cigarettes deep into my pocket and served a complete stranger with forty Marlboro in exchange for money. A packet for him and one for Lucy (pull yourself together, man). It happened so quickly that he didn't once take the lit cigarette out of his mouth, leaving behind his smoke and the smell of Lucy Hinton.

Someone else came in. *The Independent*; 20, 40, 60 Benson and Hedges and 20 pence change and thankyou most kindly madam and don't forget that Smoking Causes Heart Disease. Through the cellophane and the paper I could feel the curve of each cigarette like a cartridge.

Family Circle, Snickers, single Hamlet.

I tried to remind myself that the job was a breeze: just money and multiples of twenty, day after day. But then why did it feel like being stuck inside Lucy Hinton's mouth?

In my lunch-break I locked the shop and went to the travel agent's. Looking for my cheque-card I took the Gauloises out of my pocket, and because I was still mindful of my anxious mother, and because there was a fifty pound limit on my cheque-card, and because the travel agent was about to close up for lunch, and for several other essential reasons like these (any one of which could have been the patient and determining factor in my destiny), I bought a coach ticket to Paris.

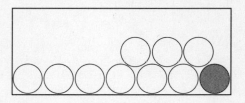

Paracelsus was born in the same year that Christopher Columbus returned from America in the listing *Santa Maria*, bringing with him the news that every established European idea about geography was wrong. Many of the more enlightened thinkers of the time then started to question other branches of knowledge, casting doubt on almost everything previously considered a certainty. Paracelsus, as doctor and alchemist, inherited this radicalism.

His unshakeable belief that the principle of all creation was separation led him to improve on contemporary techniques of distillation. However, he was always prepared to embrace a broad constituency of learning in his search for the pharmaceutical equivalent of the philosopher's stone. His expert knowledge of chemistry could therefore exist alongside a fascination for ritual incantations and sacred objects, and this modern acceptance of the notion of profusion meant that he often seemed to contradict himself. This in turn left him vulnerable to criticism. His students were known to have called him Cacophrastus and envious colleagues whispered his enviable pact with the devil.

In many ways this opposition was understandable. Paracelsus was, for example, the first European to suggest that 'miner's disease' (now known as silicosis) was caused by inhalation of metal vapours and not, as previously thought, by mountain demons who administered the disease as punishment for sin. However, it was also Paracelsus who popularized the word 'gnome' throughout Europe as a term to describe the dwarfish goblins who guarded hoards of subterranean treasure. He believed in Gob, king of the goblins, whose magic sword influenced the melancholic temperament of man, yet he also devised a radical revision of the Renaissance system of Humours to include the then startling notion of the circulation of the blood.

Like all great innovators he was prepared to examine the consequences of the unbelievable. And to Paracelsus no stories of goblins can have been any stranger than the wilder reports filtering back from America. These included eye-witness accounts of secret cities constructed entirely from gold, and solemn sad-eyed natives swallowing draughts of fire as calmly as cool water.

Uncle Gregory's money changed me. I began to appreciate how clothes and books and the food I ate could be made to speak for me. I bought a black leather jacket and Camel boots and large books about history. I lunched in restaurants on blackboard meals and drank small jugs of wine. I discovered, with something almost resembling exhilaration, that I was more than Gregory Simpson the Tobacconist's son; I was free.

At the beginning, still at the YMCA, I used to visit art galleries at random. I saw photographs by Brassai and Lartigue, and the unpublished manuscripts of Raymond Queneau. At the Orangerie I saw a kinetic installation in blue steel by Jean-Pierre Rives. In front of the Pompidou Centre an Algerian magician made lit cigarettes vanish in his bare hands and a ten-franc piece bought me a printed ticket which said there were still 512,019,580 seconds remaining until the year 2000. I remember a Seita exhibition called Ashtrays of Today where I signed the visitor's book as Grégoire Simpson, and because the book had been printed and bound in Thonon-les-Bains I

162

gave that as my address. I could be whoever I wanted to be, from anywhere.

I wanted to be the kind of person who was always on the way somewhere, or on the way back. I didn't want to repeat the empty afternoons of my months at home, lying on my bed thinking it was good enough just to be breathing. I'd learnt since then that waking up each morning could hardly be described as a triumph, so in Paris I confidently set about finding somewhere of my own to live. After that I was going to look for a part-time job to keep myself occupied, which would then leave me ideally placed to identify the beautiful woman waiting to love me.

It all sounded so simple and easy that I doubt even Lucy and Julian would have bet against it.

I suspected them of changing the recipe without telling me because I could now smoke two or three Carmens in a row and all of them tasted airy, or stale, or like somebody else's idea of extra mild. They somehow weren't as consoling as they used to be, so I'd smoke another, just in case that one or the next was different. I checked the box, but the double casta-net was unchanged, black on white, and the tar and nicotine values were the same, and there was still the promise that this particular packet of cigarettes would kill me, just like all the others.

I went outside to smoke, thinking the fresh air might help me appreciate the taste, and that's how I found him, lying on his stomach with his head behind a tree-trunk. It was nearly dusk. I called out to him but he didn't answer.

'Come on, Jamie, stop messing about.'

He scrambled up from behind the tree. 'I didn't think you could see me,' he said, looking disappointed, but he brightened up again when I invited him inside. I had to sit him on the floor because the bean-bag was occupied by Bananas, who kept one eye open while Jamie commented on my lack of furniture.

'Yes, very good, Jamie. Now tell me why you were hiding in my garden.'

'I came to see the ghost. Nice telly. Is that new?'

'Don't touch. What ghost?'

'You know, the *ghost*.'

He was, of course, referring to the mad vampire arsonist professor so vividly described by Walter.

'An arsonist,' Jamie said proudly, 'is someone who burns down houses on purpose. Walter says that's why you don't have any visitors. Is it true that bats sleep upside down?'

'Did he say that?'

'And why no-one would buy this house except you.'

'Yes, they do. Upside down I mean, I think.'

'But you weren't scared though, were you?'

'Oh no,' I said. 'Resolutely not.'

'Do cats eat bats?'

Jamie was staring alternately at Bananas and then at the burning end of my cigarette, as if at any moment the ghost might pluck it from my fingers and plunge it fatefully into the centre of the bean-bag. I didn't tell him it was fire-resistant. Instead, I asked him about Theo, in a casual kind of way. 'Still going to the Estates, is he?'

'Sometimes,' Jamie said. 'Show me the ghost now?'

'People still singing and shouting outside the flat?'

'LUNG, actually,' Jamie said. 'Does it ever *speak*?'

'What about the fierce lady with the eyes? Theo ever talk about her?'

'Maybe,' Jamie said, suddenly perking up, 'show me the ghost and I'll tell you.'

164

'There is no ghost,' I said.

'For a cigarette instead then?'

I can prove I'm much saner now than I was a few days ago. Walter isn't here.

However, I do not suspect him of dying on me. Nor have I felt the slightest urge to kill him. Contriving major disasters as an excuse to smoke is an idiocy I've now outgrown, and credit where credit's due etcetera I think it's due to me. My determination has been first-class. My strength of character has been a revelation, not least to myself. The fact that physical addiction to nicotine cancels itself out within two days is a small detail of little relevance.

As for my lung-ache, I hardly notice it now, and I shouldn't wonder if before long several of the Suicide Club take me discreetly to one side and ask me for the secret of my success. I shall tell them it may well have helped to throw away all the ashtrays, and to dispose of the disposable Bic lighters. And even though the solitude was probably useful, in the end it was nearly all a question of personality and a certain rigour of intellect needed to reconcile the body to the mind without the familiar arbitration of nicotine.

It's true anyway that I don't crave a cigarette half as often as I used to. A week ago I was writing away the cravings at least once an hour, but my attention span is now appreciably longer. There are tight green buds developing on the inside branches of the plant on the desk, for example. They look like tiny green pine kernels.

Oh, and Mum phoned up. She asked me how I was and I asked her how she was and she said everything was fine at home and I said good, I'm glad that everything's fine at home. Then she asked me if I was alright.

'You sound . . . different. You're *sighing* less.'

'I'm fine,' I said. 'I'm absolutely fine.'

I could have told her how I'd given up smoking. I nearly told her, but then I decided not to, not yet.

The room measured 2m92 by 1m63, a little over five square metres, so it wasn't big enough for my bean-bag even if I had it with me. It was in a quiet area close to the river and if I stood on the chair, put one knee on the edge of the wash-basin, and stuck my head out of the window I could just about see the radar-swollen bulb at the top of the Eiffel Tower. On account of this view the room was expensive as well as cramped, but I didn't mind because I had ten thousand pounds and no possessions apart from a few books and clothes and the twenty-one cigarettes I'd imported from England. And anyway, I planned to be out a lot.

I discovered that in Paris you could never really lose yourself. Wherever you went, no matter how wide the circle, sooner or later you were sure to come across people taking photographs of something already better photographed on postcards. The number of recognizable landmarks was reassuring; it made me feel involved in something already recorded as important. Paris immediately seemed familiar, so that I was rarely frightened by the fact that in a city this big anything could happen. It hardly worried me at all, for example, that I once saw Lucy Hinton, her white mini-skirt circumflexing between her thighs as she leant over a push-chair and fussed with a baby. She straightened to light a cigarette and turned back into someone else.

Back in my room, listening to the big city sound of sirens, I sat on the bed and handled the pack of Gauloises. They reminded me of the shop. The orange tie came to mind and I unwrapped the cellophane. A drawer opened and closed in the room next to mine and a man cleared his throat. I thought of Julian Carr and the single cigarette he used to turn upside down for luck, so I broke the duty-paid seal with my thumb-nail and prized up the edges of the silver paper.

And was surprised to see that someone had beaten me to it. I couldn't turn a single cigarette upside down, just for luck, because someone had already done it, and they'd done it all wrong. Every single cigarette was already turned upside down.

Then I remembered that the Gauloises were filterless. There was therefore no right way up and no upside down. I laughed, and took my mistake for an omen predicting the most incredible spell of good luck, times twenty.

In the beginning it was just *Tomorrow's World*. Then I watched *Top of the Pops* before *Tomorrow's World*, then *Nationwide* before *Top of the Pops* and then the local news before that. Eventually I fell into the habit of switching on the television each evening at six o'clock for the proper news, where there were often items about how many people were dying every day and all over the world from smoking cigarettes. It was a statistical epic of disaster which consistently revealed the terror to be found in numbers. Men in suits quibbled about advertising and filter-systems and amounts of money which stretched into millions. The word epidemic became fashionable. There was the first National No-Smoking day, but I missed it.

Now that I had less far to run to the Unit, they insisted I make up the distance by lapping the cinder track once I arrived. I hardly ever saw Theo, so there was little opportunity to gauge exactly how lonely and depressed he'd become since living without me. Back home, fed up, I would talk to Bananas. I read,

167

I twiddled my thumbs. I thought of taking up motorcycling, just to liven up the days.

Jamie used to visit about once a week and he told me all about Walter and Theo and Emmy and the Estates. He was a fairly unreliable narrator because he was so easily distracted, but it seemed that Theo was still giving out cigarettes and that there were more demonstrators all the time (although probably not the *thousands* which Jamie claimed). A gang of anti-vivisectionists had tried to force their way into the flat above Lilly's Pasties but Haemoglobin had chased them away.

'Bananas would have *eaten* them,' Jamie said.

He'd become a great Bananas fan ever since Bananas had lifted a dazed mouse through from the back of the house, then patted it around the rugs for a while before biting its head off.

'I'm sure there was something else,' Jamie would say, 'but I can't quite remember.'

I gave him another cigarette. He said that Theo had gone for a check-up at the hospital. As for the result . . . Jamie snibbed the next Carmen behind his ear.

'No idea,' he said. 'But there's a really cool X-ray. We stuck it on the wall in the waiting-room. It's ace.'

The X-ray was in black and white, Jamie said. Even for another cigarette he couldn't remember whether any of the black bits were on the lungs.

In English Madame Boyard said can you speak English and in English I said yes, yes I could, and the incisiveness of this answer secured me a job as part-time assistant sub-librarian in the music department of the National Library of France. I was therefore right about the Gauloises bringing me luck.

Madame Boyard, the librarian, was a stocky woman with thin lips and flat breasts and a pale complexion. She wore a beige suit and when she spoke she burred her vowels as if she was expecting a cold. She told me I was to work no more than twenty hours a week and sometimes it would be less, and I said that was fine. There was also another part-time assistant sub-librarian, with whom I would sometimes be expected to co-operate.

The work itself was straight-forward: I had to continue the task of transferring the library's Astrat Archive onto computer. The archive contained press reviews and performance programmes collected by Henri Astrat from opera houses in England and America between 1910 and 1975. Astrat had also bequested an income to finance the continuation of the archive, but the Opera Garnier had spent the money sending a team of administrators to China to explore the feasibility of in-house fireworks.

The department of music was in the basement at the back of the library, and consisted of two large adjoining rooms. Half of the connecting wall had been removed to allow an easier passage for trolleys of over-size documents. On a broad table in the centre of the larger room there were two computers back to back.

Madame Boyard went to a desk in the smaller room and glared at me until I chose the computer facing away from her. I opened a box-file marked 1940 and started to type in, very slowly but also conscientiously, the details of Mario del Monaco's debut performance as Rodolfo in *La Bohème* for the Neapolitan Opera at Covent Garden.

I occasionally glanced at the white hunch-back of the other monitor.

'She's American,' Madame Boyard had said. 'She talks too much.'

Boredom is the enemy and cigarettes can help. Fact.

I take an envelope out of the top drawer of the desk. I open it and empty the contents onto a fresh sheet of white paper. The pieces of leaf are dry now, brittling as they turn brown at the edges. I crumble some between my fingers, like a Yecuana Indian might have done, in Venezuela, a long time ago, looking for cures to boredom.

There is, say, a small village-worth of tee-pees occupying a clearing in the centre of a jungle of broad-leaved plants. In a wigwam not far away a dozen strips of dried llama and as many plump carp are being smoked in preparation for winter. All the Yecuana except one are away somewhere, down by the river probably, and the solitary Indian discovers that it is only moderately entertaining to turn one thumb over the other until the two blur together.

For something to do then, she examines the encircling bushes, wondering why such broad and inviting leaves are so bitter and useless as food. She uproots a plant and smells it, licks it, tastes it, wears it, burns it and it burns with a nice enough smell. She strips the leaves and tries cooking them in various different ways. She experiments, and in doing so she re-inforces the essential difference between herself and the other animals which stalk the plains and surrounding mountains.

Gradually, over a long period in which she learns to recognize that curiosity relieves boredom, she observes the change in the leaf as it dries. She discovers patience. She learns the skills of selection, care, and attention to detail required to cultivate tobacco for smoking. How or why it occurred to her actually to inhale the smoke remains a mystery.

Meanwhile, down at the river, the men have overcome boredom by discovering the principles of bridge-building. In the process they have become adept at modelling clay, and someone makes a pipe. The Yecuana try out smoking and several of them become ill, but this sickness is infinitely preferable to boredom and anyway, next time the leaves will be left to hang a little longer beside the llama and the carp.

And because boredom is still the enemy I find my Helix tin and tip out the pencils and dividers and protractors and replace them with the pieces of dried leaf. Then I pull the Calor Gas heater in from the kitchen and turn it onto low, placing the tin on top of the heater. I look at the leaves in the tin for a while, thinking how this act has re-inforced the difference between me and the animals, and then other things like oh what a noble work of art is man. I mean I include myself these days.

'Smoke-break,' she hissed.

'Sorry?'

'*Smoke*-break.'

Because she was the more experienced part-time assistant sub-librarian I'd had to move over to the computer facing Madame Boyard. The O on the keyboard kept sticking. For the past hour I'd been typing in the names of unsung contributors to forgotten operas, while occasionally glancing across at Ginny Mitchell, the American who was supposed to talk too much. So far she hadn't said a word. She had short hair, not quite blonde, and an interesting fine-boned face. She wore glasses with round lenses and dark frames. Not that I'd been looking, particularly, but the neck of her white T-shirt was pulled into a V-shape and she was wearing jeans cut off just above the knee. I quite liked her delicate neck and the slide of her shoulders and her white American teeth.

'Smoke-break,' she said again, pushing back her chair. There was something very familiar about her.

171

'I don't smoke,' I whispered back.

Madame Boyard was peering in our direction so I looked down and hit the O key by mistake and it stuck, reproducing at least twenty Os on the screen before I could prize it up with my thumb-nail. Then, in perfectly projected and very polite French, I heard Ginny tell Madame Boyard that we were both going to take a break to smoke a cigarette. Madame Boyard nodded.

'Make sure it's only one,' she said.

I grabbed my jacket and followed Ginny up the stairs.

At the back of the library there was a dusty courtyard with a few trees and some stone benches around a dry fountain. Half the staff of the library were milling around, smoking. We sat down on a low wall next to a green life-size statue of a shortish stoutish man wearing a long overcoat. It flapped out behind him as he strode into the wind, his hands clasped firmly behind his back like a skater.

Ginny leant forward, put her hands on her bare knees, and looked closely at the sandy gravel. Then she reached down and picked up a cigarette-end. She gave it to me.

'Really,' I said, 'I don't smoke.'

She ignored me and leant forward again until she found a second cigarette-end for herself. She held it between the very tips of her long fingers and grimaced slightly.

I offered her one of my Gauloises, which I carried about with me at all times, for luck.

'I thought you didn't smoke,' she said.

'I don't.'

'You're weird.'

'Have one.'

'No,' she said. 'I don't smoke either. What have you done with your butt?'

'I dropped it.'

'Don't you know *anything*? Just hold on to it, in case Boyard comes out. And keep an eye on the door.'

After about exactly the time I imagined it took to smoke a cigarette, Madame Boyard did come out into the sunlight of the courtyard. Ginny immediately stood up, dropped her filter, and stood on it. She then lifted her heel slightly and turned her naked ankle in both directions, crushing the filter under the sole of her loafer.

We passed Madame Boyard on our way back to the basement. She already had a Camel lit and was heading for one of the benches by the fountain, a great collar of smoke planing out behind her.

Just after six o'clock I turned on the television. A Durham man who once played inside-right for Stoke City was suing British American Tobacco because there was no health warning on his cigarette brand when he first started smoking in the early sixties. The man was fifty-seven years old and suffering from chronic lung cancer. He'd smoked fifteen cigarettes a day for thirty years and was expecting a third, possibly fatal heart attack. He was one of life's seriously low-rollers.

And then on the local news the lead story was the Research Unit and Theo. He was filmed through the wire fence walking from the Unit down towards the pond. He didn't seem to know about the cameras, because all he did was smoke and look at his feet. Then the film cut to a reporter who was interviewing Emmy Gaston outside the main gates. Demonstrators could be heard chanting Barclay Barclay Barclay, Out Out Out, and several lab-coated scientists stood at a corner of the Research Unit peeking round each other at the protesters. I recognized Theo's hair. He had a cigarette in his mouth. They cut back to Emmy, who explained very clearly that Buchanan's were

173

paying certain employees to distribute free cigarettes in order to addict new customers. It was a disgrace and something should be done.

Finally there was a studio interview with a representative of the Buchanan's company. He was young and smartly turned out in a double-breasted blue suit. He wore sincere wire-framed glasses. He said he'd been specifically sent to Long Ashton by Buchanan's senior management as a sign of how seriously the company was treating the allegations being made. He said that an internal enquiry had already begun and any necessary disciplinary action would be taken swiftly and without delay. No, it wasn't company policy to give away cigarettes to addict new users. The Buchanan's company would never, under any circumstances, approve such an initiative.

Looking admirably composed, entirely trustworthy, and all grown up, Dr Julian Carr thanked the interviewer warmly for her time.

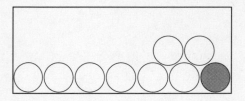

Ginny Mitchell was training to be a singer in the National Academy of Music, which was based at the opera house. She worked in the library to help pay the fees.

'Know anything about opera?'

'Not really.'

'It's simple. Everyone sings and then someone dies.'

Every hour, on the hour, Ginny told Madame Boyard we were going outside for our smoke break. As she often pointed out, it could only happen in France, and once in the courtyard we used to talk and wave around our unlit fag-ends, one eye on the door leading to the basement. Ginny told me that her first impression of Europe had been small people with bad teeth which she attributed respectively to an ignorance of dental floss and the under-development of basketball.

'I think you'll find that's a joke,' she said.

She came from Maryland and apart from buying contact lenses her most immediate ambition was to be chosen as an understudy for a forthcoming production of *Cosi Fan Tutti*. She had beautiful and slender hands, and held cigarette-ends right at the tips of her fingers, between her polished fingernails. When she talked she moved her hands expertly, flowingly, like a Mediterranean.

'I try to keep my throat and my vocal cords and my lungs in optimum condition at all times.'

Her hands lingered in front of each essential part of her singer's anatomy. 'It's like a sport. I have to train. I have to work out. I have to jog. Do you like jogging?'

'I don't know.'

'I have to keep the tiniest bronchioli as clear as glass. You know about bronchioli?'

'Little bits of lung.'

'Then I can hold the high notes. They must never be allowed to fade, not in the Paris method. I don't suppose you have any idea how large a lung is?'

'No, no I don't.'

'I mean to look after. It's quite a job.'

'Honestly, I have no idea.'

'Flattened out, a single adult lung covers about forty square metres. Imagine that.'

There was something disquieting about her. I thought it might have been her mouth, but then I really liked her mouth. It might have been the way she looked at me over the top of her glasses, or the crispness of her voice. Whatever it was, I was fairly sure she wasn't a transvestite.

'Did you always want to be an opera-singer?'

'Only when I found out I was good at it,' she said. 'It agrees with me. Here she comes.'

Ginny stood up and dropped her cigarette-end and trapped it beneath her shoe. Intent on crushing it beyond redemption she turned her heel and then her shapely leg and then her slim hips first one way and then the other. She kept on killing the cigarette long after it was dead.

Watching her ankle catch the light, I wondered if it would be a betrayal of Lucy if I fell in love with another.

'He's a great man and a great scientist. His work on the Tobacco Mosaic Virus is truly revolutionary, and we're in no hurry to lose a man of his calibre.'

Julian's arms were stretched out along the back of a

black leather sofa. His office was on the second floor of the Research Unit and it had a view over the cinder running track and the asphalt tennis court, and then down towards the pond where we'd found Bananas. His hair was darker and cut very much shorter than when I'd last seen him, in Hamburg.

I offered him a Carmen.

'You know that's not allowed,' he said, waving them away. The band of his wedding ring glinted in the sunlight. 'But have one yourself. Sure.'

In his own office, in his chalk-stripe suit, with his light-weight glasses on, it was hard to believe he was still the same age as me. I was wearing my track-suit.

'You're a difficult man to track down, Gregory.'

'You knew where I was.'

'You never answered my letters.'

'I never received any letters.'

'Must have been lost in the post then. Like the ones I sent you in Paris.'

'That's probably it,' I said.

My Carmen was turning out to be one of those which didn't taste so good. I leant forward in my chair, also black leather, to reach the onyx ashtray on the oblong coffee-table. Next to the ashtray was a glass box full of cigarettes.

'You look great,' Julian said. 'I've heard they're very pleased with your work.'

'I've been well looked after.'

He wanted to make sure I had enough money, and that I'd been offered tickets to the rugby and the Formula 3 at Brand's Hatch. Perhaps I'd be interested in Glyndebourne, where the company always liked to sponsor a marquee? I told him Buchanan's had always been most generous.

'You're worth a lot to us, Gregory,' he said, pausing accurately before adding: 'That's why I don't think motorcycling is a very good idea.'

I asked him how long he was planning to stay.

'Too dangerous,' he said, 'too much of a risk. Tell me some more about Barclay, as a person I mean.'

Ah, back to Theo then. That was easy enough. Theo had lost his mind, deserting his loyal friends for an infatuation with an anti-smoking fanatic who hated the sight of him. But I wasn't going to say this to Julian, because Theo's desertion wasn't as bad as breaking someone's heart, just for a bet. I said,

'What are you going to do to him?'

'It's not an execution, Gregory. We're all on the same side, remember? We're doing our best to protect him from these LUNG people, and we'll look after him just like we've looked after you.'

He leant over and lit my second Carmen, but despite the glass box on the table he didn't take a cigarette for himself. He said we really ought to go out sometime. I should meet his wife.

A black cotton baseball cap, fronted by JPS in gold. Walter holds the door open for Emmy, who I haven't seen since Theo's funeral. She hasn't changed. She looks fit, relaxed, as though she was still in love, and far younger than she actually is. It must be all those years without smoking.

'Walter tells me you're giving up,' she says, and I mumble a little and say hum ha I'm not out of the woods yet.

'That's why I brought you this.'

She hands me a square of green card printed with the words: Bluebell Drama Club, The Mikado, Admits Two. As I wonder what this can mean, Walter pads out to make the tea, shuffling

to the door like a man wearing slippers. I hear him put a match
to his pipe, and Haemoglobin trots out to join him.

'Thanks,' I say, 'but it's not really my type of thing.'

'You don't know.'

'Call it instinct.'

'One show and you'll be hooked. Trust me.'

Emmy goes up close to Bette Davis in *Now Voyager* and
examines her from close range. Then she moves on to the
framed print of Magritte's pipe. She smiles.

'I got that in Paris,' I say. 'How's the Outward Bound?'

'Great,' she says. 'A big of jogging, a little cycling, the
basics of Alpine parascending. Interesting people.'

She looks briefly at the acupuncture diagram of an ear and
then more closely at the cross-section of lung. She sighs
quietly, mostly to herself.

'Look at all this stuff,' she says. 'He always knew it was
killing him.'

'He didn't want to forget the risk, the gamble of it all. The
posters and everything were there to remind us. They kept us
honest.'

'It's such a waste.'

'It's always a waste,' Walter says, coming back in with the
tea. 'Think of your mother.'

'That's not the same. She never smoked a cigarette in her
life.'

Emmy glances up at the inscription from Paracelsus above
the door. 'And poor old Bananas,' she says, taking a mug from
Walter and holding it in both hands, blowing steam off the
top. She looks across at me with her convincing grey eyes.

'Theo asked me to look out for you,' she says.

'I can look out for myself.'

'Good. I want you to take my parachute instructor to see
the *Mikado*. She's very keen.'

'Emmy.'

'I'll be away and Walter's too old.'

'And it's no-smoking,' Walter chips in.

'Really,' I say, more forcefully this time, 'I don't think it's me.'

Emmy puts down her mug and tells me quite calmly that I'm in danger of becoming pathetic.

'You can't give up smoking for ever, Gregory. At some stage you have to give up giving up and go on. Take a look at what's happening outside the window. Meet some new people. Make some friends.'

'I will,' I say. 'Very soon.'

'Don't be frightened, Gregory.'

'I'm not frightened.'

'Her name is Stella.'

'Who?'

'My parachute instructor. Stella Granger. She's very nice.'

Then Emmy turns away, as if she's disappointed with me. She stares hard at the poster of Popeye, pipe in mouth, and says she often used to wonder what we did all day. 'Apart from smoking, obviously.'

'It was a club,' I say, wondering how I've upset her. 'It was just a place where people could be together.'

'How exactly?' Emmy asks, settling into one of the chairs. 'Tell me how, exactly.'

I didn't go home to England for Christmas.

Instead, I wandered the city like a superhero, on the alert for burning buildings and wailing women. Failing that, I looked out for second-hand bookshops with box-fulls of English books somewhere out of sight near the back. I browsed for anything with the word History in the title, and before long my reading became entirely determined by this arbitrary decision. I ended up with translations of Michelet's *History of France* and Fliche and Martin's *History of the Church* (Vol. VII). I read the *Unfinished History of the World* by Hugh Thomas and a *History of the New World* by Girolamo Benzini. I came across a *Know the Game History of Rugby Union Football* and *Tobacco: A History* by VG Kiernan. I became the owner of an Everyman *History of Rasselas*, by Dr Samuel Johnson. Once, when I was desperate for something to read but couldn't find any book with History in the title, I bought Raymond Aaron's *Eighteen Lectures on Industrial Society*, because it was *about* history. It served me right because it turned out to be a rejected printer's edition with page one hundred and twelve repeated one hundred and twelve times.

By coincidence, I began to find that many of the best bookshops were near the opera house, and it was always possible that I might just meet Ginny either coming or going from one of her classes. I never did. Instead, I used to see Lucy Hinton on the pillion seat of a lime-green Lambretta, in helmet and goggles, an unlit cigarette between her pouting lips and a split skirt slip-streaming past her stocking-tops. In sunglasses and a business-suit, her black hair streaming clean in the wind, striding towards the Bourse. Outside the Louvre guiding groups of Japanese photographers. In any number of cafés, partly obscured and from the side, something about the way she inhaled, and then held the smoke in her lungs for a moment before letting it slip through her lips. And I was always sure it was her, and just as surely it always turned out to be someone too old or too young, too tall or too short, with the wrong ears or nose or throat, a Canadian who spoke no English or a married Spanish au pair or a back-packing Croat looking for lifts towards Holland.

Prepared to give Lucy one last chance, I wrote her a letter

and addressed it to her Hall of Residence, where I didn't even know if she lived anymore. If she really loved me then she'd write back. If she didn't write back then it must have been a bet and I had nothing to lose by asking Ginny out. I mean I could just ask her. It would just be asking.

Opera as an art-form can be traced back to Italy and the intermissions (*intermezzi*) between acts of sixteenth-century court entertainments. During the intermezzo an allegorical or philosophical theme would be enacted to the accompaniment of music in the emerging solo virtuoso style.

The intermezzi were famous for their elegance and refinement, and as they evolved into opera their appeal was thought to lie in an aesthetic remoteness which combined with increasingly wanton displays of splendour. Eventually, opera came to depict the world as a series of possible sensual gratifications. It could fulfil the audience's desire to believe in an existence grander and more intense than their own, and the heroic gestures of the protagonists offered a clarity of emotion absent from the confused impulses and ambiguous feelings of everyday life.

The action of opera is usually dominated by a beautiful woman (the soprano). The hero (tenor) is drawn to the beautiful woman by destiny, and this combination invariably leads to disaster. Both Rossini and Verdi, for example, identify the operatic potential in the story of Othello. Wagner has his Tristan expiring in Isolde's arms, and Debussy's Pelléas and Mélisande die from frustration at the impossibility of sustaining love in a cruel and cynical world. This sense of impending disaster is pervasive. In *Eugene Onegin* both the star-crossed lovers survive, but Tchaikovsky made up for this by himself attempting suicide during rehearsals.

Ginny liked the kind of opera in which all emotion was pure, though obstructed. And in such circumstances, suicide was often viewed as the only noble response. In Donizetti's *Lucia di Lammermoor*, Edgardo the British lover is banished to France and stabs himself when he learns of Lucia's supposed infidelity. Janacek's Katya Kabanova, weary of the intensity of passion, wades into the Volga. In Verdi's *Aida* the lovers chose to be entombed together, to die sated in each other's arms, and all these opera suicides sing sublimely at the moment of death, so much so that to an impressionable mind it might seem that death itself is the key to beauty.

Of course, this glorification of death only applies to one type of opera, usually called *opera seria*. There is also *opera comique* and *opera buffa*, both of which are often no more than vulgar farces set to music. In these types of opera a brief period of discord is followed by a general resolution of conflict. Suicide is no more than a temporary threat made by conventionally disaffected lovers, and it is rare for even minor characters to die.

'My brain needed all the oxygen it could get. You know, Gregory, you've hardly changed at all. Got a girlfriend?'

'Not just at the moment, no.'

'You should get married. It's a greatly undervalued level of consciousness.'

'So my mother keeps telling me. Look, Julian, if you've given up then how come you still carry cigarettes?'

He casually flicked his packet of Centuries across the table. 'Good for morale,' he said. 'There's a chap in marketing who smokes. Embassy. Every morning he puts them into a Buchanan's packet before coming to work.'

Julian had invited me to a pub. The contents of his pockets

185

were on the table, and along with the scarlet and black box of Buchanan Centuries there was a Carmen castanet key-ring, a disposable lighter marked BUCHANANS and several coins, some of them foreign. He undid the top button of his button-down Oxford shirt and loosened his tie. I lit a Carmen.

'To be honest,' he said, leaning over the table, 'I mean out of the office and everything, I think you and Barclay are bloody heroes.'

'If you don't mind me asking, Julian, why aren't you a doctor anymore?'

He looked puzzled. 'I *am* a doctor.'

'Then why aren't you working as a doctor?'

'Jesus, Gregory, try and relax a little.'

'Or at least a medical researcher. Like in Hamburg.'

He gave me a man-to-man look. 'They were not very nice to animals in Hamburg.'

And anyway, his present position was a promotion. He told me so twice. Public Relations was the front line these days, and the money was amazing. He said that to a married man little things like cash and the year after next became important, especially now they were thinking of children. I nodded and smoked and then, instead of reminding him of the great ambitions he'd squandered since his youth, asked after his wife. Her name seemed a good place to start.

'Lucy,' Julian said.

'Sorry?'

'Lucy. My wife. Her name's Lucy.'

'Lucy what?'

'Lucy Carr,' he said, smiling broadly. He leant over the table again. 'But sometimes, just between ourselves, I call her Lulu the lover who came from the *moon*.'

186

'No,' she said, 'I can't.'

'How about Tuesday?'

'Not Tuesday either.'

I explained to her that it wasn't anything grand. I'd buy a few things from the market and we could have them in my room. Some smoked chicken perhaps. She could bring the wine. White would be best.

'I can't,' she said.

Or there was this Italian restaurant just round the corner from me, Cosini's. It was great.

'Really, I can't.'

'Of course you can. It's easy. You just say yes.'

'Gregory, I've got a boyfriend.'

I looked closely at the green statue. It was the statue of a coat, mostly, and a way of walking into the wind, but according to a plate near its base it was also Jean-Paul Sartre. His mouth was slightly open, his lips parted, perhaps a little breathless from his vigorous striding and all the cigarettes he was famous for smoking with Albert Camus.

'Of course,' I said. 'That's not what I meant at all.'

'He's in England,' she said. 'He's English.'

'I didn't mean anything like that.'

'Sure. You probably already have a girlfriend.'

I stared Jean-Paul Sartre directly in his green lapel. I stood up and brushed a leaf from his collar.

'Yes,' I said. 'I do. Obviously. She's in England too.'

Ginny's boyfriend was a medical student in London who was training to be an Ear Nose and Throat specialist. She'd met him in the Tuileries, jogging. They both jogged at the same time every morning, even though he was supposed to be on holiday, and before long they were jogging side by side. It was as if they were meant for each other.

'I know exactly what you mean,' I said.

187

My girlfriend was called Lucy. She had long black hair. She was very slim. She didn't smoke.

It wasn't really a club.

Although Theo would have let anyone join, nobody knew about it and there were no application forms. In fact, it was Emmy who'd given Theo the idea for the name, in the Estates, when he came out of No. 47 and locked the door for the last time. A huge cheer went up from the crowd of demonstrators, and under cover of *We Shall Not Be Moved* Theo stood next to Emmy and said,

'You won't.'

'I told you I would.'

'And you did. I don't suppose you ever feel sorry for smokers at all? I don't mean me. I mean these smokers?'

'No,' she said. 'All you created here was a kind of suicide club.'

'You exaggerate,' Theo said. 'It's not as important as that.'

'It's a matter of life and death,' she said.

So then when Theo moved in with me he had the idea to buy the brass plaque and the big overstuffed armchairs and the pictures to hang on the walls. It was a kind of joke, but maybe it was also to remind him of Emmy. Then Walter brought along his cigarette-card collection and then his friends and it seemed funny enough to pretend it really *was* a club.

Theo then decided that everyone ought to pass an entrance test to be admitted as a member. This was part of his constant effort to remind us all of the dangers of smoking, usually while dragging deeply on whatever brand of cigarette he favoured at any particular time. French were always his favourites, probably because they were the strongest and in this period he was always cutting down. His test questions weren't difficult. They required a basic familiarity with smoking, so as to eliminate impostors:

Which tobacco brand is associated with the final of the Rugby League Challenge Cup, which takes place annually at Wembley Stadium?

Name three often fatal diseases closely associated with the smoking of cigarettes.

What word is embroidered on the hat of the sailor pictured on packets of Player's Navy Cut?

Name any three public figures who smoked and who also died of lung cancer.

With what catchphrase did Superman defy Nick O'Teen in the 1981 television campaign against smoking?

Nearly all of Walter's friends had smoked for long enough to know these answers and many more, so nearly everyone who joined turned out to be Walter's friend. There were also rumours that Walter would happily sell the questions in advance, in exchange for tobacco. The only person ever to fail the entrance test more than three times was Jamie, even though he once got all the questions right. That was Walter again.

The women from the Estates never once came to visit, or to smoke, or to ask Theo for cigarettes. I have no idea of what happened in their homes after Theo was forced to desert them, but I believe they made no protest because they were used to having things taken away from them. It was one of the reasons they liked to smoke in the first place.

He'd met his wife at the Buchanan's Silverstone Spectacular. She'd been on the front row of the grid holding a Carmen No 6 umbrella over Rob 'King' Carter, fresh from his victories in three separate classes at the Isle of Man. From the warmth of the Buchanan's hospitality suite Julian had studied her on close-circuit television. Then, after the race started, he invited her in out of the rain. No children as yet. She was blonde.

'Satisfied?'

'I'm sorry,' I said. 'I didn't mean to shout. I'm sorry.'

'I can promise you, cross my heart and hope to die, that she wasn't at college with us.'

'I know, I'm sorry. I was thinking of someone else.'

As a way of changing the subject, and calming down, I asked him about his Enquiry. He'd been at the Research Unit for nearly three weeks and still nothing had changed, except for the local news losing interest.

'But that's the point,' Julian said, 'don't you see?'

'No,' I said, 'not really.'

Julian was in no hurry to get back to Hamburg, and even with diminished press coverage LUNG showed no signs of giving up. In their most recent protest they'd picketed the entrance to the Research Unit so that a refrigerated truck trying to get through the gates had been delayed for several hours. LUNG claimed the truck was carrying cats for testing whereas in fact, according to Julian, it was just the meat delivery for the canteen ('Why would we want to refrigerate *live cats*, for God's sake?'). This kind of thing drove him up the wall, he said.

'They should all be forced to take up smoking. Then they might learn to relax a little. I mean really,' he said, holding out his hands for the answer, 'how can they think we'd want to kill people for profit?'

And there was really no answer to place in his outstretched hands.

'That girl you liked at college,' he said, changing the subject back again. 'She was a Lucy, wasn't she? What was her name?'

'Lucy Hinton,' I said.

'Yes, I remember now. Blonde.'

'She had black hair.'

'That's right. Smoked like a chimney, sexy as hell. Do you two still keep in touch?'

'No,' I said. 'No we don't.'

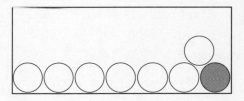

I learnt about Ginny's life in instalments, in our non-smoking smoke-breaks which always ended with her contemptuous crushing of a cigarette-end. I watched the turning of her foot, ankle, shin, knee, hip. So she had a boyfriend, but Paris was a big city and anything could happen.

She told me her family didn't understand her. She had one sister, older, who became a lawyer like their father, and to show the kind of life she was escaping, Ginny liked to cite the time her sister worked for the Philip Morris tobacco company. Philip Morris had learnt about a television documentary still in production which suggested a connection between smoking-related diseases and men who lived the lifestyle of the Marlboro cowboy. During the opening credits an ex-cowboy and ex-smoker was shown riding his horse across the sunset landscape of the midwest. He was wearing an oxygen mask connected to a tank wallowing in his saddle-bag. The film also featured a rodeo star and former cowboy, Junior Farris, who died of lung cancer in Mustang, Oklahoma before the end of filming. Philip Morris sent Ginny's sister to visit his widow. After a lengthy interview it was eventually established that Junior had spent several winters in the late seventies teaching farm management at a local high-school. It therefore wasn't entirely accurate to portray him as a Marlboro-type cowboy. On the basis of this misrepresentation a legal injunction was issued against the film, which has never subsequently been broadcast.

Ginny described a hopeless arc with her dusty cigarette-end, making it clear that no more words were necessary to explain why she'd run away to Paris in search of love and opera.

I tried to be equally open in return, and there came a time when despite countless delays and hesitations, I decided I ought to tell her the truth about Lucy.

'What I told you about my girlfriend.'

'What?'

'It isn't true,' I said.

'You don't love her?'

'No, not that.'

'She isn't in England?'

She looked at me through her eyebrows, and even though I was still trying to work out what I found so exciting about her, it wasn't her eyebrows.

'Neither of those things.'

'Well what then?'

'She smokes like a chimney.'

Otherwise, it turned out that Lucy was just about perfect. She could sing and dance and juggle. She modelled for charity magazines and was good with children. But even when I laughed out loud at Lucy's unique sense of humour, Ginny managed to conceal her jealousy. I decided to elaborate: neither of us were possessive types, we held no monopoly over the life of the other.

'I expect it's the same for you,' I suggested.

'Actually I'm very possessive,' Ginny said. 'Why do anything by halves?'

Jean-Paul Sartre listened in closely to everything we had to say, only miming his walk away from us, slippery-shoed and wily like Marcel Marceau. I often suggested we go somewhere else, after work perhaps and out of Sartre's earshot. But Ginny was always too busy with her singing, or she had to phone her boyfriend, or worst of all, she would look at me as though

I ought to know better, both me and her being in love with others and all.

'Are we friends?' Julian asked.

'Of course we are.'

'Which is why I want to help,' Julian said. 'Both you *and* Theo. How is he? Any better?'

Theo was dying.

More than a year had passed since Julian called me into this same office to announce the results of his Enquiry, when he'd explained to me at some length that in this day and age a company like Buchanan's had to be fully politicized. Every employee was encouraged to promote certain basic principles, whenever possible, like the fact that there was no demonstrable connection between cigarette-smoking and cancer, and that we lived in a free country where cigarettes were perfectly legal. Individual initiatives such as Theo's, however, were to be discouraged.

'He means I've been sacked,' Theo said.

Theo had been sitting on Julian's sofa, the black leather contrasting neatly with his white lab-coat. He was smoking a cigarette from the glass box.

'You're not really sacked,' I said. 'It's just a ruse.'

Julian had decided that in return for an undertaking to stop delivering cigarettes to the Estates, Theo could take a short holiday at Buchanan's expense. Julian would announce Theo's resignation and the LUNG protesters would go home satisfied. When everything had calmed down, Theo could discreetly return to his full salary and continue his research as if nothing had happened.

'So he's only *saying* you're sacked.'

'We did this kind of thing all the time in Hamburg.'

197

'So there isn't a problem,' I said.

'Yes there is,' Theo said. 'It's *corrupt*.'

Julian took off his glasses and rubbed his eyes. 'It's public relations. It doesn't mean anything.'

'And I was *this* close to making a breakthrough with the TMV.'

'Julian knows that,' I said.

'*Julian* is it?'

'We were at college.'

'So you know why they kicked him out of Hamburg?'

'He wasn't kicked out. He didn't like the way they experimented with animals.'

'Is that what he told you?'

'It's for the best,' Julian said. 'Think of the rent for your flat. Think of your dog. I'm being as fair as I can.'

'I could get another job.'

'You're getting old, Barclay. Be reasonable.'

'Your research, Theo,' I said. 'Where else would you go?'

He then surprised us both by smiling broadly, keeping his mouth closed of course. He stubbed out his cigarette. He stood up. 'You're both such pessimists,' he said. 'After all, I can always go and live at Gregory's place.'

Now, a year later, no matter how often I'd tried to explain it, Julian still didn't believe we hadn't plotted against him. This often made me feel as if I owed him something.

'I'm glad we're still friends,' Julian said. He offered me a light for my cigarette. 'Because there's something I want you to do for me.'

'It was a laugh, Walter, wasn't it?'

'Not all the time, no.'

'Well a lot of the time it was.'

198

He is wearing a brown pork-pie hat with a day-glo yellow Think Bike badge. He sits slumped in his chair, looking daggers at Emmy because she's here again, listening to my memories of the Suicide Club. I ask Walter if there's anything wrong.

'No,' he says.

'Sure?'

'None of your business.'

Well anyway, it was a laugh most of the time, being in a room full of fearless people every single one of whom knew what was embroidered on the cap-badge of the Player's Navy Cut sailor.

'HERO!!'

The Suicide Club reintroduced me to exclamation marks, and it was like having a second chance at an education and the happiest days of my life. My curriculum was now an alternative type of history which included any field covered by the stories of Walter and his friends, and Jonesy Paul started me off gently, on Statistics, with the story of a Japanese survey about babies of women married to smokers. One of the women in the survey gave birth to a child well below the average length and weight, but she denied she was married to a smoker. This surprised the statistician, because every afternoon the woman's husband smoked vigorously in the waiting room both before and after his regular visit. Eventually the woman was asked why she kept on denying her husband was a smoker.

'I'm sorry,' she said. 'But that man is only my lover.'

Physical Education: while playing in the 1987 Rugby World Cup, in which France reached the final, Serge Blanco the French full-back smoked an average of thirty cigarettes a day, as did a long tradition of great French players before him, including the unforgettable Jean-Pierre Rives.

English Literature: according to Lundy Foot, all the great

English novels were written with the aid of tobacco. He could quote Thackeray on the smoke of Cuba, and Kipling on the difference between a woman and a cigar. (This could also be filed under Women's Studies.) In Foot's opinion, the Death of the Novel coincided with the anti-smoking movement, whereas the Death of the Author could all too often be attributed to an opposite and equal reaction against it.

Economics: Karl Marx spent more money on cigars while writing *Das Kapital* than he earned from its publication. This might explain his strange blindness to the obvious truth that in fact tobacco is the opium of the people.

Criminology: the great Sherlock Holmes insisted that all detectives of the superior sort should be able to identify 140 different varieties of tobacco. In *ash* form.

Science and Psychology: Newton was partial to a smoke, as was Freud, who claimed to be sucking a nipple and not a cigar and eventually died of cancer of the mouth, thus demonstrating a fear of women which was entirely justified.

I loved every minute of it.

'Rubbish,' Walter says. 'You're idealizing for Emmy's benefit.'

'I do not *idealize*.'

'It was never perfect. He's lying.'

'I never said it was perfect. And anyway, since when have you been such a guardian of the truth?'

Walter lobs his tobacco pouch onto the coffee-table. Haemoglobin pads up and Walter kicks him. Haemoglobin runs away. Then Walter swipes his ashtray off the arm of the chair. It spills, bounces, settles. On the table the tobacco pouch yawns open, like a leather jaw.

It is empty.

Lucy didn't reply so I wrote to her again, gently suggesting that I couldn't wait for ever. But the only letters which came back from England were written by my mother, who'd stopped reading articles about the dangers of smoking and moved on to tragedies of more general interest. In particular, she alerted me to the terrible variety of disaster lying in wait for young Englishmen in big cities in foreign countries. The statistics made appalling reading.

Worried by her subdued punctuation, I wrote back to reassure her. I reminded her that great and wonderful things also happened, even abroad and even in big cities. *Who knows*, I wrote, *I might even be lucky!*

And on this understanding, I redoubled my efforts to meet Ginny anywhere but at the library. I asked if I could watch her rehearse for *Cosi Fan Tutti*, but she told me I'd be bored. And anyway, what would Lucy say?

Refusing to give up hope, I tried to tempt Ginny with descriptions of Cosini's Italian restaurant, and not only because it was just round the corner from my place. Cosini, the owner and chef, was famously indecisive and his restaurant kept changing. On cold days I could therefore tell Ginny there was an open fire. On hot days Cosini had installed air-conditioning. Once, after Ginny complained about how poor she was, I told her how *expensive* Cosini's could be.

She looked up, squinting against the bright sunlight in the library courtyard.

'Does it have a non-smoking section?'

'A huge one,' I said, 'always.'

'Always?'

'At least half the restaurant.'

'Sorry,' she said, 'not tonight. I'm expecting a phone-call.'

While she eyed up a good place to crush out her stub of cigarette, I wondered what I was doing wrong. I remembered it being much easier to fall in love with Lucy, so then I tried to twist enough logic to make it Lucy's fault, which was probably when I noticed that Ginny had gone.

She'd been replaced by Madame Boyard, who was now standing squarely between me and Jean-Paul Sartre, blocking out the sun. She had her hands on her hips, a lit Camel emerging from her clenched fist like a fuse. She said:

'What on earth are you doing just *sitting* there?'

'Let's put it another way,' Julian said. 'Are you better friends with old man Theo than you are with me?'

'Julian, I don't know, I don't know what you mean. Theo is *dying*.'

'I want you to bring me one of the tobacco plants he was cultivating before he fell ill.'

'I told you already. He said no.'

'And in return I'll see what medical help we can get for him. Buchanan's has been working on cancer for years. We've got some excellent people.'

'I asked him and he said no.'

'It's only a plant.'

'Julian, Theo is very ill.'

'Theo is standing in the way of progress. Help us both. You can if you want to.'

I remembered the angle of Haemoglobin's head as he watched Theo unhooking pictures in the flat above Lilly's Pasties. I remembered Popeye and the lung and Theo's collection of betting slips stacked next to the incriminating X-ray in one of the red nylon shopping bags.

'I have to have an operation,' Theo was saying. 'It's common for people my age. Nothing to worry about. It's so routine they haven't even set a date.'

And I believed him because he was already listing all the things he planned to do at my house. He made broad sweeps in the air with his cigarette as he described how he was going to convert the back of the house into a lab. As long as there was enough light, the dampness would create the humidity ideal for growing and experimenting with plants like, say, tobacco. Then, even though he'd never been there, he described my front room in some detail, including the Calor Gas heater and the bean-bag.

'And I'm not scared of ghosts,' he added, 'because Jamie told me not to be.'

Jamie had been spying on me all the time, though Theo wouldn't say whether he'd paid him in cigarettes.

'You're a corrupt man, Theo.'

'He says you've got a great TV.'

He stopped packing his bags for a moment.

'Do you really want me to come and live with you?'

'It'll be good for your work. You said so yourself.'

'But do you actually *want* me to?'

'Otherwise you'd be homeless.'

'You once said you didn't want anything. You didn't want any distractions, remember? You didn't want anything to happen. You didn't even want to talk to anyone very much.'

'I must have changed.'

'Say it then.'

'I *want* you to come and live in the house, alright?'

'Good,' he said, 'that's very good. Suddenly I feel a bit peckish.'

And there in the middle of the room he dropped everything and hopped from one foot to the other, raising his knees high and turning from the hip. I recognized the Steak and Kidney, and I liked to think he danced it partly from joy. Then I started in on my own version of the dance with a new variation of backward-rotating arms, and that really was a little bit from joy, and we kept it up until Lilly threw open the door.

'One steak and kidney pie,' she said.

'Only one?'

'And one jumbo pasty.'

I come back with Emmy from looking at what's left of Theo's lab, and Walter is sitting at my desk reading this. Or I don't know, maybe he's reading Yesterday.

'All this mulling,' he says, shaking his head.

'Who said you could read that?'

'What is it?' Emmy wants to know. 'Let's see.'

'No, please Emmy, put that down. Walter, get away from the desk.'

'Is it a diary? What is it?'

'It's a pack of lies,' Walter says. 'You get to be a hero. I'm just an old fart who wears hats.'

He waves a piece of paper at me. I grab it and eventually manage to clear both him and Emmy away from the desk.

'Most of it's true,' I say defensively.

'True?' Walter has now gone several hours without tobacco. 'I'll tell you a true story.'

'Calm down, Walter.'

He doesn't. He leans on his stick, punching the air with his finger, saying, 'There's this woman, see? And her husband commits suicide while her father murders her mother.'

'Walter, behave yourself,' Emmy says. 'Nobody committed suicide. My husband left me because he was ill and it was for the best. It was a long time ago.'

'He just left you. He used to smoke Gitanes. So you got it into your head that he killed himself deliberately. That's what you think isn't it?'

'Look, Walter,' I say. 'If you've run out of tobacco don't blame it on Emmy. It's not her fault.'

But he wouldn't let it drop. He described how his wife, Emmy's mother, died of chronic bronchitis and Emmy still held him responsible. That's why she'd made it her mission to save Walter from himself, moving in with him in his house stranded in the Estates.

'I wanted to help you,' Emmy says.

'Have a pipe, Walter.'

'But this is a true story, it doesn't just stop.'

After her husband left, Emmy hadn't found another lover until Theo. Walter said she was too busy, giving anti-smoking talks in boys' private schools with slide-shows of cancerous testicles. It was as though ridding the world of tobacco would make everything alright, including the disaster of her private life.

'I just don't like people dying, that's all.'

'Rubbish. You like complaining about one thing instead of everything. You're a frustrated old spinster.'

'That's because every man I brought to the house was disgusted by your endless smoking, until Theo.'

'So it's my fault?'

'What's got into you? Why are you saying this?'

'Because it's a true story,' Walter says. 'And next time Gregory decides to mull us all over he can put that in his pipe and smoke it.'

Emmy is close to tears. Haemoglobin is whining. My sheets of paper seem to be shuffling about the desk of their own accord. Emmy looks across to me for help and I can see we're both thinking the same thing. Theo would have known what to say and what to do.

'I'm sorry, Gregory,' Emmy says. 'My father is increasingly frail.'

If only Theo had spent less time and energy on building the lab, on courting Emmy. If only he'd gone for his operation as soon as he knew he needed it.

Still no letters.

I missed my underground train to the library because I was watching two drunks on the opposite platform. One of them was wearing a white fur coat and the other balanced a silver rucksack on his knees. On the rucksack it said Apollo Space Mission. They were sitting on a bench separated into individual plastic seats, a design intended to stop people like them from sleeping in any comfort when they were tired. The two men shared a single pistachio nut.

I have no idea what this can possibly mean.

Then they lit a cigarette. I watched them smoke, lean back, close their eyes, smile. They were utterly happy and I didn't understand why. I thought of books which might explain it to me: *A Social History of Paris Destitutes*, or *The Pistachio Nut: A History*. Then I decided they were probably just mad, a pair of old crackpots. Yes, that was it. That was all.

Because of the crackpots I was late for work, and as I jumped down the stairs, Ginny ran up in the other direction, pushing straight past me, her feet fast and urgent on the concrete steps. I had the impression she was crying.

Madame Boyard was waiting by the computers.

'Ginny Mitchell is unwell,' she said, sighing deeply.

Distracted, she pressed down the O on the broken keyboard. She watched the single letter accumulate before neatly tapping the key again to release it.

'It's broken,' she said. 'She loved him. But secretly he loved a radiographer.'

Madame Boyard had told Ginny to go outside and smoke

206

as much as she liked until she stopped crying. I wanted to help, but Madame Boyard said she doubted very much whether I could. I was a man, and the understanding of love and heart-break was almost certainly beyond me. She turned and walked back to her desk, and I watched her calf-muscles and thought she was quite attractive, in her own way. And poor old Ginny, I thought that too.

Some time later, while I was typing in the details of *Don Juan* at the Met in 1943, Ginny came back. She rubbed each dry eye with a knuckle, then with the back of her wrist, then almost with her elbow and finally on her shoulder. She sniffed. She sat down and scratched her knee and I forgot all about Madame Boyard. At last I realized what was disconcerting about Ginny Mitchell. It was the same thing which was familiar and exciting about her, all at the same time.

It was her bones. She had Lucy Hinton's sexy bones.

'Just one tobacco plant,' Julian said. 'It's not much to ask for.'

'I'll think about it.'

He looked at me as if I was making some basic and astonishing error, like encouraging children to smoke.

'I just don't understand what you've got against me sometimes,' he said.

The first time Theo went into hospital, the entire Suicide Club sat in vigil. No-one smoked and no-one talked about smoking, as if this in itself would guarantee the success of Theo's operation. It wasn't at all what Theo would have wanted, but then Theo was in hospital, his history of cigarettes opened up to strangers. We sat in silence mostly.

Old Ben Bradley raised his eyebrows, leant forward in his chair, opened his mouth, and then closed it again. He leant back in his chair, shaking his head. Then Jonesy Paul, checking each word to avoid all reference to tobacco, worked hard at a description of his baby nephews at a marionette theatre in a crèche at Great Ormond Street Hospital. There wasn't much else to say. In real life, he'd left them watching Punch and Judy while he slipped outside for a Piccadilly in Pall Mall.

Walter accepted the challenge like a man and remembered his trip to North Africa. He'd been abandoned in a desert. No food, no water. Only the sun at noon and the rare view of a horizoned Bedouin heat-hazed in the distance, slumped against the single hump of his unstoppable ... blast. Giving up is never as easy as it looks.

Finally Humphrey King, in a stroke of inspiration, declaimed at some length on the Roman Empire, including its taste for gladiatorial combat, elaborate mosaic and dormice (all of which seemed like obvious displacement activities, though no-one was going to say so). King moved on to the relationship between Romans and suicide, claiming with some delicacy that their society lacked any serene and widely accessible source of satisfaction. Walter wanted to know the exact percentage of Romans who committed suicide, and then in contrast to Humphrey King he said with no delicacy at all that if he'd been a Roman he'd have felt like committing suicide about twenty times a day.

We lapsed into silence, each one of us secretly blaming the others for agreeing to the tobacco amnesty, and then a missed cigarette later, blaming the others for Theo's illness. But still nobody smoked and nobody mentioned smoking, because Theo's life depended on it.

Haemoglobin started growling for no obvious reason. Bananas scuttled round the back of the sofa and raced himself in circles before crouching, absolutely still, facing the door at which someone was imperiously knocking.

'It's bloody open,' Walter shouted, or it could have been everyone, but nobody was quite ready for the sight of Julian, sweeping into the room with a broad smile on his face, his charcoal overcoat flapping out behind him. He looked around and clapped his hands, then looked around some more, smiling all the time.

'So this is the famous smoking club,' he said.

He pulled a carton of Buchanan's Century from the inside pocket of his overcoat. He held it up like a wand.

'Not *now*,' Walter hissed.

Julian ignored him and tried again. 'Tobacco,' he said. 'Cigarettes. And there's plenty more where this came from.'

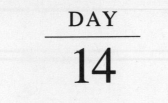

DAY

14

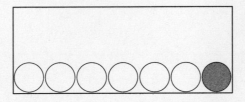

'They're absolutely brilliant.'

'So I looked ugly in my glasses?'

'No, but now. You look completely different.'

In her new contact lenses, even in the subdued light of Cosini's, Ginny looked a credit to her bones. Actually, without her glasses she looked slightly startled, but her bones were just the same. She took off her denim jacket. Underneath she was wearing a short summer dress the colour of vanilla ice-cream. Small strawberries wandered across it.

'Being a singer,' she said, 'in Italian restaurants I usually have the alveoli.'

She was wearing red lipstick. 'Let's order some wine.'

The contact lenses were stage one of Ginny's plan for life without the consolation of an English boyfriend. The dinner in Cosini's was stage two, although she'd made it quite clear in accepting the invitation that it was only because I'd been a good friend to her. Not content with this formula, she wanted me to know that she wasn't attracted to me at all, or in fact to any man just at the moment. I shouldn't worry, therefore, that she would try to seduce me. My relationship with Lucy was quite safe.

This was unfortunate because I know knew for certain that Lucy didn't plan a love-lorn move to Paris. It was Julian Carr who'd told me so, in a throwaway line between his exam results and the fact that Lucy had passed on my address. His letter had briefly revived the part of my mind reserved for miracles, and I waited for him to end the letter with a plea for forgiveness and a passionate appeal on Lucy's behalf. No doubt

213

she'd been too emotional to write to me herself. In fact, Julian was only interested in telling me about his career, and how it was all progressing according to plan. Apparently Buchanan's wanted to give him a taste of commercial research, so they'd offered him a sandwich year in Hamburg. *But no monkeys!* he wrote. I didn't reply.

'Because what does it all mean without love? What is there to defend?'

'Sorry?'

'You ought to listen, Gregory. I don't like repeating things. It puts unnecessary strain on my voice. On my throat,' she said, 'and my vocal cords.' She did that thing where she tracked her body with her hands, 'and my lungs.' It wasn't just her bones. Under her dress she had beautiful lungs, rising and falling.

I watched her breathe and asked her if she ever had the impression that anything we could do in Paris had been said and done before.

'Yes,' she said, 'of course it has. But not by us.'

Two smartly-dressed women settled themselves at a neighbouring table. One of them selected a cigarette from a silver case, tapped it on the table, and then lit it, and even though I said a silent prayer begging her not to, she exhaled the smoke in Ginny's direction.

'I thought you said this was a non-smoking restaurant.'

I shrugged, weakly, 'Cosini must have changed his mind.'

Ginny stared hard at the woman. Then she pushed back her chair and tossed her napkin onto the table.

'Well we can't just ignore it,' she said.

'Why not?'

'My larynx, Gregory, my vocal cords.'

'I know,' I said, 'your lungs.'

Walter is in no better mood than he was yesterday, probably because yet again none of the Suicide Club has turned up. Emmy is here instead, and Walter, sulking in his chair, pulls the brim of his Homburg over his eyes. After yesterday's outburst he makes me nervous, but Emmy has had to live with him between then and now, and perhaps as a kind of revenge she seems determined to talk about love, a subject we both know that Walter hates. She reminds me of the very first time she came here, when she wanted Theo to know she had nothing to do with the petrol-bomb thrown over the fence of the Research Unit. LUNG had been disbanded when the Estates business finished, and it wasn't her fault if various idiots still wore the T-shirts. She'd also wanted Theo to know she was sorry he'd lost his job.

In actual fact, all this was an excuse to see him again.

There is no immediate reaction from Walter, who has at least refilled his tobacco pouch. He has a pipe on the go.

'I loved him very much,' Emmy says, and Walter snaps open the *National Geographic* he's already read. He lifts it up to hide his face, and the dark eyes of a Yecuana woman stare out at us from the cover.

'I'm not listening,' Walter says. 'I'm not even pretending to listen.'

'Good,' Emmy says.

The unique details of Theo's life seem to reassure Emmy that he really existed. She tells me that the scar on his upper lip, for example, came from a game of roulette when the ball flew off the table and hit his lip so hard it pushed a tooth through from behind.

Walter mutters something from behind the magazine.

'Sorry, Walter?'

He lowers his screen. 'Drivel,' he says. 'Think of the chances against something like that.'

'I miss him,' Emmy says.

'We all miss him,' Walter says. 'Let's talk about something else.'

'Which is why we should all try to keep busy. Stella says she'll take you hang-gliding, to say thanks for the theatre.'

'I haven't decided if I'm going yet.'

'She's looking forward to it,' Emmy says.

And I know I shouldn't, because it's exactly what Emmy wants and all I have to resist is temptation, but I ask her about Stella anyway. Emmy is ready.

'She's a proficient parachutist, parascender and hang-glider,' Emmy says, knowing this isn't what I mean. I mean is she nice-looking and what kind of bones does she have. 'She also wind-surfs, scuba-dives and pilots microlights.'

'Superwoman,' Walter says. 'Even better, Lois Lane.' He flips back the pages of the *National Geographic* and starts again from the beginning.

'And to relax she likes to climb mountains.'

'It sounds very dangerous.'

'She's always funny and she's about your age and she has a fat black cat called Cleopatra.'

'Anything else?'

'What else is there?'

'I don't suppose she smokes?'

Walter says: 'Some people are never satisfied.' He drops the *National Geographic* onto the floor, just for effect. 'You don't stand a chance,' he says. He shakes his head. 'Ex-smoker. Homeboy.'

At which point I summon all my strength as a non-irritable non-smoker to confront this severe challenge from Walter's delinquent temper. I ask him very nicely and politely if he isn't a little hot under his Homburg.

'No,' he says, 'I'm not.'

'Isn't that your funeral hat?'

'Well spotted,' he says. 'It's because all you two ever talk about these days is dead people.'

'He means Theo,' Emmy says, 'in his uniquely sensitive way.'

'Well in that case,' I say, 'we'll talk about something else.'

I ask Emmy how she knew it was love.

Julian tapped something into the computer on his desk. It was summer outside and he'd taken off his jacket. His pale blue shirt had white cuffs and castanet cufflinks in black silk.

'My computer tells me you're in excellent health.'

'You know it's for Theo,' I said. 'I'm not going to beg.'

'I know that, Gregory, but you still haven't brought me a tobacco plant. You've been less than helpful.'

'If you're still upset about the Suicide Club, I'm sorry. It wasn't my fault.'

'I only wanted to join in. It's not a crime.'

'You failed the test. There was nothing I could do.'

'They didn't want me to pass. How was I supposed to know what they used to call smoking clubs in London? In the *nineteenth century*, for God's sake. How was I supposed to know the connection between John Wayne and Edward Duke of Windsor?'

Because to anyone but an impostor it was obvious. They both died of lung cancer, which in the Duke of Windsor's case meant he never grew up to be a King Edward. He also married a Mrs Simpson, but as she was no relation to the famous tobacconist Simpsons this wasn't relevant to the question.

'Why didn't they want me?'

'You didn't get the answers right.'

'And now you won't bring me a tobacco plant because Theo

doesn't want you to. Why not just take one? He probably couldn't care less.'

'I doubt that. You don't know him as well as I do.'

Referring to his monitor, Julian then made a big show of telling me that Theo had worked at the Research Unit for twenty-nine years, eight months and seven days. In that time he had progressed from research assistant to project supervisor.

'It's just facts,' I said. 'It's not the whole story. And anyway, you know what I mean.'

'Alright then, *you* tell me the title of his PhD thesis.'

I didn't want to argue. Most of the time, Theo was confined to his chair, even though the doctors said he would get better before he got worse, if he was lucky.

'*Deception Patterns in the Tobacco Mosaic Virus*. Did you know that? I know that. It says it here on my screen.'

Every other day we helped him into a taxi and he went to see Emmy. She was the one who took him for his cortisone injections.

'His work for Buchanan's has been an extension of his thesis, in which he noted that the symptoms of TMV remain dormant at temperatures over 27 degrees centigrade.'

His face was thinner and his hair was crazier than ever. He'd recently developed a new pain in his leg.

'His subsequent research has been designed to deceive tobacco plants into thinking that the temperature is always above 27 degrees, even when it isn't.'

Theo had no illusions about his illness. In the evenings, after everyone had gone home, he would explain to me that the problem with cancer cells was their ignorance. They had no specialization. They didn't even know how to die, which meant that they simply took over the space vacated by healthy cells. They were essentially immortal, and useless. Theo knew how it would end, with a haemorrhage or failing lungs or a fatal infection, but he still managed at least a couple of cigarettes every day.

'His final report before leaving Buchanan's suggests he was on the point of producing an inoculated strain. There's some formulas and things but I'm not a botanist, I'm just a doctor.'

'You're a PR man.'

'I'll ignore that. At the end of the report Barclay reminds us that the defeat of TMV represents an almost alchemical discovery for the tobacco industry. It makes all sorts of other advances feasible, and might even be the first step towards the development of a leaf free of the toxins which sometimes make people think that cigarettes are dangerous. Or in other words, a totally safe cigarette, which would be of incalculable benefit to the industry.'

Theo deflected sympathy by dismissing his illness as nothing more than a lost bet. God had run out of remorse for the death of his mother. God had forgiven himself. 'I feel quite flattered by how long it took,' Theo said.

'A safe cigarette,' Julian reminded me. 'Think of all the lives you'll be saving.'

'He said no.'

'One tobacco plant, just to check how close he is. Otherwise we can't help him. It's your call.'

The bed sagged alarmingly in the middle so we both sat on the floor, our knees pulled up to our chins.

'Your language was a bit strong,' I said.

'Well how was I to know she was English?'

'I thought she took it very well, considering.'

'Some people are so easily offended.'

After Cosini threw us out it seemed like a good moment to remind Ginny that I only lived round the corner. On the way we passed a shop which sold cooked chicken and wine, so we ended up eating in my place after all. I offered Ginny a guided tour of the room, and she suggested we skip the chair section if it looked like over-running, so all things considered it was turning out rather well.

We were down to the last third of the wine when Ginny said: 'You don't have any pictures on your walls.'

I wasn't really paying attention. Instead I was wondering how to direct the conversation towards the subject of destiny, especially as it might apply to me and Ginny.

'You don't even have any photos,' she said. 'Don't you like to look at photos of your family?'

I said it had never really occurred to me. Perhaps she liked poetry.

'What about Lucy?' she said. 'You must have photographs of Lucy.'

I said of course I did. Perhaps she was still hungry.

'Can I see her?'

'Sorry?'

'Lucy, I'd like to see a photo of Lucy. You know, the woman you love.'

'Oh, *that* Lucy,' I said. 'No. Actually, I. Not *here*, exactly. And she looks better in my head than she does on Kodak.'

'You mean she's plain?'

'No,' I said, 'of course she isn't. She just gets a sexier wardrobe.'

'What?'

'In my head.'

'I do believe you're embarrassed.'

'I'm not embarrassed.'

'Then why hide her?'

Ginny pretended to look under the mattress, which meant I had to lean away. Avoiding the chicken carcass, I banged my head against the door. She rolled forward onto her bare knees and the skirt of her dress flapped around her thighs. She opened the top drawer of my chest-of-drawers.

'Not in there, then,' she said. She inspected the balls of my socks.

'You have beautiful hands,' I said.

'Or you use it as a bookmark.' She picked up a couple of the larger history books and fanned the pages.

'Ginny, really, I don't have a photo.'

'Of course you have. You're in love with her.'

Eventually she seized on the Helix tin, which was the only place left I had anything to hide. She opened it up and I couldn't tell whether she was disappointed or not. She stepped her polished fingernails through the HB pencils and picked out Julian's cigarette.

She held it up, showing it to me as though I'd never seen it before. It was showing its age. It was crumpled like an old person's clothes.

'Why do you keep a cigarette in a tin full of pencils?'

'Because that's no ordinary cigarette,' I said, at last seeing my chance, 'that's a *magic* cigarette.'

'I was prepared to tell him I might have been wrong, even though I knew I wasn't wrong.'

'He said you were probably right, and smoking could be a terrible thing. But he didn't believe it. Is that what love is?'

'I came to understand why the women in the Estates might want a cigarette from time to time, as a source of comfort.'

'He said hundreds of thousands of smokers died every year, but he said it just to please you.'

'And to please him back I said a hundred thousand dead

smokers didn't mean that a hundred thousand non-smokers never died.'

'Or that the smokers wouldn't have died if they hadn't smoked.'

'Exactly. That's what it is,' Emmy said, 'that's what love is. Being prepared to change.'

'He apologized, I remember, for nothing in particular.'

'And so did I. It's not all just death and dying, or even bad lungs and bad breath, I know that now. I read a book.'

'It's not all being cool and Humphrey Bogart. It sticks in the sleeves of your clothes and causes heart blindness and vertigo. Not to mention the chemicals and the carcinogens.'

'I liked the chapter on snuff best. It could be made to smell like everyone's favourite smell. The things they mixed in with it.'

'Phenol and isoprene and arsenic,'

'Peach and lavender. Sometimes essence of geranium.'

'Sulphur dioxide, carbon monoxide, nitrobenzene.'

'Blackcurrant and raspberry.'

'Z-napthylamine.'

'Nutmeg and vanilla.'

'*N*-nitrosomethylethylamine,'

'Bergamot and cascarilla and rosemary,'

'Benzo(a)-pyrene, vinyl acetate.'

'Peppermint and sandalwood and valerian fresh from the flower.'

'Formaldehyde.'

'Menthol.'

'Methanol.'

'Cardamon.'

'Cadmium.'

'Cinnamon.'

'Cyanide.'

222

'*Cinnamon*. We mustn't forget that side of it.'

'No, we mustn't forget either side of it.'

'And that, I suppose, is love.'

'Magic cigarettes are generally in better condition than this one. Younger-looking.'

She smelled it. 'It actually smells quite good.'

'Don't be fooled. It changes when you light it.'

'In prison they use cigarettes as money,' she said. 'My sister told me.'

'I know. They have a long history of standing for something else.'

'If I kiss it do I turn into a prince?'

She put Julian's cigarette in her mouth and closed her red-sticked lips around the filter. She held it there like a drinking straw, not quite sure what was in the drink, and then rolled her eyes and pretended to inhale, before flourishing the cigarette away from her and pretending to exhale again, batting her eye-lashes like a Spanish cigarrera.

'So very elegant,' she said. 'So very unintelligent.'

Then she took the cigarette and put it lengthways under her nose, holding it there with her top lip so that it looked like a straight white moustache.

'Funny, no?' Her voice was squashed between her stretching lips, but when she tried her Rhett Butler impression the cigarette fell off, though she caught it before it reached her chin.

'Frankly, my dear,' she said, 'I can't do Humphrey Bogart.' She clamped the cigarette between her happy teeth, and I told her to be careful. She had no idea of its powers.

'Oh yes I do,' she said, 'it kills people.'

'I mean apart from that.'

223

'I ought to be going soon,' she said.

'Already?'

'Need a good night's sleep to rest the vocal cords, the larynx, you know.'

'I ought to know by now.'

'And the lungs of course,' she said.

'Are you alright?'

'Yes,' she said, 'fine.'

She handed me Julian's cigarette.

'Tell me why it's magic,' she said, but something had changed in her. She'd suddenly gone sad on me, and she inspected the hem of her dress all the time I was struggling through an explanation of how maybe, I don't know, in a parallel universe or something, if we were smokers and everything, which we weren't, but if we were, or not necessarily us, but anybody who smoked the magic cigarette, then we, or they, would fall in love with the next person they saw. Or even fall in love with the person they shared it with, if they were both smokers, in a parallel universe and so on.

'You think so?'

'You never know.'

'This is no good, I better go,' she said.

'What's no good?'

She stood up and was pulling on her jacket.

'What's no good, Ginny?'

'Don't,' she said.

I stood up. To get to the door she put her hands on my shoulders and moved me to one side.

'Don't what?'

'I'm sorry,' she said. 'I shouldn't have come. It isn't fair on Lucy.'

She didn't open the door. She tried a smile. 'There's something you should know, Gregory,' she said. She touched my

224

hand with the tip of her index finger. 'It's not really magic. It's just a cigarette.'

She reached up and took my lower lip between her teeth. Then she drew back and held me away from her.

'There, that wasn't so evil, was it?'

And then she left, closing the door behind her. Dazed, I looked at Julian's cigarette, which now carried the print of Ginny's lips on the filter.

Of course I knew all along that it wasn't really magic.

Theo's lab in the back of the house was like a last outpost of rain-forest. There were plants everywhere in bright red pots and yellow growbags, leaving greenness to express itself in every conceivable shade. Spotlights in the ceiling were overgrown by foliage but their light arrived as a kind of lime. The walls ran with damp and it was so humid there always seemed to be steam rising, just out of sight.

Emmy had taken Theo to the hospital and I tried to justify creeping around by remembering that it was my money which had paid for all this, for the double-glazing in the windows, for the work-bench and the microscopes, the slides, the petri-dishes and razor blades and glass bottles in various scientific-looking sizes. From the middle of the bean-bag, half-hidden beneath leaves, Bananas looked at me sceptically and Bananas was right. It was Buchanan's money.

I squatted down and Bananas allowed me to stroke him behind the ears. The Suicide Club had changed Bananas. It was a long time since he'd been satisfied with the delicate inhalation of ambient air above ashtrays. His addiction had grown, and now he liked to lick ash from the ashtray as well. He'd also learnt his way into Walter's tobacco pouch, where he would lie absolutely still with his nose covered in tobacco,

225

his eyes closed with contentment. Theo had even bought him his own leather tobacco pouch, filled with Latakia, and Bananas kept it close to the bean-bag at all times. When he went through into the front room he would carry it between his teeth, but most of the time he slept in the lab, and I liked to believe he had a unique talent for smelling the potential of the green tobacco leaves.

But I was stalling, partly because I'd noticed that not all the tobacco plants in the lab were the same. Not only were they all different sizes, but some had different shaped leaves, or different width stalks. In the end I took one from above the bench because it was a carriable kind of size, and left Bananas to his rain-forest dreams, where it rained Latakia from heaven.

At the Research Unit I put the plant on Julian's desk and although he'd wanted this for a long time, I was still surprised when he put his arm round my shoulder and suggested we take a walk. I asked him when I could expect to hear from the Buchanan's specialists.

We were heading down towards the pond. I lit a cigarette.

'What specialists would those be?' he said.

'I brought you the plant.'

We passed the tennis court.

'So you did,' Julian said, 'and I've been thinking about that. I can't see that Dr Barclay is really our responsibility.'

'I don't follow. His whole adult life he's worked for Buchanan's and he has a cancer which comes from smoking Buchanan's cigarettes.'

'I'm sorry, did I miss something? Has a connection between cigarette-smoking and cancer ever been demonstrated?'

'Don't be a bastard, Julian.'

He turned on me. He poked his finger into my chest and I took a step back.

'Now you listen to me, Gregory.'

He suddenly seemed bigger. He poked me again. 'Just you listen to me. I've been in this shit-hole for nearly two years. Up until today I put you on the plus side of the experience, along with my resounding success against the LUNG people. On the minus side, I managed to lose Buchanan's one of their best researchers.'

'You said you'd help him.'

'Like you helped me when I was trying to keep him at the Unit? My career is dying here, Gregory, and you're not helping at all.'

'I just brought you a tobacco plant,' I said. 'It's what you wanted.'

'You just brought me a RUBBER plant, you idiot, all the way from Barclay's own private lab, which you built for him with Buchanan's money. I have a wife you know. I have a future to think about.'

He turned and walked away, back towards the Unit, leaving me by the edge of the pond with nowhere else to go. Then he stopped and turned back, pointed at me.

'And another thing,' he said. 'Lucy Hinton.'

'What about her?'

'Of course I remember her. She had the most amazing mouth.'

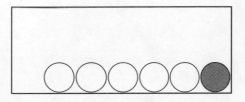

A drunk student or a disaffected librarian had jammed a lighted cigarette between Sartre's slightly parted lips. It was a fat French cigarette without a filter and every time I looked up Sartre had smoked a little more of it. Ginny said:

'I shouldn't have done it, Gregory. I'm sorry.'

The familiar sunshine of the library courtyard, mid-morning. Our friendship seemed to have stalled at these cigarette-length episodes, and any progress we might make was inhibited by the determined presence of Jean-Paul Sartre, who wasn't so much smoking his cigarette as eating it, sucking it down like slow spaghetti.

'I couldn't help it,' she said. 'It was something I wanted to do and you were there and I couldn't resist.'

She put her hand on my knee. She had beautiful hands.

'I wouldn't want to come between you and Lucy,' she said.

'Oh me and Lucy, Lucy and I.'

'The woman you love.'

Apparently I made it obvious. It was the faraway look and a certain nervousness around other women. It explained my occasional air of dissatisfaction (no Lucy). More convincingly, it was only because I was deeply in love with another that I could be so naive as to invite Ginny to dinner, share a bottle of wine with her, take her back to my tiny room (with bed), and still think we could stay just friends. That's how she knew it was wrong when she tried to kiss me. 'But you didn't have a photo,' she said.

My own idea of love was less organized. However, it now included the realization that optimism by itself wasn't enough, because hoping for a letter from Lucy hadn't made it happen. Instead, Julian wrote to me again, this time from Hamburg, a city so exciting he found it hard to describe. For the first time in his life he was being paid to do what he wanted to do, and they'd set him to work on the old chestnut of how to obtain reliable data about the health consequences of smoke-inhalation. *Smokers are still liars*, he wrote, *so we can't just ask them*. Confident that he could always have everything he wanted, Julian made it sound like a problem already solved.

He didn't mention Lucy once, not even in passing, not even to hurt me, and that hurt.

'You have it right now,' Ginny said. 'The faraway look that lovers have.'

'I was thinking of something else.'

'Let me make it up to you,' she said. 'Cinema?'

'A film?'

'Is usually what they show.'

'Fine,' I said. 'Great.'

'What about Lucy?'

'I doubt she can make it.'

'I wouldn't want to come between you.'

We decided to leave the actual choice of film to providence, so Ginny picked a day and I picked a time and Ginny picked one of the cinemas near the Sorbonne which replayed classics. By the time we'd done that, Sartre had swallowed all of his cigarette. On his lower lip, as evidence of the miracle, there lay a single golden flake of unburned tobacco, which I presumed he was saving for later.

No human being deserved to burn horribly in hell. Theo was trying to convince me of this so that we could talk reasonably about Julian Carr.

'They say he has terrible problems with his wife,' Theo said. 'Poor thing.'

'And that explains why he had someone break in and steal one of your tobacco plants?'

'I don't think so, Gregory. That was more because you cocked up and took him a rubber plant.'

Theo was standing at his broad work-bench, inspecting the lower branches of a plant which was about a metre high, produced white flowers once a year, and whose broad leaves were commonly dried and shredded into smoking material. These were just a few of the botanically accepted methods often used to differentiate a tobacco plant (*Nicotiana affinis*) from a common rubber plant (*Ficus elastica*). Theo said he missed his rubber plant.

'Gave the place a homely touch,' he said.

He was having a good day. His face was less haggard and he was moving more freely. I sat on the floor to watch him, my Twenty Centuries T-shirt sticking to my shoulders because I'd just run back from the Unit. Bananas turned sleepily in the bean-bag, rolling onto his back.

'Buchanan's is like any other big company,' Theo said. 'It's very protective of its position. If I solved the problem of the virus I could sell the discovery to someone else, who could then grow tobacco wherever they liked.'

'But this is stealing,' I said. 'It's Julian's personal vendetta against us.'

'I thought you two were friends?'

'He's a mean, lying, two-faced, smarmy, deceitful, revengeful, bitter, betraying, begrudging bastard.'

Theo stopped what he was doing. He lowered himself into

the armchair we'd brought through from the front and lit a cigarette. I lit a cigarette. Bananas slid off the bean-bag, took his Latakia pouch between his teeth and jumped onto Theo's lap.

'Well now,' Theo said. 'I wouldn't call him *mean*.'

'He never sees the human angle. It's always money and statistics. He thinks we should disband the Club.'

'Of course you could always stop smoking.'

'Apparently he sees Walter as a fire-risk. Sorry?'

'Just an idea.'

Theo stroked Bananas behind the ears, between the two bald spots on the top of his head. 'Then it wouldn't matter what Julian thinks.'

I watched Theo calmly enjoying his cigarette, and tried to read his expression. He was joking, surely. He said,

'If you don't like the situation as it is then you have to take some of the blame.'

No, Theo was wrong. I now knew as an absolute fact that everything without exception was Julian's fault, ever since he'd drawn my attention to Lucy Hinton's mouth. It shocked me to realize I couldn't remember her mouth, and then I discovered I'd also lost her lips. I could remember her cheek-bones and her jaw, but these were now separated by a grotesque pair of all-purpose red lips, stuck in a pout directed at Julian.

I'd accused him of knowing absolutely nothing about Lucy Hinton's mouth. 'You even thought she had blonde hair,' I said. But he shrugged it off, and then taunted me some more by suggesting I find a new girlfriend before the results of my tests only applied to celibates. Well ha bloody ha, Julian.

'Think what you like,' I said to Theo, 'I've known Julian a long time.'

'He's frightened. He works for Buchanan's, who imagine

people like me growing tobacco in allotments, between the carrots and the onions.'

'Which would be bad news for Buchanan's.'

'Exactly. The market suits them as it is, so they resist any sort of change.'

'You're sure it's not just Julian?'

'Of course not. It's Buchanan's and the other tobacco companies. They all have the same vested interests and they generally co-operate to protect themselves, which includes suppressing a TMV-immune plant, if it comes to that.'

He wouldn't tell me if he'd actually created an immune strain. He said it hardly mattered. And even if he had, then one plant in a single Research Unit wasn't going to help Buchanan's very much. If they really wanted to be certain that nothing would change, they'd have to destroy his whole lab.

Deerstalker. Greenish tweed. Flaps up and tied over the top.

We also have Jonesy Paul, old Ben Bradley, Whittingham, Dr Hacket, the Pole Jan Peto and Lundy Foot, who between them ought to be doing a better job of cheering Walter up, even at the expense of driving me rapidly insane. They are all smoking except for Lundy Foot, who often loses track of conversations while wondering which of his addictions to service next. He chews on some nicorette while trying to remember if he's taken his royal jelly supplement, and which desire it is exactly which gives him that faint but unmistakable feeling of discomfort. I know that feeling: it makes my hands nervous.

In a room-full of smokers, my blood tries to circulate in a reverse direction. It crashes back into itself, desperate to return to the time when I could say sure you're a good man Ben Bradley and I don't mind if I do take a light, but without the Irish accent, which is just another symptom of not feeling

235

myself today. My lung-ache is back and so is the pain in my arm, and my impatience towards stupidity like Jonesy Paul telling me I've left the Calor Gas heater turned on in the kitchen with a tin of bark or something on top of it and should he turn it off and I was about to suggest should he put his head in the oven when Walter in his truly absurd deer-stalking hat bangs the bowl of his pipe like a gavel against the edge of his ashtray on the arm of his armchair.

He announces an extraordinary meeting of the Suicide Club, to commence immediately. Then he proposes the motion, without more ado, that Gregory Simpson have his membership revoked.

Well now. I take the communal silence that follows as an expression of support.

Old Ben Bradley says: 'But he lives here.'

'Beside the point,' Walter snaps, checking his hat is still tied on top. 'The point is,' and here he gavels the ashtray again for good measure, 'that Simpson is no longer a smoker, so therefore how can he still be a member of the Suicide Club?'

Actually, I'd be willing to correct this ommission almost instantly, because Bradley's JPS are only inches away, next to my invitation to *The Mikado*, saying *Hi There!*, saying *Hello Baby!*, saying just smoke me for God's sake what difference does it make?

Jonesy Paul says: 'He might start again.'

Walter shakes his head regretfully. 'It's been more than two weeks.'

Now they all take a good look at me. Two *weeks*?

'But it feels like a lot longer,' I say.

'Well I don't smoke either,' says Lundy Foot.

'That's different,' Walter says slowly. 'You would if you could. You're true to the *principle* of the thing.'

'What about Haemoglobin?'

This is exactly the sort of digression the Suicide Club likes best, involving a detailed assessment of whether Haemoglobin counts as a member at all, or whether he is less of a member than Bananas, whose commitment to tobacco was altogether more intense. There follows a moment's silence and eyes down in honour of Bananas, undoubtedly the greatest cat who ever lived, before Walter petulantly calls the meeting to order again with his pipe, insisting on someone telling him how I can still be a member.

More silence.

Jonesy Paul says: 'He's a friend of ours?'

'But it's not a club for people who *write things down*, is it?'

'It keeps my hands occupied,' I say.

'If you took up writing to give up smoking,' Lundy Foot asks, 'how are you going to give up writing?'

'We could make him an honorary life-member,' Dr Hacket suggests.

'It's the *principle* of the thing,' Walter insists.

Jonesy Paul comes over and offers me a Lambert and Butler. He pulls two cigarettes out of the pack in stages, like in all the best adverts. I say no thanks, and then start writing like fury, hearing old Ben Bradley saying he didn't see me smoke at Humphrey King's funeral, and Well Done Quite Right Gregory Dr Hacket says, and Jonesy Paul puts his fag in his mouth and starts clapping, and then someone else, but I have no idea really because my head is down and the Pole Jan Peto is silently emptying his pockets onto the desk, and here is a pipe, and a packet of pipe-cleaners, and four cigars from a Panatella six-pack, and a plastic pouch of Erinmore, and a box of Chesterfield, and a twisted pack of Golden Virginia, and a single sheath of red Rizla papers with a corner torn off and he's saying, in the middle of all this, I Give Up Too, Good Man.

At last I look up. Jan is standing there, smiling encouragingly, knowing it's a nice gesture he's made. He does this all the time, but it's still a nice gesture. Walter, admitting defeat, slumps sulkily back into his chair, crosses his arms.

'We're supposed to *like* it,' he says.

Julian said I wouldn't give up smoking in a million years, so when I arrived home from the Unit, out of breath from running, I asked Theo if he thought it was true.

'If you've got that long I wouldn't bother,' he said.

'Really.'

'I don't know, I'm late.'

He was going to visit Emmy in the Estates. He gave me a tobacco plant and a red nylon shopping bag to carry outside to the taxi. The bag was full but surprisingly light, like in the old days, but now it was full of flowers laid lengthways, huge orange and white daisies for Emmy. Theo had managed to change, so why couldn't I?

I went back into the front room, where Walter was discussing domino strategies with Jonesy Paul and Humphrey King, and I asked them if they thought I could give up.

'What would you want to do that for?'

'But do you think I *could*?'

'Search me,' Walter said, and then he was pulling on his coat and so were the others. Humphrey King said 'Giro day,' and as the door closed behind them I took out a cigarette, but then remembered the self-satisfied look on Julian's face when he told me I'd never give up.

'You can't afford to,' Julian had said, 'not with the upkeep of the house and everything. And anyway, you're not the type.'

238

'I might be the type.'

'You're not, believe me. That's why we picked you.'

Ever since the break-in, everything Julian said could be made to sound sinister. I remembered the way he'd talked about the house, just before he called Walter a fire-risk.

'It's not very well *protected*, is it?'

At the time I'd imagined he was worried for us, but now, after what Theo had said about the lab, I wanted to find a way to hurt Julian, if only to prove we weren't entirely defenceless. I said the first thing which came into my head.

'I could give up smoking.'

He laughed out loud.

Back at the house now, someone was banging the brass knocker at the front door. I still hadn't lit my cigarette so I was glad for the distraction. It was Jamie.

'Where's everyone else?' he asked, surprised by the empty room.

'Out, about. Jamie, do you think I could give up smoking if I wanted to?'

'Sure you could. Can I do the test again?'

He jumped into one of the leather chairs and I asked him what vegetable was known to counteract cancer. That ought to keep him quiet for a bit, at least while I smarted at the memory of Julian threatening me that I shouldn't try to threaten him. He said I was weak, and indecisive, and full of anxiety. I had no discipline. I had no qualifications and nothing to look forward to. 'You'll never give up,' he said. 'You need us as much as we need you.'

'Carrots,' Jamie said.

'Have you been talking to Walter?'

'Everybody knows that.'

'Alright then. Who sponsored one-day international cricket in Australia in the nineteen seventies?'

Julian said I wouldn't be able to concentrate. I'd remember every cigarette I ever smoked. It would mean completely changing the way I thought, and I just wasn't the kind of person who did that. I was obsessive, and repetitive in my habits. I was anxious about making decisions, which reinforced my attachment to the decisionless rituals of addiction. Julian told me there was no substitute. He said I didn't stand a chance, and I think he quite enjoyed saying it.

'Benson and Hedges.'

I didn't enjoy hearing it. It felt like an affront to my manhood.

'*Benson and Hedges.*'

'Yes, quite right, Jamie. So you really think I could give up if I wanted to?'

'Do I get to join?'

'Would you say I was a weak person?'

'Give me another question. Any question.'

'Jamie, has no-one ever told you that cigarettes damage your health?'

'Harder than that.'

'What do you most want in life?'

'Money, fast cars. Cigarettes.'

'Whatever it is you want,' I said to him solemnly, 'you can't have it. Not exactly how you want it. My mother taught me that.'

'All I want is a cigarette,' he said.

I gave in and tossed him a Carmen. We shared a match.

A belly of low cloud flattened the glare of the street-lights and trapped the day's heat into the city. I was on my way to the cinema, wearing my black leather jacket and my Camel boots and my most communicative clothes in between. I had a comforting wad of Uncle Gregory's money in my back pocket, and dreaming of eloquent purchases I could make for Ginny I passed an old lady in a blue duffel coat who asked me a question I didn't understand. I wasn't in a hurry, so with the decency I'd inherited from my parents I stopped and asked her if she could kindly repeat herself.

'A few francs,' she said.

I flustered through my pockets, avoiding Uncle Gregory's money, and inside my jacket my hand fell on the pack of Gauloises. I held them out to her, meaning she should take just one, but she thanked me and took the whole pack, with no idea at all of how lucky they were. She walked away before I could explain.

When I arrived at the cinema Ginny was already queuing. She was wearing over-size dungarees and the white sleeves of her long-sleeved T-shirt overlapped her knuckles. She was wearing her round-rimmed glasses. In need of solace as I was, I could easily have chosen this moment to fall in love with her, but I was distracted by a non-smoking fat couple standing in the queue behind her. They were sharing a baguette and a Camembert cheese, which they spread on the bread with a pen-knife. Lucy's parents, I thought, on a gastronomic week-end away.

Assuming they had instructions to report back to Lucy, I made a point of kissing Ginny on both cheeks. Her dungarees gaped at the side when she leant forward and I saw her hip-bone naked below the seam of her T-shirt. I think I must have blushed, but I tried to hide it by saying I hadn't seen *Now Voyager*, either, at which point, thankfully, the queue began to move.

I soon found out that anyone trying to forget the loss of a pack of lucky cigarettes should avoid *Now Voyager*. The cigarettes in this film are uniquely expressive, managing to communicate lucidly in the awkward territory between language and action. In the very first scene, for example, Bette Davis smokes secretly in her bedroom, thus signalling her inhibited and even suicidal nature. Davis looks terrible at this stage, and there seems to be something wrong with her upper right incisor. However, the power of tobacco means that as soon as she smokes in public, Davis blossoms. Even her tooth heals up. She then finds love in the figure of Paul Heinreid, who seduces her by putting two cigarettes in his mouth, lighting both, and then handing one of them over. Although by the end of *Now Voyager* both Heinreid and Davis have suffered for love, neither of them noticeably suffers from lung cancer.

Cigarettes aside, it's a simple tale of a European man who falls disastrously in love with an American woman, and I suppose Ginny and I were wondering what to make of this as we later strolled down towards the river. There was no romantic moon, but it was still warm. We stopped half-way across the Alexander Bridge and looked down at the slow-moving water, where the lights from the bridge crazed like fire-flies.

Ginny's elbow touched mine. She pointed upstream to where a perfect circle expanded on the sparkling surface.

'Fish,' she said. She took my arm. 'Look, another one.'

She pointed out the ripples where several more fish were breathing, and then the river started to fill with fish, all of them breathing perfect circles. They gradually spread down-river, swimming towards us and as they came closer we leant further over the parapet to keep track of them, and one raindrop fell, and then another, and then many, and we realized it was raining.

Ginny laughed and put her forehead against my arm. We looked at the sky and then we looked at each other. She licked some rain from her lips and took off her rain-dropped glasses. And it was there, standing in the middle of the Alexander

Bridge, an instant ocean of fish leaving Paris beneath us, that we kissed for the first time.

Then we stopped kissing. I said I had to go. I blamed it on the rain, but it had nothing to do with the rain.

Of course I could, if I wanted to. But it was important not to be simplistic about such things. It wasn't a straight-forward choice, and there were many and complicated issues involved. There were convincing arguments both for stopping (think of your health), and for carrying on (what to do with your hands).

Stop: I knew all the facts and the figures. I knew the statistics and the death-count.

Smoke: I liked it. And besides, statistics never told the whole story.

Stop: My aching lungs and the way I sometimes had to hold my heart in my hand. Think of the worry.

Smoke: Think of the worry, and the crematorium gardens full of roses dedicated to non-smoking dead people. Keep in mind, at all times, the distinction between life and survival.

Stop: It would upset Julian, but Julian aside, Theo wasn't a statistic and he was dying. Remember Uncle Gregory and Walter's wife and John Wayne. Remember the preference for funeral number 2 in the middle of the next century, and not funeral number 1, sometime soon. Think of all those liberated minutes to spend doing something else. Anything else. And. But.

Smoke: Up at the Unit, week after week, they declared me fiddle-fit, and causality was yet to be scientifically demonstrated. It could be one particular brand which was responsible for the death-count, or a not unusual combination of cigarettes with something else. No-one knew. The cancerous cigarette might be an independent event, so that each smoke was like a separate bet, having nothing to do with the last. The dangerous smoke might be number three on the second Tuesday of each month, or the one you didn't smoke because you were too drunk to pull it from the packet, or the one you saved especially for your best friend at the end of a long day. And anyway, I liked the money Buchanan's paid me. And the Chinese might drop a bomb. And it had to be better than Roman discontent and twenty dormice a day.

Stop: Okay then. Forget everything else. It would really upset Julian if I gave up.

Smoke: Everything else. The importance of showing my solidarity with the Estates and with Theo. The taste of Lucy Hinton in every fresh cigarette, and like Paracelsus said, it's the dosage which counts. The way I could light a match and openly hold the danger in my hand in otherwise banal and wholly tamed places. The fear of fattening up. Bogart, and the little bit of Bogart that rubs off. The chemical satisfaction and the seven seconds. The less certain satisfaction of openly defying mortality. And beyond even that, a deeper fear that without cigarettes I might be left with no desires at all.

Stop: Imagine Julian's reaction, and how wrong one man could be.

I lit another cigarette. Surely there must be other ways I could fuck Julian up.

DAY

16

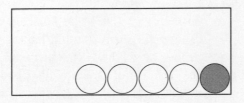

'You can't love her that much or you wouldn't have kissed me.'

'It's not as simple as that.'

'Why not?'

'It's very complex.'

I decided against a smoke-break. Ginny then decided she was also off cigarettes for the day, even though Madame Boyard had told us twice that we could go out now if we wanted to. By the middle of the morning Madame Boyard was chewing the end of her pencil and flicking angrily through Kobbé's opera guide, wondering how long we could keep it up.

Ginny kept on peering at me over the top of her computer, until I felt like a rat in one of Julian Carr's experiments. In another letter from Hamburg he'd assured me that rats didn't count as animals because they were vermin, and anyway, not all animal-testing was the same. Then he described a test he'd developed involving a single rat and a maze with six different exits, where each route to an exit posed a different problem for the rat to solve. Whenever the rat succeeded in reaching an exit, it was rewarded with a piece of cheese. However, as soon as the rat discovered that the reward was always the same, it lay down in the middle of the maze and refused to move. Eventually it died. Julian therefore replaced the cheese at one of the six exits with a chamber full of tobacco smoke. He then replaced the rat. The second rat learnt the routes to all the exits, and then made regular visits to the five containing cheese. It seemed motivated and happy, even for a rat. Julian's conclusion: *What a wonderful world.*

247

Madame Boyard pushed back her chair and accused us both of being crazy, and then English. She can't have been more than half-way up the stairs, Camels just opened and a filter pinched between her fingers, when Ginny said:

'One moment you like me, the next you don't. Didn't our kiss mean *anything* to you?'

'Of course it meant something.'

'You obviously don't love her.'

'You used to tell me I did.'

'That was before you took me to the cinema and kissed me afterwards.'

'I can't just leave her.'

'Why not?'

Because since my kiss with Ginny on the bridge I thought about Lucy all the time. At night, lying on the narrow bed in my tiny room only an eighth the size of a human lung, I tried to think about Ginny but I couldn't. Instead, there was now no moment in the day which didn't somehow remind me of Lucy. I would see a young Parisian, of either sex, smoking in the street. I would notice their unmistakable air of defiance and understand immediately that they were defying me personally, the cigarette they were smoking a direct result of their recent seduction by Lucy Hinton. I tried to keep in mind how banal a version of happiness was offered by cigarettes, but I wasn't sure I believed it anymore.

I'd lost touch with my idea of myself as super-hero, and now it felt as if every day I lived had been handed down to me used and slightly soiled. Kissing Ginny had brought back the memory of my failure to climb a mountain, kill a dragon, smoke a cigarette, and if I couldn't do any of these things what could I usefully do? Now, whenever I caught sight of Lucy in the street, she would take a drag on her cigarette and

248

stare me down disdainfully, her face heart-shaped and full of scorn. It was even worse when I didn't see her. Then I would find myself worrying what kind of shoes she was wearing and whether she'd changed her brand of cigarettes, and if she had, what colour exactly was the packet she held in her hands day after day. I mean right now, today, wherever she is.

It was exhausting. It made me nostalgic for the amniosis of home and the easy defeat of lying on my bed all afternoon, happy just to be breathing. I hadn't forgotten the feeling that waking up every morning was no victory in itself, but now I imagined waking up every morning with Lucy, which wasn't the same thing at all.

'You can come and watch me rehearse, if you like,' Ginny said. 'It's nearly final selection time.'

'Sorry?'

'For the understudies for *Cosi Fan Tutti*.'

I tried to concentrate, and briefly wondered how opera would sound in an American accent. But then Madame Boyard came back, smelling of tobacco smoke, and I remembered why I wouldn't be going to find out.

I crushed my Carmen to death in the large onyx ashtray on the coffee-table in Julian's office. Then I placed the empty box of Carmens carefully beside it, the double castanets facing upwards and the health warning turned away from me. I took a fresh box of Carmens from my shirt pocket and unwrapped the cellophane, which I placed next to the empty box next to the extinguished cigarette. Holding the bottom of the new box in my left hand I took the top section of the flip-top box between the fingers and thumb of my right hand, and flipped it back. I pulled out the slip of gravelled silver paper which said PULL. I placed it on top of the cellophane in the ashtray.

From the new box in my left hand I pinched two new filters from two new cigarettes between my fingernails. I extracted both of the cigarettes from the box. One of them, I put in my mouth. The other, I turned upside down and replaced in the box, tobacco upwards. Finally, using Julian's underused lighter, I lit the cigarette in my mouth and even though it was only mid-afternoon, I began to enjoy my twenty-first cigarette of the day.

Julian asked me why I was trying to provoke him.

Theo had recently spent the night in hospital for the removal of a cyst which was thought to be the immediate cause of the pain in his leg and lower back. The doctors had also performed a biopsy, which revealed an inoperable tumour in his lung. Theo himself had stayed remarkably calm, even cheerful, claiming that his years in the Unit had taught him how adaptable the main organs of the human body could be. Not to mention the organs of Syrian Hamsters, domestic cats, and eagerly amenable beagles. I found it hard to share his bravado, especially when he started calling the tumour his internal tattoo, a swirl of indelible cancers etched across the inside of his chest. *Mother*, it said.

I blamed the cancer on Julian Carr. If only he'd offered us the medical resources available to Buchanan's as soon as I'd asked. If only he hadn't mentioned Lucy Hinton's mouth. I stubbed out my twenty-first cigarette of the day and lit my twenty-second.

'Give me the pack,' Julian said. 'You know it's wrong.'

'I'm not your statistic, Julian.'

'Give me the pack.'

'I'm not your controlled experiment. I have a certain amount of free-will.'

'No you don't. That's why we pay you.'

I took another drag and Julian sighed deeply and then swore.

He lurched forward and grabbed one of the cigarettes from the glass box on the table and lit it, inhaling deeply. He told me not to look so surprised.

'You're supposed to have stopped,' I said.

'I'm murdering a cluster of brain-cells,' he said. 'To bring myself down to the common level.' He exhaled smoke through his nose. 'You think I'm all suit, don't you? You think that's all I've become. Well I've got problems too, you know.'

'Sure. Like whose life to ruin next.'

He looked at the end of his cigarette and made a face and crushed it out in the ashtray. 'God knows how long they've been in that box. Give me a Carmen.'

I gave him a Carmen and watched him light it. 'I really thought you'd stopped,' I said.

'I'm having a hard time.'

'I weep.'

'Please, Gregory, be a bit nicer.'

'Why?'

'My wife left me.'

I went to light another cigarette, but Julian had the box of Carmens now and I didn't want to ask for it back. 'I'm sorry,' I said.

He shrugged and said, 'That's love.'

'And marriage,' I said.

'So we're the same now, Gregory. We're both alone.'

'Speak for yourself.'

'Can I ask you something?'

'I'm not alone, Julian. It's not the same thing.'

'What do you do in the evenings?'

As he said it he inhaled sharply on his cigarette, so I couldn't tell if he was being serious or not. 'You could come round sometime,' Julian mumbled, and now I thought he really meant it. 'We could order pizza.' It was as if a layer of pain was coming to the surface, forgetting its own weight. 'Isn't that what single men like to do?'

'I don't know, Julian. I live with Theo.'

'You're my oldest friend,' Julian said. 'And you don't even like me.'

'I never said I didn't like you.'

'Tell me why you don't like me.'

'Alright then. Lucy Hinton. Lucy Hinton's mouth.'

'She had an amazing mouth.'

'Don't do it, Julian. Don't taunt me. What did she do with her mouth?'

'She ate, she spoke, I don't know, she smoked. It was amazing, that's all.'

'So you kissed her?'

'No. I wanted to, but I never did. She spent most of her time kissing you.'

'So you never kissed her?'

'Never,' he said. 'But I always wanted to.'

And the way he said that made me believe it was true. For the first time since I'd known Julian I felt superior to him, and it was a feeling I knew I could grow to like. I even felt slightly sorry for him, but I rose above it.

'Lucy Hinton,' I said. 'She was one of the great kissers of all time.'

'I did terrible things,' Walter says. 'I rolled cigarettes in the pages of my army issue bible.'

'You can't have been the only one.'

'I smoked the whole New Testament. And I should never have killed Emmy's mother. I killed my own wife, for heaven's sake.'

252

'No you didn't. Don't be silly.'

'Passive smoking.' Walter looks grim. 'She didn't stand a chance.'

Without Emmy or any members of the Suicide Club, the posters and the photographs and the Paracelsus inscription above the door come into clearer focus. It's the first time in several days that Walter and I have been alone, and because he asks me nicely I give him something to read. Unfortunately, under his cream-white stetson, he now seems no happier than he was before. He looks up and says:

'This girl Lucy. You shouldn't have done what you did.'

'I know. But that's finished now, like cigarettes. It's all in the past.'

'You should get out more, like Emmy says.'

'And you should stop smoking like Emmy says.'

'Well she's right. That's another terrible thing. I was forty-five when she was born, but I'd have changed if I was younger. I'd have given up. She was such a pretty girl, just like her mother.'

'It wouldn't have made any difference.'

'Who knows? We all want to be better than we are, even Stella.'

'Please, Walter, I've heard more than enough about Stella.'

'Sharp as a tack.'

'Nobody can force me to meet her.'

'Pretty too.'

'Not if I don't want to.'

'Delicious as an MCC.'

'Walter. Manners.'

'Alright then, she's ugly.'

'Is she?'

'Find out for yourself.'

'She probably won't even like me.'

'You're probably right. She's not a cigarette. There's no satisfaction guaranteed.'

'I want a cigarette.'

'You want satisfaction, it's not the same.'

'No, I really want a cigarette. I mean right now.'

Walter tosses back the pages I gave him earlier and tells me to write something down instead, so I ask him to tell me a story, and without hesitation he starts 1916, the morning of the Battle of the Somme.

He is a private in the Black Watch and his platoon is ordered into line by a second lieutenant from the Blues and Royals. Cold and wet and miserable the platoon is marched away from the trenches. At an abandoned farm-house Walter and the other men are ordered to make their weapons ready, while a deserter from the Catering Corps is pushed towards them. His hands are tied behind his back and he is made to stand against the battered wall of the farm. He is blind-folded. His whole body is shaking and he is not offered a last request. He is given a cigarette. His teeth chatter so violently that when the cigarette is put between his lips he bites it in half. Horrified, he spits out the loose crumbs of tobacco, narrowly missing the officer, who steps back in disgust and gives the order to fire.

Walter, along with the rest of his platoon, shoots the unknown deserter dead. There is no justice involved. The officer doesn't collapse from passive smoking. Nor does he make the war-time mistake of striking the third match. He hands out the extra tobacco ration which pays off the Firing Squad.

Walter remembers smoking his Firing Squad cigarettes, and he did it for the same reason as everyone else, because whenever he wasn't bored he was scared of dying, like everyone was. It was because in the middle of a war there was nothing else which he wanted which he could also have. It was because only the very secure and the very stupid could ignore any opportunity for comfort.

People nowadays, they imagine they'd act differently.

Dr and Mrs Julian Carr used to live in a street of detached houses like an evolved version of the street where my parents lived. Now Julian lived there alone. Although I'd learnt that possessions themselves didn't generate happiness, in Julian's house they provided a fairly convincing imitation, and I had the feeling that he paid someone to keep the house exactly as it was when his wife left. That was sad, I think. Julian was on the phone when I arrived so while he talked I took a close look at the wedding photographs on the mantelpiece. Lucy Carr had shoulder-length hair and a spectacular smile, but her eyes were too blue and her hair was very blonde.

'Sorry about that,' Julian said. 'Hard to get away these days.' He was just loosening his tie when the phone rang again.

There was a *Tobacco World* magazine on a coffee-table. I flipped through it and found an article praising the way Julian had undermined the LUNG demonstration. The magazine was more than a year old, and a photo made the Unit look grey like a nuclear installation. I tossed it back onto the table and wondered exactly why I was here. Partly, it was because I'd been invited, and with the inconvenient decency I'd inherited from my parents I didn't know how to refuse. But it was also because I was keen to cultivate my feeling of superiority over Julian, knowing that he'd never kissed Lucy Hinton.

Julian came back, apologetic. He took off his suit-jacket. He'd invited me to eat but he didn't have any food in. He did, however, have some beer, so he lit the gas coal-imitation fire and we sat facing it, drinking little bottles of French beer and leaning back against the sofa. He rolled up his sleeves and matched me cigarette for cigarette, not seeming to care how many I'd smoked already that day, and he offered me more beer as if the speed we drank each bottle was a direct measure of how much we were enjoying ourselves. Theo was right. Julian had never been mean.

He gestured casually towards the magazine and asked me if I'd seen the article.

'No,' I said.

'It doesn't matter. All that LUNG business was just a side-show. You were always the main reason I stayed here.'

He opened another two bottles and said he was sorry about Theo. 'Really I am,' he said. 'I wanted to help him but they wouldn't let me.'

'Who wouldn't?'

'The company. You've built me up into something I'm not. I'm just an employee, and I do what I'm told. You should have brought him along this evening.'

'Who?'

'Theo.'

'He's with Emmy.'

'Not at the house, then?'

'No, at her place, Walter's place. Why?'

'I'd like to get to know him better.'

With each bottle of beer, I found it harder to dislike Julian. He apologized for the way he'd talked to me about Lucy Hinton, blaming it on the breakdown of his marriage.

'It isn't as if I did anything wrong,' he said. 'We wanted children.'

Julian went quiet. He closed one eye and looked down the neck of his beer-bottle while I noticed that every picture in the room was either a photo or a painting of his wife, mostly publicity shots from race-tracks with Lucy Carr perched high on the seats of numbered motorcycles. She had interesting knees. A series of pastel portraits brought out the delicate angle of her elbows.

'I tried,' Julian said. 'I even gave up smoking for the sake of the baby. But nothing happened.'

'I didn't know,' I said, automatically wondering how many other things I didn't know about him.

'It was those tests I did as a student. Gregory, have you ever been in love?'

'I think so,' I said. 'I don't know.'

'Probably not then,' he said. 'I'm lonely on my own.'

And I nodded sympathetically, calmly swallowing some beer, increasingly confident that along with superiority I could safely allow myself to feel a little pity. Poor old Julian.

'At least you have all those old guys,' Julian said. 'They all go home at night, I suppose?'

'Of course they do.'

'So both our houses are empty. We're just the same really.'

I assumed that Julian's self-pity was making him ramble: my house was nothing like his. It was never empty. Even without the Suicide Club and Jamie there were always the animals, and also the ghost of course. Theo was never away for long, and Walter had a key which he often used when he wanted to give Emmy and Theo some time alone. There was always something happening, even if that wasn't the way I'd planned it, and it occurred to me, without regret, that I'd failed miserably in my attempt to keep the world at bay.

Julian was saying that these days he only had one ambition left.

'It's more of a dream really,' he said. 'I want to help create a cancer-free cigarette. That's why I wanted one of Theo's plants. Imagine it. Imagine smoking as much as you liked without ever having to worry.'

'Buchanan's would make a fortune.'

'Buchanan's couldn't care less,' Julian said. 'If the market slips here they just concentrate on the millions of non-smoking women in China. They don't know the meaning of worry.'

The phone rang again, and Julian went to answer it. This time when he came back he was still holding the telephone, and he looked puzzled. He held out the receiver.

'It's for you,' he said. 'There's been a fire.'

'What has she got that I haven't? What do I have to *do*?'

Ginny was following me home from the library. I walked no slower than I'd normally walk which was a little faster than Ginny would walk if she wasn't trying to catch me up. This meant that sometimes she had to break into a run to keep up with me, for which she was well prepared by all that jogging. I didn't tell her when I was about to change direction so sometimes I bumped into her, or left her stranded on the opposite pavement. I rarely looked back but it hardly mattered because before long she always caught me up again.

This had all started because I didn't do smoke-breaks anymore. I hadn't been to the opera to hear her rehearse and I'd refused her invitations to the cinema and even to Cosini's.

'I don't greatly appreciate your behaviour,' she said.

And eventually she was willing to prove it by grabbing hold of my arm and forcing me to stop. I gave up and agreed to a coffee, even though I had no idea of what to say to her. I remembered once finding her attractive, but that was before the kiss on the bridge, and since then I'd found myself hoping desperately for implausible encounters with Lucy. I started watching out for travelling productions of *The Magic Mountain* (Shenandoah version), or fly-posters announcing the imminent European tour of Lucy Lung and the Carcinomatones. But still I never woke up to a letter from her, and I had to accept the increasing likelihood that I might never see her again.

It was like losing the organizing principle in my attempt to make sense of anything, meaning there was no destiny, no process beyond our control leading us always closer to an inevitable reunion. At the same time, looking back over the details of my recent history, I found no significant connections and none of the consolation of meaning offered by history books. I discovered, without great surprise, that I knew nothing of the laws which presided over the events of my life. I didn't know how to live and I would never know.

It wasn't an easy thing to explain to Ginny. She looked very sad and beautiful in the softened light beneath the Carmen Blonde awning which shaded our table. She was wearing sunglasses and a tartan shirt I hadn't seen before, but it was all too late. Our clothes wouldn't speak for us, I knew that now, so I avoided her eye and watched the street beside us move one way and then the other. My eyes stopped at the solid familiarity of numbers, from the cc ratings on parked motorbikes to the number 20 sub-titled on a stretch of bill-board opposite, beneath images of desire distilled into fearless people subduing wild places. On the back of a *Figaro* being read at the next table I registered the date and the edition number, and the race-times for a meeting at Vincennes.

'I'm thinking of going back to America,' Ginny said, watching me closely. I tapped my coffee spoon against my saucer and then against the table-top. 'I didn't get the understudy part.'

The man reading the newspaper lit a Gauloise, and Ginny glanced across at him. 'They wouldn't allow it in America,' she said, but her heart wasn't in it.

'They have guns instead,' I said.

She looked at me over the top of her sunglasses, hoping it was a joke. At that angle I could see the raised edge of a

259

contact lens. 'I mean for killing people,' I said. 'They don't need cigarettes anymore because they have guns instead.'

She smiled because she wanted to have something to smile about. Then she sniffed, and pushed her sunglasses back up her nose.

'You're really quite hung up on cigarettes, aren't you?'

'Well so are you, with your singing lungs.'

'I guess we both are.'

'I wouldn't say that.'

'Hung up, I mean. Maybe that makes us compatible.'

She covered my hand with hers to stop me tapping the spoon, and I realized that for at least a few moments I'd forgotten I had no idea of how to live.

Ginny leant over the table towards me.

'I don't plan to just let you go,' she said.

She took off her dark glasses and I looked at her lips, then at her eyes, which were aimed down at my mouth. I could already taste the blandness. I could already anticipate the same disappointment as last time, on the bridge, when it had hardly tasted like a kiss at all. It didn't compare. It didn't even come close to the unforgettable sensation of kissing an ashtray.

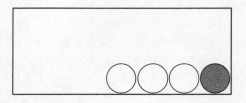

Walter wants to know if I believe in the human soul.

'Does it exist, how big is it, what does it mean?' he asks, making sure to include all the essentials. 'Because I wouldn't want to blame everything on tobacco. That really would be sad.'

He is wearing a black beret, flattened over one ear like the sculpted hair of a lounge-singer. It is a beautiful blowy spring day, and we've just come in from the garden. Walter is recovering from taking wild swings with his walking stick at the potato-like plants which are over-running the grass, and Haemoglobin is slumped at his feet, bewildered by his inability to remember the map of where he last urinated. After bounding about idiotically he'd eventually decided on the gates, almost hidden behind the trees which were beginning to bud.

Walter and I have been taking a look at the gorge, where Walter crossed his hands over the crook of his stick and peered out over the edge.

'Remember the ashes?'

Of course. And in particular the way they'd blown upwards and outwards and away from us over the gorge, like seeds, with no immediate intention of settling. I gazed down at the faraway mud-flats and the slow brown river.

'Good old Theo,' Walter said. 'Always up in the air.'

The gorge had its usual hypnotic effect. It appealed alternately to my urge to jump and my fear of jumping, leaving me in a state of suspension somewhere in between. I agreed with Walter and disagreed with him. I was happy to remember the flight-path of Theo's ashes, and I was sad. I was excited about getting out more, like Emmy said I should, but I was also terrified. What if Stella didn't like me? What if she did?

I turned away from the gorge and looked at the wreckage of the house. At the back the brick was charred black, and broad leaves were starting to crawl from the empty window frames. The fire, which had started in the lab, had eventually been defeated by the humid walls, dividing the house almost exactly in half. The brick at the front was still bright and the colour of cigarette filters.

Looking at the two-tone house, Walter asked me if I believed in ghosts, but he was shivering and he looked miserable so I suggested we come back indoors, for Haemoglobin's sake. Walter now has a pipe and a cup of tea and looks just about warmed through.

'What I mean is,' Walter says, waving his pipe at me, 'is there a part of all of us which is durable and unique?'

I'd like to give Walter more of my attention, but I have work to do with the Helix tin. It has now been on the Calor Gas heater for three days and the leaves have dried and browned.

'I can't believe only chemicals rule the way I am,' Walter says. 'And I like to think I'd have been the same if I'd never smoked. Are you listening to me, Gregory?'

These pieces of leaf are evidence that I can do something constructive with my hands. It doesn't have to be all torching and burning and the scorched earth of smoking. Instead, in the spirit of creation, I shall now tailor the pieces of leaf into thin strips, about as long as a fingernail.

'I prefer to believe that I have a soul,' Walter says. 'And that my soul is impervious to nicotine.'

Into the Helix tin I pour a quarter-capful of 8-year-old whiskey, a present from Julian on the eighth anniversary of our meeting in Hamburg. The whiskey is supposed to soak into the strands of leaf and then evaporate, moistening the leaf while at the same time giving it a distinctive flavour. I want this to be my idea, but I expect it's been done before. Moistened, the strands of leaf look like threads of wool from a miniature brown tank-top, but I'm going to leave it alone now. I don't want to meddle and overdo it.

Finally, however, and this is simply to ease the process of evaporation, I prop open the hinged lid of the Helix tin with Jan Peto's pack of red Rizla papers.

'Sorry, Walter,' I say. 'I didn't quite catch that.'

'Since you stopped smoking,' Madame Boyard said, 'your work has deteriorated considerably. In the past three weeks, between the two of you, you've only recorded six operas.'

Madame Boyard was sitting at right angles to our two computers and leaning forward across her elbows, squashing her breasts even flatter than usual.

'And two of those were short and comic,' she said. 'So either smoke some cigarettes or concentrate a bit harder on your work. Do I make myself clear?'

'Perfectly,' I said.

'You're lucky to have these jobs at all.'

I thought of Julian, designing his own projects in Hamburg.

'And I'd also appreciate it,' Madame Boyard said, 'if you'd stop whispering all the time.'

'Fine,' I said.

It wasn't me who whispered. Now that we'd given up smoke-breaks, Ginny would hiss messages at me while we were typing: why was I ignoring her, why didn't we go for a cigarette, what was wrong with me?

'Unless of course,' Madame Boyard said, 'the two of you have some other problem which I don't know about?'

The whole thing was absurd. I'd only taken the job to keep myself occupied, and now I was being told I wasn't any good at it. It made me envious of Julian, who described his life in Hamburg in great detail, in long letters to which I still didn't reply. This was partly because of Lucy Hinton, but it was also because I felt distanced by his obvious success.

He was now concentrating exclusively on the problem of data collection. He told me that tests could be carried out on people after all, subject to strict contract, of course, and that the well-known tendency for smokers to lie could often be corrected by the offer of large amounts of money. I was amazed by the figures he quoted, but then I'd never realized that Buchanan's were selling 12 billion cigarettes every year in Europe alone. Julian: *We don't give* all *the profit to the opera*.

'This is exactly what I mean,' Madame Boyard said. 'You're not concentrating, Gregory.'

'I'm sorry,' I said. 'It's the withdrawal.'

'Liar,' Ginny said.

Madame Boyard looked at her expectantly. Ginny shrugged. 'It's very simple. I love him and he doesn't love me. And it's the opera archive which suffers.'

In a matter of fact kind of way, as if she was tired of whispering, Ginny then told Madame Boyard everything. She moved from splitting up with her boyfriend to our evening out at Cosini's, passing *Now Voyager* on her way to our fateful kiss on the bridge, which had grown so passionate and prolonged I hardly recognized it. I felt sorry for Madame Boyard. I assumed she'd be embarrassed, forgetting that she was French. She was also, like Ginny, a lover of opera.

'No wonder you're getting no work done,' she said, patting Ginny's arm. Then she turned on me and asked me what was wrong with me. 'It's not every day that someone falls in love with you,' she said, before listing, with great precision, all of Ginny's accomplishments and attractive physical features, including her bone structure.

English and embarrassed, I mumbled something into my keyboard about liking Ginny very much, in fact she was brilliant, but I already had a girlfriend, in England, so it was completely out of the question.

'He doesn't even have a photo,' Ginny said. 'And he refuses to talk about her. All I know is that she has black hair and she smokes.'

'He could still love her,' Madame Boyard suggested. 'To be fair. It's still possible.'

'But that's not what love is, in my opinion,' Ginny said, and Madame Boyard nodded. 'It's more about totally changing the way you think. It's irresistible. It's addictive and compulsive. It's intoxicating. If she was offering him this kind of love he wouldn't be here. Right or wrong?'

I told them both, as briskly as I could manage, that nobody could ever prove they loved anybody else and anyway, it was none of their business. 'This isn't an opera,' I said.

Both Madame Boyard and Ginny reflected for a moment, and then agreed between themselves that I was wrong and love in the modern world *could* still be like an opera. You just had to make room for the big feelings these days, that was all.

Julian Carr didn't have this kind of problem. Julian Carr had everything. He had responsibility: he was running his own series of tests. He was a decision-maker, specifying exactly how many cigarettes should be smoked each day. He was a problem-solver, deciding that each person should fix their nicotine and tar intake by smoking a single brand to the exclusion of all others. He was forceful, insisting on regular monitoring sessions to ensure that his data was superior to anything inferred from monkeys. But he also turned out to be resilient, especially when he found out that the constraints of his system deterred all but the most desperate. *Wasters*, he wrote, cursing them for their random and unscientific lives. They were always dropping out of the programme. They missed appointments and admitted to accepting cigarettes from strangers. They smoked too many cigarettes when they were drunk, and too few when they were hungover. More significantly, they'd all been smokers before starting the tests, so Julian could never know how far their previous cigarettes distorted his results.

Nevertheless, he remained resolute. He was sure he could find a reliable non-smoker, given time and the financial backing of Buchanan's for his new salary-plan. This involved a small initial fee which would double each year. The longer the test-course lasted, the more value the data would have to Buchanan's, and the larger the fee would become. Obviously this would depend on the fulfilment of all contractual requirements, probably to include living near a Research Unit, but then after the first few months the nicotine itself would add its own unique enticement. *All I need to be happy*, Julian wrote, *is to find my Mr X.*

I envied him for knowing what he wanted. And he'd almost certainly get it, probably before I ever progressed from staring at computer screens, recording lost operas while women discussed my incapacity for true love.

'Men can't change the way they think,' Madame Boyard said, 'because they mostly believe they're perfect already, or at least half-way serviceable. They can't accept that love is a kind of death, with an after-love after-life which is different from the life they know.'

'We should ignore them,' Ginny said. 'But you start loving them and then you can't stop.'

'Of course you can,' I said. 'Just do something else instead.'

'Nothing else matters anymore. Not even my singing. I've given up jogging.'

'You can't be in love then,' I said. 'It's supposed to be good for you.'

Madame Boyard and Ginny sighed in unison. They were flawlessly in tune. Then Madame Boyard asked me if I was frightened of women, at which point I stood up and put on my jacket.

'Now then Gregory.'

Madame Boyard stood up and blocked my exit. 'Calm down,' she said. 'Here,' she picked up her bag and I thought she was going to offer me some money, but she took out two cigarettes and put them on the table. 'Have these,' she said. 'And calm down.'

'I've given up, remember?'

'I won't tell anyone.'

I should have told her in no uncertain terms that it had absolutely nothing to do with smoking. But I was distracted by Ginny, who deftly picked up one of the cigarettes and dropped it into the top pocket of her denim jacket. She looked up at me innocently, and whatever the differences between Lucy and Ginny, I now suspected one essential similarity. All women, without exception, were mad. That would explain many and mysterious things it was otherwise impossible to understand.

'It was supposed to be fire-resistant,' I said. 'It had a BSI label.'

I closed my eyes, hoping it hadn't happened, but along with the bonfire stench of burnt wood and charred bricks, there was the distinct smoulder of green tobacco. I could hear steam hissing and men shouting. I could hear Haemoglobin barking. I opened my eyes and saw Haemoglobin turning excited circles in the headlights of a fire-engine parked between us and the

269

house. Bands of blue light rolled around the dark garden, colouring in Emmy and Theo and Walter as they washed past. Only Julian was immune, standing in the shadow of a fire-engine talking to a fireman, trying to find out what had happened.

'He might still be in there,' I said.

'No,' Theo said. We had to shout above the wind and the hissing of the fire-engines. Theo turned up the collar of his raincoat.

'Maybe he found some shelter?'

'No,' Emmy said. She was re-zipping her oilskin jacket. She was wearing Theo's jeans.

'There must be *some* hope, surely?'

Theo came very close to me so that he didn't have to shout. His face had grown thin, the scar on his lip more visible. He put his hand on my shoulder, as if to steady me. He said:

'Tobacco burns at a temperature of 800 degrees centigrade.'

Emmy reached out and held my hand.

'We know how you feel,' she said.

'I lost a pet macaw once,' Walter said, but Emmy gave him a sharp look and he stopped. Disorientated, I did my best to focus on Walter's yellow storm-hat. It made Walter look like a fireman.

'His name was Mac,' Walter said.

I wanted to blame someone. Then it would somehow make sense. I stared hard at Walter's bell-shaped hat, wondering if a man his age would remember dropping a lit pipe into a waste-paper bin full of paper. Dry paper. And old wooden pencils.

'It's not Walter's fault,' Emmy said. 'He came up to the Club so that we could have some time on our own.'

'He did all the right things,' Theo said. 'He called 999 and then he called us.'

270

'You don't understand,' I said. 'My mother only bought it because of the label.'

However much I blinked it kept on happening, over and over again. Bananas asleep in the bean-bag. The tobacco starting to burn. Bananas waking up, sitting up straight, breathing in deeply. His nose twitching and his green-marbled eyes smiling themselves Chinese. His back straightening. His tail sweeping slowly one way and then the other, brushing the old black corduroy of the bean-bag.

'The bad news or the good news?'

Julian had to shout to make himself heard. He was the only one of us properly dressed for the weather, in his charcoal overcoat and black leather gloves. 'The back of the house is burnt-out,' he said, in a more normal voice now that he was closer, 'but the front is almost completely untouched.'

'Fancy that,' Theo said.

'They're looking for clues as to how it started, but the main thing is that nobody was hurt. Thank God.'

'Gregory has had a shock,' Theo said.

'We've *all* had a shock,' Julian said.

When nobody disagreed with him, he walked back towards the fire-engines.

'I loved that cat.'

'He wouldn't have suffered,' Theo said.

'We don't know.'

'800 degrees centigrade.'

Trembling with pleasure, perched on the bean-bag, his body alive with sensual satisfaction. He is always about to jump, to escape, but the smell of burning tobacco changes slightly as different plants reach different stages of combustion, a little more interesting, a little more intense. The work-bench flames then collapses and the arm-chair explodes, but the bean-bag remains cool and intact, living up to its label. Bananas, eyes

271

wide and green, inhales deeply, smiles, disappears slowly behind veils of blue-green smoke.

'He's dead, isn't he?'

'It's never easy,' Emmy said.

'I blame myself.'

'There was nothing you could do.'

'I shouldn't have introduced him to ashtrays.'

'He would have died happy,' Theo said. 'Charged up with nicotine. He beat the discomfort that comes from knowing that satisfaction never lasts. He was satisfied without end. It was the perfect death.'

'Not dead but happily sleeping,' Walter said.

'Dead, burnt,' I said. 'Gone forever.'

Against 800 degrees of heat the bean-bag had been defence-less. It had forgotten its promise to my mother. It had been no help to Bananas. It could do nothing to protect its memory of Lucy's back and buttocks. The frailty of the bean-bag led to an eradication so thorough I was left stunned, unable to think clearly.

'It doesn't make any sense.'

'Death is natural,' Walter said.

'And it really is possible to die happy,' Theo said. 'I promise you.'

'He'll always live on,' Emmy assured me, 'in our memories.'

And I was just beginning to consider believing them when Julian came back.

'Damp in the wiring,' he said. He looked at Theo. 'This wouldn't have happened if you'd stayed at Buchanan's. Your plants would have been safe.'

'I don't want to argue,' Theo said. 'Not here.'

'Why should we argue? This isn't your problem. This isn't even your house.'

'I was thinking of Gregory.'

'Anyway, it could have been much worse.'

Julian then told us that the front room wasn't even water-damaged, and still not thinking properly all I could say was thankyou. He said that's what friends were for.

'I loved that cat.'

Julian slapped me on the back.

'Cheer up, Gregory,' he said. 'It might never happen.'

'You look dreadful,' Ginny said.

'Why did you come?'

'Madame Boyard said I should. What happened to your shirt?'

I looked down and saw it was full of tiny burn-holes.

'You didn't think I'd just let you go?' she said.

It was more than a week since I'd been to the library, and I'd spent most of that time walking around Paris. Each morning, to give myself a sense of purpose, I devised a complex itinerary, bristling with rules. I had to make long detours, for example, to avoid the red diamond signs outside tobacconists, or I would set out for Montparnasse at night-time, never deviating from a route which connected every cinema on the Left Bank showing a black and white film, preferably in French, but always with a W in the title. Wherever I went, following whatever rules, I boldly tested the theory of love at first sight by looking at a lot of girls for the first time.

I started counting churches, equestrian statues, Italian restaurants, anything to distract my mind from the need to make decisions. I stared at monuments until they all became alike. I walked like a man asleep, simply an occupied space which no-one approached, drifting along behind black-haired girls and old ladies smoking lucky cigarettes. Gradually, I began to lose the forward momentum in which life could be recognized, but I never let myself go completely: my touristic itineraries were a source of vigilance, a tabling of time. They were an effort at containment and gave me an easy, easily achieved sense of satisfaction, however temporary.

I could have gone on like this indefinitely, sleeping and walking and continuing to live, not insensitive but neutral, meaningless, like a rat abandoned in a lab. My mother was wrong, and nothing terrible happened to me. Disasters didn't exist, or they were elsewhere, even though the tiniest catastrophe might have been enough to teach me what I wanted to defend, either Lucy, or Ginny, or my imaginary magnificent future. But I wasn't ill and my days weren't numbered. In fact, if anything, each day still seemed used, peeled back at the edges, like a page which had already been written, bound, published, studied, studied again, dog-eared and over-read until nothing could be learnt from it. It left me with a sense of dissatisfaction so vague I was almost ashamed.

I didn't read history anymore, because life wasn't a conundrum I could solve by reading. Instead, I collected books of matches from careless restaurants, and back in my room, late at night, I practised striking them into my cupped hands like Humphrey Bogart in Paris in *Casablanca*. I burnt holes in my shirts. I held burning matches upside down and watched the flame climb towards my fingers, thinking that the match was an honest object. It made no pretence at being solid or dependable in my hands.

'You've got holes all over the front of your shirt,' Ginny said.

And I hadn't shaved and I wasn't wearing shoes or socks. But then Ginny wasn't going to the opera either. She took off her denim jacket and hung it on the door-handle. She was wearing her vanilla ice-cream dress, the short one with the strawberries. No glasses.

274

'I told you I wouldn't give up,' she said, and I remembered that while walking it had always been in the back of my mind that Ginny had an answer to all this. She believed in the absolutism and the absolution of love, and there was always the possibility that she was right.

I moved further along the bed to make room for her, but when the soft mattress sagged us together we both leant the other way, resisting the tendency of the bed. Ginny kicked off her trainers and drew her legs up beneath her, and we both bounced softly on the soft mattress. She blinked brightly.

'Contact lenses,' she said.

'You should wear your glasses.'

'Do you prefer me in glasses?'

'Ginny.'

'Do you like me at all, Gregory? You've treated me appallingly.'

'I haven't been feeling very well.'

She pushed herself up onto her knees and turned to face me, balancing herself against the wall until the bed stopped moving. She sat back on her heels. Then she crossed her arms over her chest and between the thumb and forefinger of each hand, and she had beautiful hands, she took hold of the thin straps which held up her dress.

'I have everything Lucy has,' she said.

I could think of nothing to say back to her. Slowly, she peeled the straps off her shoulders and rolled the dress over her breasts until it lay crimped around her stomach. She abandoned the straps at her elbows. She was wearing nothing under the dress, but I didn't let that impress me. It was all meaningless, and a little sad, because I wasn't going to let her excite me. It wouldn't be fair on Lucy.

Ginny knew what I was thinking. She took a deep disappointed breath and her lungs filled with air, lifted her upturned breasts, held them trembling for a second, and then let them fall again.

She pulled the straps of the dress free of her arms. I looked closely at the material gathered around her stomach. I didn't know how to tell her it wasn't working, but then she leant over to the door-handle and reached into the pocket of her denim jacket. She brought out a single cigarette and a lighter, and swayed back to face me again, still kneeling. She put the cigarette between her lips.

'Your larynx,' I said, pushing myself upright on the bed, pulling my feet up beneath me.

She wiped an eyebrow, and then moved the cigarette to the side of her mouth. Her lips relaxed and the cigarette dropped to a rakish angle I recognized from old films. I knelt in front of her, fascinated.

'Your vocal cords,' I said.

The cigarette twitched when she breathed.

'My lungs,' she said, the cigarette jerking. 'Is this how Lucy does it?'

I nodded.

She held the lighter in both hands and scratched a flame from it. She raised it towards her mouth, and the white insides of her arms pushed against her breasts.

'Watch me,' she said. 'Watch me do it too.'

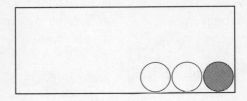

Each week Theo smoked fewer cigarettes, and we all knew he was dying. Indomitable, Walter went out of his way to find the Celtiques he used to like, and then pointed out the significance of winter in relation to Theo's cough. As winter moved towards spring, Walter started blaming the house: the toxic dust created by lab-building, or microscopic ash residue from the fire.

Emmy told him to stop.

'Theo is dying of lung cancer from smoking cigarettes,' she said.

Love had changed Emmy, as if she'd eventually accepted her destiny always to fall in love with smokers. She thought it might be an oedipal thing. Once, she even confessed to a grudging respect for the recklessness needed to smoke. It was like an appeal to God for special consideration, and although there were other ways to appeal to God, like mountain-climbing and motorcycle-racing, neither of these had ever interested the men she loved.

Theo made it absolutely clear that he didn't want to spend his last weeks in hospital. He didn't like the way doctors poked at him and drained him, as if measurements would explain everything. He especially didn't like the eager young housemen who asked him very politely whether he'd mind his lungs being preserved for use in lectures to school-children. After he was dead, of course.

He preferred to be at home, among unreasonable people.

We now lived exclusively in the front of the house, and

279

from his chair in the Suicide Club Theo would sometimes send Jamie to the bookmakers. He still bet on the favourites, but now he always lost. It made him happy, confirming that he'd understood something of the laws which governed his life, and each failed bet temporarily restored his strength. It was at times like these, when twenty-to-one outsiders romped home ahead of champions, that Theo and Emmy cheerfully sorted out money and the cremation and what would happen to Haemoglobin when Theo was gone. Theo gave me the key to the flat in the Estates.

'What should I do with this?'

'I don't know,' he said. 'It's up to you.'

As Theo's cough became worse, Jamie started running faster to the bookies, scared that Theo might die before he made it back. But Theo, whenever he felt strong enough, seemed less concerned with his own health than he was with mine.

'You could give up, you know, if you wanted to.'

'I know I could.'

'Tomorrow, if you wanted.'

Jamie had just rushed back from the betting shop with the astounding news that Wales, the worst team in the Five Nations tournament, had beaten the favourites France in Cardiff. Theo was feeling good.

'It's not the same for me,' he said. 'Smoking wasn't a retreat. It was a kind of contest.'

'Theo, you're dying.'

'So I lost. But I still took Him on.'

'This is to do with Julian, isn't it?'

'You're more than a statistic, Gregory. You're better than that.'

Before the effect of the Welsh victory could wear off, I told Theo that Julian still blamed him for holding back the plants he'd cultivated in the lab. 'He reckons they could have saved thousands of lives.'

'And him being such an expert on life and death.'

But then his chest began to hurt him again and he didn't elaborate.

I tried not to think too much about life after Theo. Instead, I found comfort in my weekly routine, glad that some things stayed the same. Twice a week, every week, I ran up to the medical-room at the Unit, where strangers plugged me into machines to see exactly what cigarettes had done to me. They swabbed my eyes for amblyopia and inspected my sweat for alkalis. They examined my blood for its measurable O's of oxygen, and asked me if I ever felt anxious. And no matter how worried I said I was, they always gave me a clean bill of health. They told me that nothing was wrong with me, and then handed over enough cigarettes at twenty a day to last me until the next appointment. The whole procedure was familiar and consoling, and in need of such comfort, I continued smoking exactly 20 cigarettes a day, the same as always.

Naturally, Julian always knew where to find me. He would sometimes dawdle around the medical-room, examining wall-charts and testing the sharpness of scalpels against his thumb.

'It's nearly ten years since Hamburg,' he said.

I watched dark blood leave my arm by fat syringe.

'We should think about a new contract.'

'If that's alright by me.'

'Well obviously,' Julian said. 'I'll forgive you for the day you smoked more than twenty. You've been under a lot of stress, what with Theo and everything.'

Julian looked at a screen and tapped some keys. 'Hardly a day of illness in almost ten years,' he said. 'You've been a great help, Gregory. We'd like you to continue.'

I appreciated Julian's more cautious approach. It proved that my fighting talk about giving up must have made an impression, even though the truth was I'd become so used to smoking I could hardly imagine what not smoking would be like. Theo was dying, and my Carmens were too valuable a comfort to think of discarding. And anyway, nothing was wrong with my health, and my income depended on it. There was no pressing reason to stop.

'So I'll draw up the paperwork then?' Julian said.

'Yes,' I said. 'Fine.'

I didn't tell Theo. He was hardly smoking at all now and I didn't want to upset him, but then Jamie burst in, waving Theo's betting slip, gabbling the news that an overweight forty-five-year-old Seventh Day Adventist had just become heavyweight boxing champion of the world.

Inspired, Theo sat up in his chair and remembered some Buchanan's gossip he'd always been meaning to pass on, about the Hamburg labs. It was some years ago, and there was a refugee from the Ukraine, a former Olympic gymnast, who'd developed a cancer during some tests designed by Julian. Carr always claimed that the cancer pre-dated the tests, but after questions from the German press he eventually admitted that the Ukrainian, among others, was being paid to smoke cigarettes. Buchanan's immediately issued a statement denying responsibility. They entirely agreed that exposing human subjects to potentially cancer-inducing agents, merely to establish causality, was morally and ethically unacceptable.

Julian was then publicly dismissed from his post.

'As for the gymnast,' Theo said, but the effect of the bet was wearing off and he couldn't finish the sentence.

His lucid moments became increasingly infrequent, no matter what shock defeats Jamie brought back from the betting shop. On March 2 Theo laid no bets and smoked no cigarettes. We took him into hospital, and he died the next day, at twenty past eight in the evening. He had a bet with Walter that he'd last at least another week.

She lit the cigarette and puffed out a little smoke without inhaling.

'Lucy doesn't do it like that,' I said. 'She breathes it all in.'

She took the cigarette out of her mouth and checked it was still alight. I was breathing heavily, trying to inhale any smoke which side-streamed towards me.

'She inhales as deeply as she can into her lungs,' I said.

Ginny put the cigarette back between her lips. Smoke swirled into her eyes and she blinked hard. She should have worn her glasses. I concentrated on the tip of the cigarette and Ginny's face lost focus, merging into the pale background behind the ember beneath the ash at the end of the burning cigarette.

It lifted slightly as she sucked on it, favouring her lower lip. The cigarette paper crackled, burned, and the red ember chased a centimetre closer to the filter before it was surrounded again with ash, white more than grey. Ginny took the cigarette out of her mouth, closed her lips around the smoke. I imagined it settling behind her teeth, on her tongue.

I wanted to kiss her.

Her lips, pursed closed over the smoke, made her look determined and a little frightened. They slipped open, closed again, and an orphan wisp of smoke floated up past her cheek. She took an inward breath, short and sharp like someone bee-stung, pin-pricked. She swallowed a cough at the back of her throat. And then, her eyes crossing at the wonder of it all, she watched the smoke she breathed out through her nose.

I put my right hand on her left breast. She looked at my hand and then into my eyes and then she inhaled again on the cigarette. A tear tracked down from her left eye.

'Contact lens,' I said.

'Smoke,' she said.

The tear shrugged over the ledge of her eye-lid and slid towards the ridge of her cheek-bone. It fell onto my hand and dripped through my fingers.

She smoked the cigarette all the way to the filter, and the only movement in the room was the regular travel of lit cigarette from hand to mouth and the upward waver of smoke. When the cigarette was finished, she leant over and stubbed it out on the metal lid of the Helix tin. She blew the last of the smoke out of the side of her mouth, and kept on blowing long after it was all gone. Then she took a deep breath of clean air, and her breast rose in my hand. I leant towards her and we kissed, and this was exactly how it used to be, in the good old days, tasting Lucy Hinton. Everything was alright, and nothing had ever gone wrong. I opened my eyes and saw the yawing cheek-bone of Ginny Mitchell, kissing me. I closed my eyes again.

Some time later, out of breath, we pulled apart.

Ginny smiled. She bit her lower lip.

We started again. Her fingers were on my face, on my back, pitching into my ears. Then they were under my shirt, but I wasn't much interested in any of that.

I wanted to steal the taste of the cigarette from her tongue. I wanted to lift every last trace of nicotine from her gums and the smooth enamel behind her perfect American teeth.

I have no idea how much time passed before I noticed the taste of the cigarette was fading. I pulled away and was surprised by the hold Ginny had on one my wrists, my hand threaded beneath the skirt of her dress. She bit my neck. I leant away from her. The bed brought us together again.

'What's wrong?' she said. She kissed the side of my mouth. I freed my hand and then held onto her shoulders to keep her still.

284

She tilted her head, aiming her next embrace.

'Nothing,' I said.

She flapped her head onto my shoulder.

'I feel a bit light-headed,' she said. 'I'm not normally like this.'

'That's the nicotine.'

'I like it.'

She aimed a kiss at my chin, but pulled up short.

'There's something wrong, isn't there?'

'No,' I said. 'Of course not.'

'What is it?'

'It's to do with the cigarette.'

'I thought I was pretty good at it,' she said. 'For a first timer.'

'You were brilliant,' I said. 'Have you got any more?'

She put her hand under my shirt and rolled a finger on a rib.

'No,' she said, 'I haven't.'

I looked over at the Helix tin, but that was different.

'Let's manage without,' she said, pulling her finger across to my navel.

I caught her hand and held it. 'I can't,' I said.

'Why not?'

'I just can't. It excites me.'

'More than this?' She bit my earlobe.

'More than that,' I said.

'I suppose I could go and get some more.' She sounded doubtful. 'If you really wanted me to.'

I kissed her lips, and the taste of cigarette had definitely faded. 'Just one more,' I said. 'I'd like that very much.'

She swivelled off the bed and rolled the dress back up over her stomach and then her breasts. She threaded her arms through the straps and said:

'You're still weird, but I love you.'

She settled the straps on her shoulders and reached for her jacket. She kissed me on the nose and said she wouldn't be long, and then closed the door behind her without nearly enough force to mean good-bye.

I had no idea what I was doing. Ginny was a singer and she had lungs as clean as glass. I reached out for the Helix tin and picked it up, exploding the ash from her cigarette. It settled on the bed and on me and on the floor. The ash from a whole packet would probably cover everything I owned.

I tried to work out what was happening. I was asking Ginny to smoke cigarettes. Lungs ruined, her singing career would collapse. Her whole life would change. Presumably, at some stage, I would also encourage her to have sex with a man with no qualifications and no future who lived in a room the size of a shrunken lung. I should never have acted as if the cigarette Ginny smoked was magic. It wasn't. It had once belonged to Madame Boyard who had bought it in a shop, and it wasn't right to let Ginny believe that magic cigarettes were available in shops in exchange for money.

The fact was: cigarettes made no difference. This was just another dog-eared day which had been lived before, and I was suddenly aware of the disappointing truth, as sad and ridiculous as a dunce's cap, that I had no desire to carry on. I had no desire to change or defend anything. I wanted to forget hope, enterprise, success, perseverance. I was letting myself go, and it came easily.

I stood up and locked the door. I sat down again. I opened the Helix tin. I took out Julian's cigarette, and the writing above the filter which used to say Buchanan's, and which I once thought such a clever idea, had almost worn away.

I could crush this ragged cigarette between my fingers like Superman crushed the cigarettes offered to children by the evil Nick O'Teen.

It was a novel idea, which had never really occurred to me before. The cigarette was such a fragile object, so easy to break, and I wanted all it stood for to disappear. I wanted to begin my adult life again from the beginning, avoiding pointless obsessions and this persistent habit of disappointing women.

But I wasn't Superman. I put Julian's cigarette between my lips and it tasted like the unlit cigarettes in a cigarette shop. The filter was firmer than I expected but otherwise it was all so familiar, as if I recognized it from another life. Now, not that it made any difference now, it seemed an obvious and absolute truth that I should have smoked when Lucy asked me to. I grabbed a book of stray matches from the floor and curled up on the bed, Julian's unlit and battered cigarette hanging from my mouth.

Ginny was hammering at the door.

'It's a packet of twenty!' she said, excited, but I didn't move from the bed. I told her I was sorry. She called out my name. I told her I was sorry. She demanded to know what was going on and I said I was sorry. With my face turned to the wall and the cigarette in my mouth she might not have heard me. She kept calling out to me. I covered my ears with my hands. Sometime later, or perhaps it was earlier, she slumped down with her back against the door.

'I won't give up,' she said, over and over again, but in the end she did.

'I want to go home.'

'Have another pipe,' I say. 'I'll wipe your ashtray for you.'

'Alright,' Walter says. 'But this is the last one, and then I'm going.'

He picks fresh tobacco from his pouch and tamps it down

into the bowl. I watch his practised hands because his face is hidden by the broad brim of a huge sombrero. Haemoglobin turns in his basket, snores, settles. The ghost imitates the wind, scratching against the corners of the house.

I ask Walter if he believes in ghosts.

'You mean seriously?'

'Seriously.'

'Of course I don't. Do you?'

'No,' I said. 'Probably not.'

Walter puts a match to his pipe, and a cloud of smoke billows up from beneath the brim of the sombrero. I ask him where he got the hat.

'It's a long story,' he says, but for once he shows no inclination to tell it. 'Involving Fidel Castro, the CIA, and an exploding cigar.'

Actually, Walter is sulking. I should have remembered his competitive streak from the way he plays dominoes.

'In Cuba,' Walter says, glancing out from beneath the sombrero so that I see he hasn't quite given up, even now. 'Where the girls who like their fellas,' and here he quite deliberately tips the ashtray off the arm of the chair, just to annoy me, 'always light their panatellas.'

None of his ploys are going to work. I shall clear up the ashtray later, calmly and without fuss. It's not a problem, and to be perfectly frank, without wishing to blow my own trumpet, Walter never had a chance in a million of beating me at Tempting Gregory, a game I invented some hours ago to pass the time. Walter had wanted to stay a little longer, mostly because Emmy is still away on a course, devoting the surplus energy she once invested in LUNG into learning about the dangers involved in nuclear fuel. 'Still fighting the good fight,' I said, and she said, 'Still fighting, anyway.' Before coming back she intends to make her first parachute jump.

288

Anyway, Tempting Gregory is a very simple game. To win, Walter has to make me admit that I want to smoke. The only rule is that he isn't allowed to stop me from writing, but apart from that, anything goes. So far he has recounted all the times when smoking saved his life. He frequently refers to his venerable old age. He has reminded me of irrational wars, random buses, escaped radiation, over-powered motor-cycles, undetected asbestos, lethal sand particles, passive smoking and, imaginatively, the possibility of being eaten by lung-fish. He has placed his lit pipe in my hand and blown smoke in my face. He has described Tahitian maidens rolling cigars along the insides of their honey-brown thighs. He has evoked jazz basements and cowboy camp-fires and Rick's Casablancan bar. Varying his attack, he then tried to irritate me towards the delirium of a cigarette-craving, only coming close once when he read a page from yesterday and snorted with derision while threatening to set fire to it with his lighter. Close, Walter, but no cigar.

As a last resort he's been trying to bore me into submission. I'm not allowed to look at a book or the television, or to move from my chair, while he sits in front of me handling moist tobacco from his pouch. Now, at last, I think he accepts defeat, though not at all gracefully.

'You know,' Walter says, pointing at me with the stem of his pipe, 'you're lucky to live in this house.'

'Thankyou, Walter,' I say, even though it has nothing to do with luck. This house is the positive evidence of my ten years working for Buchanan's, always hoping there's no other evidence lurking inside my body, no internal tattoo, no patient message.

'I've thought of something else,' Walter says.

'Last chance.'

'If you've really given up,' he says, pausing, timing the

strike, 'then why haven't you told your mother?'

Walter was always good at games. I pretend I have something very important to write down.

'I could tell her if I wanted to.'

'But you haven't, have you?'

'Maybe I don't want to.'

Maybe I don't know how. My mother thinks cigarettes are dangerous, and important. She can't be expected, as a lifelong non-smoker, to grasp that the reasons for both starting and stopping are equally absurd and entirely reasonable. The world remains the world, and I remain me, in the same relation to everything else as I ever was, except with a tube of burning leaves between my teeth, or not, as the case may be.

'It proves you're not going to make it,' Walter says.

'I could tell her anytime.'

Walter goes through the familiar ritual of refilling his pipe.

'I thought you wanted to go home.'

'The other thing,' Walter says, enjoying himself now, 'is what happens when you stop writing? Does that mean you've started smoking again?'

'It could mean anything. I could have joined Emmy's Outward Bound club and taken up hang-gliding, or mountain-climbing. I might have fallen in love at first sight.'

'With Stella?'

'I don't know who. It's first sight.'

'That's good,' Walter says, 'because Stella won't look at you more than once.'

'She might.'

'She won't. Mostly because you can't make up your mind about anything. You haven't even decided to go to the show yet. For all we know, the moment you stop writing you'll run up to the Unit and plead with Julian to take you back. You know Julian offered money to Jamie?'

290

No, I didn't, and it was almost a shock to think of Julian still out there, in his suit, smoking, offering money to strangers. For the last few weeks I've only ever imagined him sitting in the dark in his front room, fuming. He crushes out half-smoked cigarettes on the glass frames of photos of his wedding.

'I bet Jamie said no.'

'Surprisingly, he did.'

The last time I'd seen Jamie, at Theo's funeral, I'd explained to him as simply as I could that Theo had died because he smoked too many cigarettes. I could see how determined Jamie was to understand this, even though he'd always known about the connection between cigarettes and cancer. It was like switches and electric light, or taps and water, but before Theo's death he'd never needed to think it through.

'But why would they sell anything which killed people?' he asked.

'I don't know,' I said.

'But *why* do they kill people?'

'They're made that way.'

I recognized Jamie's confusion. It reminded me of the foul taste of Miss Bryant's cigarette, and the end of my sense of the certainty of things.

I pick up the phone and dial a number.

'There's no need, Gregory,' Walter says. 'I believe you. You win.'

I motion him to be quiet. The phone is answered and I say hello and out of habit, though sleepily, Mum asks me if I'm alright.

'I know it's late,' I say, 'but I've something to tell you.'

And then, even though Walter is watching me and I know it would make Mum very happy, I find I can't say it. It's as hard as telling her I love her.

'Tell me,' she says, 'now you've started. Have you found a girlfriend?'

'Maybe I'll come over,' I say.

'What?'

'Maybe at the weekend. I'll come over.'

Both of us are happy with this idea, so we say goodbye before I can ruin it. I'll just turn up and not smoke until someone notices. After lunch, most probably, when I don't head for the garden as soon as Dad offers to show me the photos from his OBE day.

'Never mind,' Walter says. 'I still think you've cracked it.'

'You think so?'

'Yes. I believe you're going to stop.'

'For good?'

'You've proved you can do it. You've made it, and frankly I'm impressed.'

'Well thanks, Walter.'

'I suppose it can't have been easy.'

'Thanks very much.'

'But you are now officially an ex-smoker, and I take my hat off to you.'

'You really mean it?'

'I really do. I take off my hat.'

And quite amazingly, he does just that.

DAY
19

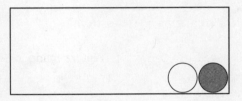

Second class, Smoking. It had been building up to this since the Gare St Lazare, presumably to continue all the way to Hamburg. The train had found its voice and all it ever said was cigarettes tch tch, cigarettes tch tch.

Diagonally across from me sat a girl in a black dress and tortoise-shell sun-glasses. She placed a yellow soft-pack of Ernte 33 on the table-top, next to a book in Flemish which might have been a novel. When reading, she sometimes tapped her teeth with a slim metal lighter, but I tried to ignore her because all that mattered was that time should pass and nothing should get through to me. I gazed out of the window, then down at the quick silver of a parallel track, liquid in the sunlight.

She lit a cigarette. Tobacco. Smoke. I thought I might have met her somewhere before. Inhaling, exhaling, reflected in my window, her transparent lips and her fingertips. Since smoking a cigarette she wouldn't notice, were we to kiss, that I tasted like an ashtray.

Cigarettes tch tch, Cigarettes tch tch, and telegraph poles wiping past the window.

That morning I'd packed my possessions into a single suit-case and set no itinerary besides buying a train ticket that would take me to Hamburg. On the way to the station, in the bright morning sunshine of the city, Lucy Hinton was everywhere, lighting smoking extinguishing her cigarettes, sitting standing kneeling by the river, littering the pavements with crushed butts, killing passers-by. Could I have known that this one girl would become the template for every girl

295

I'd ever meet? I should have paid more attention. I should, obviously, have smoked a cigarette.

Reflected in the window, against a background of rapid greenery, repositioning her sun-glasses, tapping her teeth, smoking her cigarette, turning her page, coughing occasionally.

Of course it was possible, given the small choices I was still free to make, that I could leave the train at any of the stations before Hamburg. I could recover my senses in a remote guest house (No Smoking Please), before returning to Paris refreshed, lungs intact, and from there perhaps to England. I could find Lucy Hinton and assess the probability of living happily ever after.

Touching the middle of her top lip with the tip of her tongue. I could ask her for a cigarette.

I realized I must have forgiven Julian. I imagined him in his lab, pacing up and down between burning Bunsen-burners and frothing test-tubes, beside himself with the seemingly impossible task of finding his Mr X. I assumed he'd still recognize me. I trusted his letters, and the trouble he'd taken, and I wanted to believe this made him my friend. He'd written so often that I couldn't believe in a bet between him and Lucy. In fact, Lucy had really loved me, that was the truth. She left me because I broke my promise to smoke a cigarette. It was all my fault and I ought to be dead.

Shifting in her seat, re-positioning her bones. I was an idiot even to think it. Her bones were nothing compared to Lucy's bones. And Ginny's bones. Ginny's back-bone curled against my door, Ginny in tears. I was an idiot and I ought to be dead. Which was why, the night before, I'd smoked a stale Buchanan's Century which had once belonged to Julian Carr, a very good friend of mine.

Ginny had given up, slammed her fists one last time against the door, gone home. I lay on the bed, the unlit cigarette in

296

my mouth and a book of matches in my hand. I stared at the wall. I thought hard about Ginny's heartache, which had nothing to do with cigarettes. I explored my own cruelty. I decided, without too much difficulty, that I really ought to be dead.

So I struck a match, but not into my cupped hands, and not like Humphrey Bogart. I watched the flame climb towards my fingers. I could make excuses. I could blame it on Uncle Gregory, and his easy charisma impressing my young mind with the attractions of an adventurous life, full of trouble and tobacco. Or, on the basis of a single half-overheard conversation, I could speculate that Uncle Gregory was secretly my real father, and this adulterous mismatch had scrambled my genes, leaving me incapable of kindness. Or I could blame my parents, citing their failure to buy me a top skateboard or a decent stereo or a motorized go-kart, and for giving me nothing to rcbcl against except their decency.

My fingers were burning. I tossed the match onto the floor, and waited. Nothing caught fire.

I struck a second match and watched it burn. It was my own fault for thinking that I arrived in Paris a free man. I'd cast myself as the centre of the universe, poised to rescue beautiful women, destined to live forever. With luck and time and the headstart of Uncle Gregory's money, I'd expected to stumble across everything I wanted, just by stumbling along. Disappointment was inevitable.

I threw away the second match. No fire.

My mother had been right all along. There was always something missing, and I had to learn to accept dissatisfaction, like everybody. I was no different, and I should never have laughed at her exclamation marks. She used them because what she was saying was important and she was teaching a slow learner. She only wanted me to take notice, but I never had. I ought to be dead.

I lit a third match and brought it close to the end of the cigarette. I thought of Uncle Gregory in Adelaide and monkeys in test-stations and cowboys in the desert with oxygen in their saddle-bags. I thought of 20% of all British deaths, and Buerger's disease, and benzo-a-pyrene, and tobacco heart, and the inefficiency of filters, and every threatening headline my mother had ever sent me. I searched out every positive assurance that Julian's cigarette would definitely kill me.

I lit the cigarette and drew in deeply and it tasted so vile I didn't doubt it was fatal. I inhaled again, even though each time I brought the cigarette to my lips it felt like holding nausea in my hands. I finished it and still I wasn't dead. I threw it onto the floor. Nothing caught fire.

Nothing was happening. I'd smoked Julian's cigarette and it wasn't lethal. It was just a big disappointment, like everything else, like my mother had always warned me. Julian's cigarette had no special message, no particular moral, and my life was no less fragile than any other. I was not the centre of the universe and everything was expected, unoriginal, unsurprising.

The girl on the train, unharmed by the cigarettes she'd already smoked, lit another. She pushed her glasses back up her nose.

Of course it hadn't killed me. There was no reason why my death should be any more extraordinary than my life. I had to grow up, and fast, which was partly why I hadn't brushed my teeth. I wanted to keep the taste of tobacco alive in my mouth. It reminded me that it wasn't my destiny to live forever.

From now on, I intended to replace all my heroic and ineffective desires with the simple and achievable desire to smoke. The unique and the operatic had escaped me, so instead I would set myself a derisory task which would determine everything in advance. I would accept the inevitability of repetitive days by committing myself to cigarettes, and any other constraints which Julian specified. It wasn't the future I'd planned for myself, but I preferred it to a life of re-living the dissatisfactions of others.

I'd thought it all through. Every cigarette was bound to remind me of Lucy, and Ginny, but that was fine. It would be a kind of unending penance, making me remember and suffer, just like I deserved. And as a smoker I'd have to find a new way of showing my mother I loved her, even though it probably wasn't love which made me want to die before her. At least I presumed I would. It was no great secret that cigarettes were about to seriously damage my health.

The girl in the black dress was tapping her enamelled finger-nails on the laminated table-top, drawing my attention to the single Ernte 33 she'd rolled slightly towards me. Her eyebrows arched above the tortoise-shell frames of her sunglasses. I could take the cigarette. I could start a conversation. I could find out where she came from and what she did and what we had in common apart from smoking. I looked away. Her reflection shrugged and carried on reading.

I intended to withdraw my affections and detach myself from everything. I would be indifferent to the weather and the time of day, remaining impervious to any sensation except the hourly swell between deficiency and satisfaction offered by cigarettes. No doubt the external world would continue to address information to me, but I'd no longer be inclined to receive it. Instead, I imagined myself surviving without joy and without sadness, without a future and without a past, simply, self-evidently, like a drop of water forming on a tap, like a rat. I would ask for nothing, accept nothing, and make no impositions. And all in return for smoking a fixed number of cigarettes, each and every day.

Gradually, my life would empty itself of any activity beyond this imperative routine. It would be free of all crisis and all disorder, a life with no rough edges and no imbalance. I would have no projects and feel no impatience. I would exist without desire, without resentment and without revolt. Hour after hour, cigarette after cigarette, day after day, something was going to start which would be without end: my cancelled life.

From Paris to Hamburg, interrupted only by station-stops where I failed to alight, and in the background, cigarettes etcetera.

The Suicide Club was packed. All the regulars were there, as well as Emmy and Jamie, and a large number of scientists and technicians from the Unit. I offered round a tray of sandwiches, studiously avoiding Julian Carr who was representing Buchanan's and paying his respects on behalf of the company. He was also watching Jamie, who'd been trying to convince Mrs Cavendish the Unit receptionist that Theo's lung photograph, if she only stood close enough and crossed her eyes, was actually a hidden 3D image of a red Indian chief. Behind them, Walter was arguing with Emmy. He refused to pass round any sandwiches.

'I am increasingly *frail*,' he protested.

Lundy Foot was trying to persuade tea-drinkers to try a drop of sherry, and Julian Carr was now glaring at me over the top of Jamie's head.

Theo, restored to full health, appeared from nowhere. He smiled his closed mouth smile, made a space for himself, and danced an intricate jig which involved precise hopping and not infrequent skipping.

'Theo,' I said, 'stop that right now.'

'Why?'

'It's your own funeral for goodness sake.'

'Exactly,' he said, moving to his left, jumping to his right. 'And this is the best way to communicate with the people below.'

It was less than an hour since we'd all come back from the mid-day service at the crematorium, and I'd already smoked 27 cigarettes. I hadn't eaten all day, and I felt distinctly light-headed.

Theo was now standing at my shoulder. Even though he was only a hallucination, brought on by too much nicotine, I wanted to be polite.

'So then,' I said, 'how's heaven?'

'Mustn't grumble.'

'God smoke?'

'Not that I've noticed. Watch out,' he said. 'Here comes trouble.'

'Gregory.'

'Julian.'

'On behalf of Buchanan's, my deepest commiserations.'

'Sandwich?'

'I couldn't help noticing,' Julian said.

'I know,' I said, 'too many cheese, not enough ham.'

'That you seem to be smoking too much.'

'It's the occasion,' I said. 'Helps me get a grip.'

'Of course, I understand that,' he said. 'But maybe you could slow it down, just a touch.'

'Thanks, Julian. You're a good man.'

'It may not be the best time,' he said, glancing over his shoulder. 'But your new contract is ready.'

'Later,' I said, and went to offer sandwiches to a medical researcher I recognized from the Unit. I lit another cigarette. My head started to spin, and I sat down in one of the armchairs we'd pushed against the wall.

'That man has a one-track mind,' Theo said. He was making

himself comfortable on the arm of the chair, just behind Walter's favourite ashtray. 'He's not going to like it when you give up.'

I nearly choked on my smoke. 'I've no intention of giving up.'

'If you say so.'

'I'm in the middle of smoking more cigarettes than I've ever smoked in a single day before. It doesn't suggest I'm about to stop.'

'Smoke another,' Theo said. 'I can feel myself fading.'

I lit another cigarette. Theo now had a tan. He was wearing a lab-coat and Bananas was sitting on his shoulder, peering at my cigarette with green eyes.

'It's not as though there's anything wrong with me,' I said.

'How do you know?'

'Because I have a full medical check-up twice a week.'

'Ah, I see,' Theo said.

'What does that mean?'

'Well,' he said, 'if there was anything wrong with you, do you think they'd tell you?'

'Gregory!'

It was Emmy, leaning towards me holding a tea-pot. She wanted to know if I was alright. 'I'm fine,' I said, even though I could be dying of lung cancer and heart disease and of *course* they wouldn't tell me. I felt a dull ache in my chest, near my heart. Pull yourself together, man. 'Emmy,' I said, panicking slightly, 'do you ever have the impression that Theo is still with us?'

'Of course I have,' she said, 'all the time.'

She wanted me to know that Julian Carr was starting an argument with Dr Hacket about Romans, and I promised to go and calm them both down. I took a glass of sherry from

302

Lundy Foot, and found Julian leaning menacingly over Dr Hacket.

'His middle name was Bombastus,' I said, correcting them both before leading Julian away. He said:

'What are you playing at? Sitting in that corner you smoked at least three cigarettes. I saw you.'

'It's the grief,' I said, 'and the worry. I'm sorry, Julian. It won't happen again.'

I left him with Emmy, because there were still several things I wanted to sort out with Theo, and in the nicotine daze of the rest of the afternoon I hope I managed a fairly convincing impersonation of a normal person. I handed round sandwiches, added sugar-lumps to cups of tea, proffered my lighter to unlit cigarettes. If I didn't always follow the flow of conversation it was only because I was concentrating on Theo, and to keep him clear I constantly had a fag on the go, either wedged between my fingers or stuck between my lips.

'I'm not giving up,' I told him. 'Julian wouldn't let me near a one-day international ever again.'

'You never go anyway.'

'No opera. No motor-cycle GP. I'd lose my income.'

'It's only money.'

'The practical consequences are unthinkable.'

'Unpredictable.'

'Incalculable,' I said. 'I don't even want to think about it.'

But Theo insisted that I couldn't go on living in retreat. I had to move on. Listening carefully, I smoked my Carmens one after the other and his voice never wavered. Stop smoking, he said, Meet some new people, which was all very well until my 37th cigarette of the day, which turned out to be one cigarette too many. I started to feel unwell, and even though Theo was still talking, I had to go outside for some air. I stood in the driveway and took deep breaths, which seemed to help.

I was about to take a walk, up to the gates and back, when Julian put his hand on my shoulder.

He pulled me round so that I was facing him, and then he slapped the pack of Carmens from my hand. Immediately it hit the ground he stamped on it. Then he stamped on it again, and then he crushed it with a swivel of his foot, even though there were still three cigarettes left inside, including the one I always saved for last, turned upside down for luck. Julian said:

'20 cigarettes a day. You know the rules.'

'I'm sorry,' I said. 'I need to sit down.'

'What about the contract?'

'Fine,' I said. 'I'll sign it.'

I was still feeling groggy. Theo and Bananas popped up behind Julian's back and I looked at them and thought a single word. Advice. Over Julian's shoulder Theo mouthed: 'Don't be frightened.'

'Alright then,' I said to Julian. 'I'll sign it. But not here.'

Julian followed me back inside, and waited while I called a taxi. He hardly raised an eyebrow when I told him we were going to the Estates. All he wanted was for me to sign his contract, and he kept quiet in the taxi, across the waste-ground, in the lift, and only spoke when I opened the door to flat number forty-seven.

'What a dump,' he said.

The flat smelt familiar, of stale tobacco and dust, and in the room which used to be the clinic I told Julian to make himself comfortable. He wiped the dust off Theo's chair and sat down behind the table. I sat in the patient's chair. He took an envelope out of his suit-jacket and put it in front of me.

'Let's not waste any more time,' he said. 'It stinks in here.'

He handed me a pen and I took the contract out of the envelope. I read a few lines. I noticed I was holding the pen like a cigarette.

'Oh, I get it,' Julian said. 'You're pretending to hesitate, winding me up for old time's sake.'

'You always said I could stop whenever I wanted.'

'Of course I did. But you're so obviously Mr X it should never occur to you to stop. Stopping just doesn't apply to your personality type.'

'It's a bit stupid though, isn't it? I might get lung cancer.'

'And you might not. Anyway, in Hamburg you said you wanted to die. I thought that was the whole point.'

'Well it was,' I said. 'But then I met Theo.'

I couldn't see him anymore, but I knew he was still with us. I could feel him urging me on. I said to Julian:

'You knew he could immunize against TMV, didn't you?'

'How would I know that? All his plants were destroyed in the fire.'

'What about the one you stole?'

'It died,' Julian said, straight-faced, even though we both knew that immunized tobacco plants were just about indestructible. 'The contract, Gregory.'

'Why did you burn down the lab?'

Julian's eyes went blank. He brought out his packet of Centuries. He selected a cigarette and lit it, and then held the smoke in his lungs for a long time, as if this was an admissible reason not to reply.

'You were with me at the time,' he said, smoke surrounding every word. 'You were in my house. You were drinking my beer.'

'You wear a suit, Julian. You give orders. That's what you do.'

'Why would I set fire to Theo's lab? There were plants in there which could have made a safe cigarette.'

'I don't believe you. And anyway, how would you know? The tobacco would have to be tested, and the tests could take

305

forever and still be inconclusive, just like they are already.'

'You think I made it up?'

'It was an excuse to get your hands on one of Theo's plants. Theo was right. You wanted nothing to change. You found out about his discovery and you were scared he was going to sell it.'

'I promise you,' Julian said. 'I know nothing about this.'

'You invited me to your house to keep me out of the way.'

'Who told you that?'

'Then you destroyed the lab to protect Buchanan's. Theo actually beat the TMV years ago, but he knew this would happen. He never told anybody because he knew someone like you would come and destroy it all.'

Julian glanced down at his packet of Centuries. He slid them towards me. 'Let's resolve this like adults,' he said.

It was some time since Julian had stamped on my Carmens. I took a Century out of his pack. I turned it carefully in my hand, and read the writing above the filter. I put it back in the box, upside-down, and slid the box back across the table.

'For luck,' I said.

He took out the upside-down cigarette and lit it.

'But only if you save it until last.'

'Stop fooling around, Gregory. What else would you do with your life?'

'I could do anything. I could buy a motor-cycle. I could go to New York.'

'With whose money?'

'Where as a non-smoker I will rarely be treated as a pariah.'

'Yes, very good, Gregory, but the joke wears thin, even by your standards. Including the farce of bringing me down to this dump in the first place. Now sign the contract. You know what's in it.'

Another ten years of retreat and the dangerous illusion that I was impenetrable, that I offered no purchase to the outside world, and was inaccessible behind my smoke-screen of cigarettes. Only now I'd learnt that refusal was impossible. Nobody could remain completely detached and incurious because the world was always offering itself to be unmasked, and it couldn't do otherwise. It was time to stop being a statistic, and prove I had more than collective significance.

I tossed Julian the key to the flat. 'Keep it,' I said. 'In exchange for the days left on the first contract.'

Julian sighed. I could see he felt sorry for me.

'Remember the monkeys?' he said. 'They never set them free, you know. They didn't send them back into the wild with a gross of Carmens each and a typewriter between every thousand, to spend their retirement writing *Hamlet*.'

'I once had respect for you, Julian. Can you believe that?'

'We kill them, Gregory. At the end of the tests we kill them all, and then we have a very close look at what the cigarettes have done from the inside out.'

'Are you threatening me?'

'Of course not.'

'You've changed, Julian.'

'I'm a fully qualified doctor.'

'You're like a low-tar version of your former self.'

'I have a first-class degree. I get results.'

'You're filter-tipped.'

'Everything you have is because of me.'

'And aerated.'

Julian stood up and leant over the desk, his weight spread across his splayed fingers. 'So sign the damn contract,' he said.

'No.'

He lunged at me across the table. I swayed out of his reach, stood up, opened the door to the waiting-room. I was nearly at the outside door when he said:

'Lucy Hinton.' I stopped where I was. I turned round. Julian hadn't moved. 'She only slept with you for a bet.'

I opened the outside door and went out onto the walkway. I started walking towards the lift.

'Lucy Hinton!' he shouted out, his voice carrying clearly from behind the table, through the waiting-room, following me along the walkway. 'I fucked her. I fucked her all the time!'

I made it to the lift. The door opened on a woman holding a sleeping baby wrapped in an anorak. The woman had a fag in her mouth. She stepped out of the lift.

'Three weeks!' Julian screamed. 'I give you 3 weeks, *maximum*!'

The lift doors shuddered closed, shutting off Julian's voice. Sooner or later, inevitably, he would have to notice the queue which had formed outside the flat. He would know what to do. He was a doctor.

DAY
20

I've made a big mistake.

Inside the house, on the desk in front of me. A Helix tin, originally designed to hold scientific instruments, now containing tobacco leaf. Stripped, cured, shredded and flavoured by my own hand.

A packet of cigarette papers.

I must have misunderstood. It's highly unlikely that Miss Bryant would have said the narrator can never die. More reasonably, she probably taught us that the narrator can't describe his own death. Not all of it, not to the very last moment, for obvious reasons. According to Miss Bryant then, the narrator either lives to see another day, or dies silently.

Outside the house, the early morning blue of a bright spring day, this day and no other. Outside my window right now. High white clouds. Hang-gliding weather.